ALL
THESE
PERFECT
STRANGERS

AOIFE CLIFFORD

SIMON &
SCHUSTER

London · New York · Sydney · Toronto · New Delhi

A CBS COMPANY

First published in Great Britain by Simon & Schuster UK Ltd, 2016
First published in Australia by Simon & Schuster (Australia) Pty Ltd, 2016
A CBS COMPANY

1 3 5 7 9 10 8 6 4 2

Simon & Schuster UK Ltd
1st Floor
Gray's Inn Road
London WC1X 8HB

www.simonandschuster.co.uk

Simon & Schuster Australia, Sydney
Simon & Schuster India, New Delhi

A CIP catalogue record for this book
is available from the British Library

Paperback ISBN: 978-1-47115-362-4
eBook ISBN: 978-1-47115-364-8

Typeset in the UK by M Rules
Printed and bound by CPI Group (UK) Ltd, Croydon, CR0 4YY

Simon & Schuster UK Ltd are committed to sourcing paper
that is made from wood grown in sustainable forests and supports the Forest
Stewardship Council, the leading international forest certification organisation.
Our books displaying the FSC logo are printed on FSC certified paper.

For Richard, Aidan, Genevieve & Evangeline

With thanks to Garry Disher and the Australian
Society of Authors' Mentorship Program
supported by the Copyright Agency

ALL
THESE
PERFECT
STRANGERS

'This is about three deaths. Actually more, if you go back far enough. I say deaths but perhaps all of them were murders. It's a grey area. Murder, like beauty, is in the eye of the beholder. So let's just call them deaths and say I was involved. This story could be told a hundred different ways.'

Prologue

I am sitting in the waiting room looking at the painting on the wall. It has different-sized circles splattered all over it, every single one of them red. The first time I saw it I was worried it was one of those inkblots where you have to say whatever comes into your head. Stupid, I know, but I was only fifteen. All I could see was blood, which I knew was not a good answer. I decided if anyone asked me, they would be balloons because no one could make a big deal out of that.

The Rorschach test is what those inkblots are called. I looked that up at the town library straight after my first appointment. The only thing that painting actually reveals is how untalented Frank's wife, Ivy, is. She did it at an adult education class. Frank had an affair with her when his first wife had cancer. The whole town knows that, and they haven't forgotten. Neither has Ivy. That's why she's the receptionist and glares at all his female patients, including me.

Today, Ivy is wearing lipstick the exact same colour as the circles, but her mouth is always a thin straight line. She is making me sit in reception for ages, before letting Frank know I am here because I called her 'Ivy' instead of 'Mrs Hennessy'. I wanted to show her that I'm different this time around and I guess she wants to show me that she isn't.

While I'm waiting, I pull out the criminal law textbook from my bag. I'm reading about police cautions today but I'm not really in the mood to take it in. On afternoons this room is chock-full of school kids and parents from all over the district. Mostly anorexic girls. Occasionally you get a gay boy with his mother hoping that it's just a phase.

It is much quieter this morning. Ivy is sorting the mail and there is a farmer with a crumpled brown-paper face, staring into the middle distance. A shotgun accident waiting to happen. His pear-shaped wife, with a tight twisted mouth, almost sits on top of him, worried he might make a bolt for the door. She recognises me and pokes her husband in the ribs, but Frank appears, and I slip the textbook back into my bag without him noticing. That's the sort of thing he'd ask questions about.

2

Ivy announces, 'Doctor will see you now,' as if Frank is a train about to leave the station. Standing by the reception desk, Frank brightens, the way you do when you see a friend, and a smile leaks out of me in return. Frank is thin and wiry. His mouth stretches all over his face, so even a small smile from him is a broad grin. He looks like a farmer, but that's probably because everybody looks like a farmer around here.

'Hi, Frank,' I say to wind up Ivy, who insists upon 'Doctor'. She opens the next envelope as though she is gutting a fish.

'Penelope,' Frank says in return. He knows what I am up to.

His office has a new plant, but the same old chair. He doesn't have the fancy ones that you lie down on. It was a deliberate choice, he told me when I was fifteen, but now I think they probably cost too much.

'So, Pen, how are things?' he asks, as he closes the door behind me. Frank never asks 'how are you?' because he says people automatically say 'fine', which must be a lie, because you wouldn't be seeing a psychiatrist if everything is fine.

'Fine,' I say.

Next to the box of tissues for patients who cry is my file, fatter than I remember it. Frank has the patient file in his office for appointments but usually it's locked away in a cabinet in the kitchen. No one can access it but him, he claims. I don't believe that for one second. I bet Ivy spends every lunchtime reading all about Frank's patients.

Frank opens my file and looks at the first page.

'October 1987, not so long ago,' he says.

He's wrong, of course. October 1987 is a lifetime away. Everything has changed since then. For starters, I don't need treatment, not like when I first arrived here. Today's session is about money, a tactic. My lawyer, Bob Cochrane, has arranged it. He's talking about suing everyone, the college, the university and anyone else he can think of. I've been a victim of a terrible crime. All Frank needs to do is write a report demonstrating my pain and suffering and then I'm out of here.

'When did I last see you, Pen?' asks Frank, shuffling through the pages. 'July 1988, just on two years ago. You stopped treatment quite suddenly, if I remember correctly.'

I don't see why we are going over ancient history. None of this is relevant to what we are supposed to be discussing now, so I tell him that actually the last time we saw each other was just before Christmas, when he wrote a reference for my bursary application for college.

He nods his head slowly, like he's taking my point, and then starts with the standard questions and I play along. Am I living back at home? Yes. How am I sleeping? All right. He pauses before asking if I'm taking any medication.

'No painkillers?' he says, and he gestures towards my face. I have taken the bandage off so he can see the cut. I thought it might be helpful for the report. When I tell him no, he nods his head.

He puts down the notepad, and resettles himself in his chair, like we are in a game show and the next round of questions will be more difficult.

'We are going to have to discuss those murders at university and your involvement.'

I am surprised by his bluntness. Other than the police, hardly anyone else has tried to talk about it with me, as if it would be bad manners to pry. But that is what psychiatrists do best, find pressure points.

He waits for me to speak, but I can't quite form the words for this conversation, so I look out of the window to avoid his gaze. There is a giftware shop across the lane that Tracey used to steal from. She said it was easy because the owner hated working and never paid attention to the customers. But the owner's mother did and that was the start of the trouble.

After a couple of minutes, Frank says, 'Pen, by the end of this session, I have to decide if I am the right person to make the assessment your lawyer is asking for.'

I turn away from the window. Frank is the only psychiatrist in my town. Frank is the only psychiatrist in the district.

'I have an arrangement with a colleague who travels to this clinic once a month to see . . . particular patients. It may be more appropriate for you to see her.'

I shake my head violently. I don't want anyone else to read my file, to ask me questions, to make judgments.

He leans back on his chair, pressing his fingers together, which he always does when things are serious.

'Then we are going to have to go through what's happened. I understand parts may be difficult to talk about so I am proposing that you write it down.'

'What?' I ask.

'I want you to put in writing what happened at university, the events, your thoughts and feelings, so we can discuss it.'

'But how does that have anything to do with your report?' I try to keep my voice light and conversational, like this is an interesting development, rather than something really annoying.

'Bob has asked me to evaluate if I think a return to treatment is warranted. Between that and the report, it's going to take at least a couple of sessions before I'm prepared to make that assessment. It will require your commitment to cooperate. No disappearing acts or long silences this time.'

The only appropriate answer to this is a long silence as I try to work out my strategy. Frank eventually interrupts.

'And don't worry, I'm sure the university will cover the cost.'

That isn't what I am worried about. I remember what I was reading in my textbook when I was waiting.

'You are not obliged to say or do anything unless you wish to do so, but whatever you say or do may be used in evidence. Do you understand?'

The police say it whenever they arrest someone. Three years ago, they said it to me. But what is more interesting was the footnote at the bottom of the page. It cites a study that found, despite the warning, almost no one stays silent. People feel compelled to talk, to excuse, to explain or confess.

I know that is right because I talked last time. I still don't know if I talked too much or not enough.

'It doesn't have to be anything special,' says Frank. 'It's a technique to assist our discussions. A simple exercise book will do. Bring it along with you and read out what you have written. I don't even need to look at it. It will just be the starting point for each session.'

I wonder if this could be a way I can tell my story and be silent as well. Could I write down *'the truth, the whole truth and nothing but the truth'*? That phrase isn't in my criminal law book. I expect it's in the evidence textbook, which you don't need until your final year. Telling the whole truth means more than just an absence of lies. It means revealing

7

all the secrets you know. I didn't tell the whole truth when I was sixteen and went to court. I haven't told the whole truth about what happened at uni. Perhaps I could tell it this once and then never again. Write it down but only read out the parts I want Frank to hear.

It's risky.

He must sense my weakening because he makes it a condition of continuing to see me.

'We will explore what you have written and then you can take the book home with you.'

In other words, Ivy won't get her hands on it.

So I give in.

When I get home, Mum is still at work, so I hunt around for some paper to at least make a token effort because I need that report from him. I'll rewind the clock to six months ago when I left for university and start from there to keep him happy.

Eventually, I find a diary that belongs to Mum. It has a hard blue cover, a day to a page and holidays I've never heard of. Her work gave it to her as a Christmas present last year. She says they're cheapskates and could at least have bought a ham or some chocolates.

I'm still not sure how I feel about this but I take it to my bedroom and lock the door. Propped up against my bed, I start writing on the page that has 1 January 1990 at the top of it, even though today is Tuesday, the 17th of July and the first event I am going to write about happened at the end of February. Still, New Year's Day feels right.

After some false starts, words crossed out, sentences left abandoned, I begin.

'This is about three deaths ...'

Chapter 1

It was Mum's new boyfriend who drove me to the Carillon to start the long bus ride to university. The bus stop was across from the court house, right in the middle of town. Terry's a long strip of beef jerky with an IQ to match. Like lots of people in my town, he was glad to see the back of me.

I said goodbye to Mum before she left for work. She had used up all her sickies and couldn't take a day off from the Cannery but she gave me a couple of hundred dollars she'd been saving up, which was a nice surprise. Terry drove me so he could use Mum's car to pick up some building supplies for his mate. He didn't believe in material possessions such as owning a car or actually paying for things himself.

He pretended it was because he was a hippy but really he was just another sponger. Mum only met him two weeks before and she was already lending him our car.

Terry watched me haul my bags out of the boot, mumbled something that could have been goodbye or good riddance and jumped back in and drove up the main road.

Getting on the bus, I turned up my Walkman loud enough to be an annoying buzz to the other passengers, as I gave a mental two-finger salute to the place I had lived in all my life.

We drove from my town, through even smaller towns, on potholed dusty country roads, until we came to a smooth black highway leading to the horizon. The university was in a city I had never been to before, far beyond the edge of my known world. The air-conditioning packed it in halfway into the trip but the bus kept going until, at the end of a sun-soaked afternoon, we entered the city interchange. From there, I hauled my luggage onto the bus to the university, taking up the entire seat with my belongings, which threatened to topple over as we began to navigate the labyrinth of internal campus roads.

Passing sports ovals, manoeuvring through round-abouts, I pressed my face to the glass. Green leafy trees lined the streets, welcome banners were up and people were dotted around large buildings. The bus slowed as we reached a pedestrian crossing. Groups of students spilled across the road, mooching their way to the grassy river-bank. As the driver pressed on the horn to hurry them along, I caught sight of a girl with dark hair falling to her shoulders, not curly, not straight, but somewhere in between. There was a glimpse of her fringe as well, all flicks and cowlicks that wouldn't lie flat. It was Tracey. I knew it was Tracey. Instinctively, I raised my hand to the glass to slap it and get her attention before she walked past, but then she turned to talk to a person behind her, and it was the wrong nose, different sunglasses and I realised that the girl outside was at least two inches too short. I fell back on my seat and felt upset and stupid all at once. The whole point of coming here was to escape from what had happened with Tracey, and yet it was as if I had packed her in my luggage and brought her along with me.

I didn't look out the window again until Scullin Hall loomed into view and the bus shuddered to a stop.

Clambering off the bus, gleaming with sweat, I stood and took it all in. There were two squat towers of grey brick, four storeys high, joined by a concrete wedge at ground level with the charisma of a nuclear bomb shelter. Months later, one of my lecturers told me it was a leading example of brutalist architecture. I could never tell if that was a joke or not.

For a moment I thought I had made a terrible mistake. That I didn't belong here and I should get back on the bus and go home. But too much had been sacrificed for that. Gathering up my bags, I went to the only door I could see. It was locked. Hearing voices, I trudged around the perimeter, until I discovered the main entrance on the far side, where a boy and girl were arguing while they dismantled a fold-up table.

'Welcome to Scullin. I'm Toby.' Slim, with milky-brown skin and a gold hooped earring like a pirate, the boy stopped what he was doing and grinned at me. The girl frowned. Her dark-brown long hair was so straight it looked as if she had ironed it that morning along with her perfectly creased blouse. I felt even more crumpled looking at her.

'My name is Leiza Parnell. Did you have any trouble finding us?' she asked, while shooting a sideways glance at Toby next to her. He gave an almost imperceptible shake of his head. 'Because Toby was supposed to have spent this morning putting up signs letting people know to come around the back.'

I decided to support Toby, who at least had a smile on his face. 'No trouble at all.'

Toby looked at the girl in triumph. 'See, I told you, Leiza, it's an intelligence test. If you can't find us, then you shouldn't be here anyway.'

Unconvinced, Leiza responded, 'Really? Because you're very late. The Welcome barbecue has finished.' Behind them

14

I could see a handful of people milling about picking up litter and packing away chairs.

'That's true,' said Toby. 'Everyone's inside getting depressed at the size of their rooms.'

'I only just got off the bus,' I explained.

Leiza was still sceptical. 'Anyway, we need to mark you off. Where did you put the list, Toby?'

'Signs were my job. Everything else was yours.' Disgruntled, Leiza began to hunt through the pieces of paper lying on the ground.

Toby made no effort to help her. 'Is this all you brought?' He looked at my bags. 'You pack light. I've nearly done my back in carrying people's junk up and down the stairs. You should see the shit they pack. No parents either?'

I shook my head. Toby nodded his approval. 'Mum's in the Philippines visiting relatives this year, but my first year she was here, sobbing her eyes out.'

Leiza interrupted. 'You could actually help me find the list, Toby. The Sub-Dean was asking for it before. If you've lost it ...'

'I have the list here, Ms Parnell,' a voice said. 'I thought registration had closed for the day.'

Standing behind us was a round-faced man in an ugly brown suit, with a petulant mouth. A chubby finger pushed his glasses up his nose as he looked at me. 'And who do we have here?'

'I'm Pen Sheppard.'

With a shrewd look in my direction, he drew a line on the piece of paper and I noticed circles of wet under his armpits.

'Ms Penelope Sheppard,' he said aloud. 'I am the Sub-Dean of Scullin, Bryan Keyes.' He seemed to imply that I should have known this already. 'You would be our bursary recipient, if I am not mistaken.'

'That's right,' I said, quickly, trying to stop him from talking about it in front of Leiza and Toby. I didn't want to be pigeonholed as the 'poor girl' on my first afternoon but the Sub-Dean didn't notice and went on. 'Our new Master's first initiative, but one I fully support. So important to lend a helping hand to those less fortunate.' Though from his face, he still needed convincing that I fell into this category. 'I believe that was the reason the Master wanted to personally welcome you, Ms Sheppard.' He said this as though it was a great honour. 'Tobias, as you are her residential assistant, you may wish to show her to the Master's office.'

'No problem,' said Toby. 'Leiza, are you sure you can manage without me?'

Leiza rolled her eyes, muttered 'unbelievable' under her breath and went back to folding up the table.

Toby grabbed my smallest bag. Walking through the entrance, we moved through a dingy reception area, past walls of marked mint green and along long halls of grubby linoleum, the black scuffs recording the migrating patterns of generations of students. Toby led me past family groups of nervous parents and kids my age wishing they would leave. Noisy later-year students yelled and ran past like they owned the place.

'I owe you one,' he said. 'Leiza was driving me crazy. She's a slave driver.' At the end of the second corridor, he knocked on a door with the words 'Master Marcus Legard' scribbled on tatty cardboard and stuck on the brick wall beside it, as if it were a temporary exhibit.

Toby pushed on the door and stuck his head in. 'No one's here.' Dropping my bags, I followed him inside. It was exactly what a place of learning looked like in my dreams, a complete contrast to what I had seen of the building so far: floor to ceiling bookshelves which gleamed in the subdued light, deep oxblood walls with lines of leather-bound books and an ornate Turkish rug on the carpet. If it hadn't been for the strong smell of fresh paint I would have thought this room had been untouched for decades.

'Check this out.' Toby stepped forwards into the middle of the room, slowly spinning around with my two bags. 'Completely different from last year. Carpet's new, and so are those bookshelves. The Sub-Dean has been going on all day about budgetary concerns. No one allowed to have a second sausage at the barbecue and now I see where all the

17

money has gone. This would have cost a bomb.' He put his finger up to one of the walls, and the faintest red smear came off. 'Not even dry,' he said.

I moved towards the bookcase, conscious of not touching anything for fear I might break something or smear dust across it. There were silver-framed photos of people in dinner suits and formal dresses, perfectly placed on a bookshelf so that all of them were easily visible. I recognised some politicians and an enormous opera singer who was always on television singing about dying while looking in the best of health. There was a man who was common to all of them. His hair, shaped dramatically like a cockatoo crest, changed from black to silver to white as he got older and fatter. Next to the photos, hanging on the wall, was a large blue and gold coat of arms of a book superimposed on the Southern Cross. It shone as if it had been recently polished, in contrast with a jumble of pine-framed pictures, carelessly propped underneath it.

'These don't look very expensive,' I said. Reproductions of fruit bowls and flocks of sheep, gambolling in meadows, they were the stuff people from my town thought of as art, and hung on their walls for generations.

'Belonged to the former occupant,' Toby explained. 'Guess they're on the way out. Not good enough for our Marcus with his happy snaps of the rich and powerful. That emblem is his old fancy university. Bit rude to be rubbing our faces in it.' He wrinkled his nose. 'This paint smell is unbearable.'

Moving past the bookshelves, I found a recessed wall, hidden from the doorway. Hanging from it was a large rectangular photograph that fit the space so perfectly I wondered if it had been bought for it. Or had the space been created with the picture in mind? It was over a metre long and at least that wide, with bleached white mounts, and a frame as sharp as a scalpel. It seemed at odds with the expensive clubbishness of the rest of the room because of the subject matter. It was of a nude boy lying down surrounded by darkness. A cold light caught only the right side of his body, leaving his face, genitals and feet in shadows. A white hip bone jutted out and you could count ribs, see the outline of a bent knee, part of a hand, a portion of thigh. The rest of his body dissolved into the blackness. It was as though he had been carefully cut into pieces. I was transfixed and repelled by it all at once.

Toby came to see what I was looking at.

'Definitely new,' he said. 'Still, better than the fruit, I must say.' He checked his watch. 'Tell you what, I've got to go and pick up some keys from Carol, the Master's PA. How about I get yours and meet you back here?'

'How about I come with you?' I asked, unable to take my eyes off the broken boy.

'No, you should wait for Marcus. Don't worry about

him,' he said, gesturing to the picture. 'I think he's quite cute.' He gave me a half smile as he slouched out.

I stayed watching the boy for a long time, wanting him to wake up or turn over. I was still waiting when a man, dressed in an artistically crumpled linen suit, meandered in through a side door that I hadn't noticed, puffing on a cigar.

'I do apologise,' he said. 'Been here long?'

It was the face from the photos, sunburnt with even more chins. When he took off his hat, a jaunty straw Panama, I could see that the white sails of hair had become old-man wispy. His eyebrows were still impressively black, though, as if he spent every morning putting them on with pen. This must be the Master.

'I've been sitting outside escaping the smell of paint.' He spoke in a powerfully projected baritone as if a crowd of students was listening to every word. 'They finished yesterday but it's as if I'm drinking the stuff. Keep tasting it in my mouth.' He gestured expansively with the cigar. 'Don't usually smoke these but thought it might help. Let's adjourn outside to my garden.'

Once outside, he headed towards two wrought-iron chairs under a lemon tree. One had a tumbler and a half-emptied whisky bottle underneath.

Pouring himself a drink, he told me to call him Marcus. 'Titles are for small people to feel important, and Master makes me sound as if I'm planning world domination.'

Unable to bring myself to call him anything, I settled on, 'It's a lovely garden.'

'Courtesy of the last inhabitant.' He smiled and I caught a flash of small, uneven, grey teeth. 'Much better than his interior choices, I will admit, but I am tempted to rough it up a little, plant a big cactus in the middle or perhaps install some confronting phallic water feature. Something to offset its *loveliness*. If I could give one piece of advice to students of this wonderful institution, it would be to avoid the lovely in life, so often synonymous with the dull.' There was not the slightest expectation that I might disagree. I didn't bother telling him that I had managed to avoid the lovely so far, though not by design.

'And what do you think of the rest of Scullin?' he asked, motioning at the building with his cigar, loose ash shimmering through the air.

'I haven't seen much of the inside yet.'

'But the building itself, don't you find it has a certain totalitarian charm? That it exudes Five Year Plan? I have a notion to get enormous banners of myself to display at the entrance. Something in a bright communist red would stand out so nicely.' He inhaled deeply on his cigar. 'Sadly, I suspect the *Sub-Dean* would not approve of the expense.'

The emphasis suggested the Sub-Dean was one of the little people. Leaning so far back on his chair that it was in danger of toppling over, he continued. 'I wanted to meet and congratulate you as our first bursary recipient. An idea of mine. The first of many. I must say your application interested me. I can see that you're a survivor, a trait I value highly. So easy to play the victim. So much harder to make a comeback.'

I sat up a bit straighter at this. I wasn't used to people praising me for anything, let alone for the very events most were so critical about.

He exhaled, a spiral of smoke snaking upward. 'Some might see the bursary as misguided *noblesse oblige*. Certainly the Sub-Dean thinks so. He doesn't come out and say that directly of course. Being forthright is not his style, but that's what he thinks. I prefer to see this bursary as an endorsement from one survivor to another. I see potential in you. Don't disappoint me.'

I didn't intend to. That bursary paid all the accommodation and food costs. It was the only reason I could stay at a residential college. Frank had been my referee for the application, detailing all the personal history that the bursary would help me escape from.

'Consider this a fresh start, Ms Sheppard. For you, for many of your colleagues. University is an excellent place to reinvent oneself.'

I opened my mouth to say thank you, but he was still talking.

'Anyway, we need a photograph to record this happy

occasion. Always publicise one's successes because no one else will.' He heaved himself out of his chair, ignoring my half-hearted protests that it really wasn't necessary, and began striding back towards the office, bellowing, 'Carol! Carol!'

A woman, who looked like other people's mothers, in sensible trousers and neatly cut dark short hair, eventually appeared. 'Yes, Master?'

'The camera. We must have a photograph.'

Carol scurried back inside the office, with Marcus close behind. I was unsure whether to get up or stay put, so I waited, pretending to admire the roses before following. By the time I reached the room, there was still no camera but Toby had appeared with a handful of keys.

'You finished with Pen?' Toby asked Marcus. 'She hasn't been to her room yet. Still time to get unpacked before dinner.'

'Aah, it seems the photograph will have to wait. Perhaps tomorrow,' said Marcus. 'It will be an excellent year, Ms Sheppard, certainly not dull. I'm sure as the first bursary recipient you will achieve great distinction for yourself and this college.' Picking up his cigar from a large ashtray, he put his head close to mine and said, 'University can be an expensive place. I'm sure we can find you some gainful employment if needed.' Waving away my thanks, he headed back out to the garden.

'You're bloody lucky,' Toby said in an accusatory tone, once we were far enough away from the office. 'I didn't even know there was a new bursary.' But he didn't seem to hold a grudge because he quickly defaulted to tour guide mode. 'Dining room is that way,' he said, pointing through double glass doors, 'and public telephones are down there, if you need to call home saying you got here in one piece. Take a book. There's always a queue.'

I made a non-committal kind of sound, as I had no intention of calling home. We passed a set of stairs. 'Page Tower's up there. That's where the non-smokers live their boring healthy little lives. You're in Forde with me, where happiness is a lit cancer stick.'

I had put down smoking on my application form, not because I actually smoked, but because I had some vague idea that smokers were a more tolerant group, on the whole.

'We're on the third floor,' Toby said, hoisting one of my bags onto his shoulder, as he began to climb the second set of stairs. 'This is the only exercise I do.'

'Why Forde and Page?' I asked, trying to squeeze past two girls who stopped on a landing to let us pass.

'Don't you know your history? Prime Ministers, same as Scullin,' Toby said, nodding at the girls. 'Most of the places on campus are named after Prime Ministers. Forde and Page are the Patron Saints of Failure. Didn't even last a month between them.'

We arrived at our floor and Toby ripped off a piece of paper stuck to the first door which said, 'Back in 5'. He pulled out a key that had been hanging on a string around his neck and unlocked it.

'I'll make you a cuppa first and then you can start unpacking.'

The room was large, a double room in fact.

'Don't get too excited,' Toby warned, as I looked around approvingly. 'Your room's a coffin.'

Music posters covered every inch of the walls. Wild hair, extravagant eye shadow, velvet and black, lots of black. The faces glared down at me, as if they weren't nearly as impressed by Toby's room as I was. The double bed near the window was barely visible under a mound of clothes, paper, junk and a large billiard ball bean bag. In the middle of the room, shrine-like, was an enormous stereo, a mountain of CDs piled next to it. I had seen CDs before, but never so many together, outside of the music store in our town. As Toby disappeared through an internal door into a tiny bathroom to fill up the kettle, I started to count them.

'Dave, my boyfriend, is an airline pilot,' he said, catching me in the act, as he came back into the room with the kettle. 'He buys pirated CDs in Bali for me. You can get them for a couple of bucks each.'

Where I came from, old people still used 'gay' to describe being happy, and young people used 'faggot' and beat up boys they suspected of being one. Toby must have guessed something from my face. 'Would you like me to hide in a closet to give you time to get used to the idea?' Then he told me he had actually climbed into his neighbour's closet in his first year and frightened some poor girl's mother half to death when he burst out of it. I made him promise that if my mother ever came to visit, he would do that to her.

We had tea and biscuits while Toby showed me the floor plan. 'Bedrooms run down either side of the corridor with a basic kitchenette and bathrooms in the middle. Only residential assistants like me get their own ensuite.' He looked pretty happy about this. 'I decided to put all the floor's first-years near each other because you tend to hang out together at the start anyway.' He pointed to a little square on the plan. 'That room's Joad's and next to him is a girl called Kesh. Her real name is Marrakesh, can you believe it? She said she grew up in a commune. Anyway, they have both picked up their keys.'

'Where am I?'

Toby moved his finger further down the corridor. It was just a box like the others but I still felt a thrill. My own room in college, where I was surrounded by other people roughly the same age as me. This was the beginning of something new and we were all at the starting line together.

'You can have that one. It's pretty good. Not next to the bathrooms, might have to give that one to Michael because he's the last to check in. You can hear the toilets flushing and people vomiting. Breakout area is worse though. Drunken first-years talking rubbish all night and it's also where the phone is. Incoming calls only but still. Can drive you mad having to answer it all the time. Gave that room to Joad.'

'Why?'

Toby flashed a wicked smile. 'Seemed appropriate.'

'Who's next to me?'

'Rachel. She's a second-year. Probably make her grand entrance tomorrow.'

Sounds of people moving echoed up from the stairs. 'Must be dinner time.' There was a knock on the door and a solemn-looking boy poked his head through. Square head, John Lennon round glasses, light brown hair that looked like he cut it himself, he was wearing woven leather sandals that would have spelt social death in my town.

'I was told you had my key.'

'Michael Doherty?' Toby guessed, after checking his list, and beckoned him in. 'We were about to send out a search party. You are the lucky last!'

'There was a note on the door.'

'That's right,' said Toby.

'It said you'd be back in five minutes but you were gone for over an hour.'

Turning to hand me my key, Toby arched an eyebrow.

Michael was definitely getting the room nearest the bathroom. I decided to make my excuses and left.

My room was the last one along the corridor. Even though it was still bright outside, the room was subdued. I switched on the overhead fluorescent light, but it buzzed so loudly I turned it back off.

I shut the door and locked it, a good strong lock, and immediately the thought entered my head that Tracey would have approved of it. She put a lock on my bedroom door for me when Mum was dating Gary.

Dumping my bags on the industrial bristle floor, I lay down on the bed and took it all in. Toby's description of the room captured its ambiance, if not its shape. More square. The walls were mouse-coloured, a depressing grey-brown. Blobs of old Blu-tack from the last inhabitant were still stuck on them, and I could smell the ghosts of thousands of cigarettes in the air. It was sparsely furnished with a wooden bookcase, a plastic chair, metal bin and a large laminate desk. There was a mirror over a sink with a small cupboard underneath. Next to it was a much larger cupboard, which later I would be told was referred to as a 'Tardis', because of the incredible amounts of junk that could be squashed inside it, and that was it. Better than a prison cell but not by much.

I lay down on my bed. The blanket itched my skin. I was going to stop thinking about Tracey. I was here and she wasn't. That was the end of it. I would make new friends even if I wasn't used to making polite conversation with strangers. There wasn't much call for that at home. Even less, if you were the town pariah. I had talked to more people today than I had in months. It was exhausting. My mouth hurt from smiling. I decided to skip dinner and stayed where I was, staring up at the ceiling. It was nicotine-stained with funny yellow clouds, round like squashed thought bubbles.

In the end, I sat up and read the information that had been left on my desk. There was a brochure on the history of the college, claiming this was the home of 'high achievers'. The only one I had heard of was a TV show host, who got axed when he had appeared on air drunk. The next piece of paper was headed UNI-SAFE – IT CONCERNS U, about a recent attack by someone wielding a screwdriver. I was used to my mother's gun-loving boyfriends. A screwdriver didn't even seem like the person was trying. I threw all of it into the bin, stood on my bed and gazed out of the window at the empty car park below. The sun was setting. I could see past where the bus had dropped me off and back along to the other residences. Then I turned to look at the river which ran roughly parallel to the road. The noises of the college receded as the buzz from the cicadas swelled, and the world slowed until it was neither day nor night, but something in between.

Chapter 2

Today, I am early for my appointment with Frank, so I sit on a bench near the bus stop where I left from six months ago. That feels like ancient history and it feels like yesterday. Second semester starts next week but I won't be there.

The bench is in the square with the Carillon on one side and the black bones of cherry trees on the other. There is a new tourist information board next to the trees, stating they are a town feature.

It is a raw winter day with a weak sun and there are not many people about. Even the court house across the road is quiet. Just a couple of utes are parked out the front of it. Most of our town is a sprawl of bad 1960s architecture and cheap fibro housing, but the court house was built in good times when people and money sluiced into town and before they slipped away with all the wealth. It's made of faded yellow sandstone with columns, a massive green octagonal dome and a large clock in the centre that probably stopped working last century. Sitting back from the road, behind a wrought-iron fence with stone pillars, it presides over our town. I like to look at it because it doesn't belong here and neither do I.

In primary school we went on an excursion to the police station around the corner and the court house. I was allowed to sit in the judge's chair. Tracey was the accused, standing behind the wooden bars in the dock, telling jokes and cheeking our teacher. Mrs Kelly told me to bring my court to order. I held the gavel in my hand, my fingers still inky from the fingerprinting. It was lighter than I had expected so when I tapped it onto its wooden block, I thought no one would hear it. But it sounded as if I was thumping the bench with a hammer and the result was immediate. Complete silence. I had the power for there to be noise, or for there to be none. Everyone was listening to me.

When I came back to court for Tracey's committal, people were supposed to listen, but it was the lawyers who talked the most, interrupting, objecting and telling me to keep to the question. I realised important people are the ones who ask the questions, not give the answers. But still my answers were enough. During my evidence, Tracey's mother fainted in the court room and the case was adjourned while an ambulance was called.

By then, I was a couple of months into my sessions with Frank and it would be another year before I decided to stop. We often discussed Mrs Cuttmore fainting in the court. She was the only one who believed that the police had the wrong person, and she kept believing right up to the point she heard me, Tracey's best friend, say that they didn't.

I don't like thinking about those days but having to see Frank again brings them back.

A dumpy track-suited woman comes past, pushing a pram with a small child trailing behind her, wailing.

'C'mon Amber,' she yells over her shoulder and I recognise the voice.

She turns to look at Amber, who has thrown herself down on the path in silent protest. 'If you don't get up, I'm gonna belt ya one,' she threatens, but her heart isn't in it. Instead, she jerks the pram to a halt and walks towards the child.

As she comes marching back, child wrestling under her arm, she looks my way and stops short in surprise.

'Penny Sheppard,' she says.

I try to think of her name. She was the year above but left school to have a baby. She is fatter than I remember. Maybe she is pregnant again. Maybe that's just how she looks now.

'I can't believe it. I saw you on telly.' Her eyes widen, rimmed with black eyeliner, as the kid scrabbles down her side and starts playing with the pebbles. Despite the make-up, she looks washed out and faded, but seeing her face properly, I remember day-glo socks and a 'Choose Life' t-shirt and 'Kim' pops into my head.

'I was makin' the kids' tea and the news came on and there you were ... I never have it on that channel, but the kids lost the remote ... and it was you. I wasn't sure at first, but you were in the paper and that. Couldn't believe it. Mum says trouble follows you round like a bad smell, but I said this time wasn't your fault.'

Not like last time are the unspoken words that curl around us.

The little girl stares up at me, trying to work out the reason for her mother's excitement, but soon gives up and begins singing quietly to herself while picking up pebbles.

'Been back long?' Kim asks.

'A few weeks.'

'Where you stayin'?'

'At Mum's. How about you?'

'Lee's working up at the abattoir, two hours' drive away. Told him I'm not leavin' town. So, I'm back home and all.'

There is a shared moment of resignation. She sits down on the seat next to me and pulls a packet of cigarettes from her handbag. The name Lee brings a memory of a large, dark-haired sullen boy. He used to get into fights on the football field. Tracey once kissed him at the Blue Light Disco.

'Wanna smoke?'

I shake my head. There is a whimper from the pram, and Kim grabs the handle and rattles it back and forth.

'Teethin'.'

I nod. She is the first person my age I have spoken to since I left university.

'Youse seen anyone from school?'

That she even asks this question, that she has stopped to talk to me in the first place, makes me hope that perhaps people have forgotten about what happened three years ago and have moved on to hating someone else. And I wonder if that could really be possible.

Kim is a font of information. Girls, whose names I remember but faces I don't, were having babies. A boy we both knew got killed in a car accident. Another has been busted for growing cannabis. Mostly she whinges about hardly ever getting to go out. Tracey and I used to make fun of people like Kim who spend their whole lives in this town. Now, I am happy to listen all morning.

'It's footy season, so we only see Lee if we visit him. Plays for his town's team. Might as well be a single mum. I mean the pay's good and he wants to save up for our own house and get married, but what's the point if you never see them? I'm gonna find someone else and the first he'll know about it is when I leave the kids on his doorstep.'

Amber comes over and starts tugging at her mother. 'Need to go wee, need to go wee.'

But it is all too late. The little girl stands there bow-legged, a wet patch at her crotch and a small puddle underneath her. She looks up at her mother fearfully but Kim sits there, ignoring her completely and Amber goes back to playing with her small pyramid of stones. When Kim finishes her cigarette, she sighs, crushes the end of it on the bench and flicks it onto the gravel, near her daughter.

'Anyway, couldn't believe it when I saw you on the news. Nasty scar you've got but get a fringe and you won't even know it's there.'

I automatically pat my forehead and feel the long pucker under my fingers.

Kim stands up and releases the brake of the pram, when I say to her, 'Maybe we could meet up at the pub.' But even before I finish the sentence, I can see that I'm wrong. She fusses around, cigarettes back in the handbag, checking if the baby is still asleep, not looking at me.

'Na, not this weekend. Catching up with Julie ... Julie Cuttmore. Getting married in a few weeks, so it's kinda like her hens' night.'

She is beginning to regret her decision to stop and talk to me.

'Seeyathen.' She speaks too quickly as she grabs Amber's arm. 'Muuum, that hurts.'

'At the pub sometime,' I find myself saying, and she tries to smile with her mouth, but her eyes look frightened, and she hurries away.

I have seen that look before.

It was in the senior locker room. The only time they got me. Almost a year after the committal. Lying on the floor, my nose bleeding after they had pushed me into the lockers. Julie Cuttmore was sitting across my chest, her knees digging into my arms.

She leant down near my ear, so close I could feel the words on my skin. 'It was your fault she did it. All your fault. You fucking murderer.'

A ring of girls surrounded us, an early-warning system for teachers. I squinted up, to concentrate on something that wasn't Julie, thinking I deserved this. It was Kim's face that was blurred and then came into focus, biting her lip as she stared down at me, trying to be tough, but looking close to tears.

Chapter 3

'What on earth are you wearing?' asked Toby, as I walked past his room on the way down to dinner. 'You look like Little Bo Peep.'

It was the Thursday night of Orientation Week and I was wearing a dress I hated. A floral print in blue and pink. It was maiden and matron all at once, a dress that good girls wore, a dress that you wore to court to put all the blame on someone else. It was the only dress I owned.

'Rachel told me we had to wear something formal to dinner before we got changed for the bar crawl. She said it was college tradition.'

I met Rachel the day after I arrived. Ballerina-scrawny, bobbed hair that couldn't quite decide if it was red or blonde, frecklish skin, she had knocked on my door, scrounging a cigarette. By the time I explained I didn't smoke, she was sprawled across my bed, telling me all about herself.

A walking exclamation mark of a person, she was Australian, but had grown up in the United States, which explained her accent, a fluctuating mix of drawl and twang. Sometimes it was almost all Australian, missing consonants and drawn-out vowels, then it would revert and sound exactly like the American accents you hear on TV. This was her second year at university and most of her schooling beforehand had been private tutors. Her parents were divorced and both had remarried. Her father, a rich businessman, lived in a mansion on a harbour while her diplomat mother worked in embassies around the world. She was enrolled in Asian Studies and learning Japanese.

She had been curious about how I had scored the bursary but I deflected the conversation back to her.

'Diplomats' kids are always fucked up,' she told me with an odd note of pride. 'Myself included.'

'Well that explains it,' Toby said now, eyeing the dress with distaste. 'Rachel's a lot of fun but don't believe a word she says. She's just taking advantage of innocent little first-years.'

I felt a flicker of annoyance. Trying to fit in at college,

while suffering from a continuous hangover, was hard enough without someone deliberately trying to trip me up.

'Get changed before anyone sees you. Then burn it.' Toby pushed me back but I wasn't quick enough. Joad was coming out of his room as I walked past. He was a rich farmer's kid from up north, biding time at university before returning to the landed gentry to continue the family fortune. I was prepared to try and not hate him on principle, but my good intentions didn't last long.

Smirking, he stood in the middle of the corridor. 'I didn't know you were Amish.'

I tried to walk past, but he moved quickly to block me.

'The Laura Ingalls look suits you. Maybe you should plait your hair or wear a bonnet,' and he moved closer and touched one of the flower-shaped buttons near my chest.

'That's not funny,' I said, pushing his hand away.

He tried again, but this time it was more of a grab for the general area.

'Don't touch me,' I said, louder now.

'You saving yourself for marriage to some first cousin or are you here to have some fun?' Close up, his face was a series of razor-sharp points, an angular chin, a tapered nose, a serrated tongue.

'I don't think Pen's finding it fun,' said a deadpan voice. It was Michael, who had been sitting in the breakout space and was now leaning around the corner, looking at both of us.

Joad turned towards him. 'So what? I was.' His attention off me, I quickly scooted off in the direction of my room, nodding my thanks to Michael as I left.

When I eventually got downstairs, now dressed in the standard student uniform of t-shirt, ripped jeans and Doc Martens, I saw Rachel was reading the blackboard menu outside the dining hall.

'Not chilli con carne already, I am definitely going vegetarian this year,' she said loudly, and pushed her way into the queue for dinner, in front of two first-year girls, who scowled, but didn't say anything.

I decided to pretend I hadn't been fooled by Rachel. She had meant it as a joke. That was all. I was just out of practice with this sort of thing. It wasn't her fault that Joad was a jerk.

I stopped and read the blackboard. Chilli con carne sounded all right to me. When I headed to join the back of the queue, Rachel noticed me walking past, and pulled me into the line, behind her.

'Come on, they won't mind if you cut in.' But when I turned around, their faces told me they did.

'Last year, all I ate the whole frickin' time was salad,' Rachel continued. 'And I know for a fact that Maggies are having pizza tonight.' An all-girl Catholic residence, Magdalene College was the concrete cloister next door.

The queue shuffled forward, moving through a side entrance into the cafeteria-style serving area.

'And he's the reason why I almost got malnutrition last year. I was sure they were going to fire him.' She pointed to a guy behind the counter, wearing a splattered apron, his stringy hair pulled back in a ponytail. Serving another student, he was within earshot of our conversation. 'My father always told me never to trust a thin chef or a man wearing a bow tie.'

The chef turned to Rachel, glaring as though his father had warned him about skinny girls with big mouths.

'What are you having?' Under his hairnet, he had the face of an albino ferret.

'Vegetarian.' Rachel affected a bored drawl.

'I don't remember you being vegetarian last year,' he said.

'Yeah, well I converted to Buddhism in the holidays and I'm a vegetarian now.'

'Buddhism,' he repeated sarcastically.

'Richard Gere, Dalai Lama, that kind of shit.'

He narrowed his eyes and pointed his tongs at her, splattering greasy droplets over the countertop. 'I'll be keeping my eye on you, Sunshine. I only make a set amount of veggie meals here, orders of the Sub-Dean. So, there'll be no going back to meat when it suits you.'

Rachel gave him a 'whatever' look, grabbed the plate

and put it on her tray. Wincing, I glanced at the chilli con carne, the consistency of wet cement, and decided to turn vegetarian as well. The cook committed my face to memory, before handing me two blanched white slugs of cannelloni in a sea of pink water, without comment.

We found a couple of empty seats near Toby. The dining room was a football pitch of a room with exposed beams and wooden floor. Long rectangular tables were lined up in regimental rows. Noise bounced around it and when it was busy you had to lean in to hear what your neighbour was saying. The scraping of cutlery on plates and chairs on the floor coming from around us echoed through my skull. Toby gave a knowing smile at my clothes and then went back to assaulting his plate with double helpings of everything. With a full mouth he asked, 'Did the budding attorney-at-law enjoy her introductory tutorial?'

Lectures didn't start until the following week but I had attended the getting-to-know-you session that afternoon at Law School. The place was overrun with people I despised, mostly rich private school kids trying to disguise the fact that they would, one day, inherit the earth, directly from their parents.

'It was all right,' I said.

'Did you smell the fear?' he continued. 'That you're no longer the smartest person in the class?'

That was an altogether too accurate description of how I

had felt, but I tried to pretend otherwise, because sitting next to Toby was Rogan. Broad shoulders, high cheekbones and dark hair, he was poster-boy handsome. The type of boy every girl in the room knew the name of within minutes.

'There was a policeman in my tutorial,' I said, trying to be fascinating.

Rachel, who had been nibbling around her dinner, was instantly horrified. 'Really? In a uniform?'

I shook my head and instantly regretted it. Everyone at college had been drunk since Sunday and I was hung over almost to the point of dumbness. Sudden movements hurt.

'Did he have a moustache?' asked Toby.

'Neat and regimental.'

'Shame,' said Toby. 'I prefer mine a bit more rugged lumberjack.'

'What was he doing in your tutorial?' Rachel asked suspiciously.

'Taking notes, of course.' Out of the corner of my eye, I noticed Rogan was listening.

'You're kidding,' said Rachel. 'What sort of fascist state is this university? There should be laws against it.'

'Perhaps there should be police in every tutorial ensuring that the police don't enter,' I said innocently.

'Very funny.' Rachel gave me a shrewd look which she converted to a mulish pout for the rest of the table.

Toby asked, 'But what was he doing there?'

'He's a student.'

Almost giddy with relief, I smiled down at my dinner. I was in a place where I could say the word 'police' without a stunned silence following and people beginning to whisper about me the moment I turned away. That realisation more than made up for the pain in my head.

Rachel changed the subject. 'Anyway, who has their outfit ready for tonight? If I knew we were wearing red again, I wouldn't have traded my favourite bra last year.'

She frowned, but was distracted by Kesh, who beetled her way across to our table, head bowed, eyes on the floor. A round girl dominated by enormous breasts, I had only seen Kesh in baggy t-shirts and shapeless dresses, but tonight she had squeezed herself into a tight red singlet which threatened to disintegrate. Appreciative hoots, whistles and applause came from the surrounding tables and embarrassment stained her face, neck and the more than ample portion of skin on display.

The theme for the bar crawl was the Rubik's Cube. Each college had been given a particular colour to wear. We were supposed to wear six items of red to swap with strangers from the other colleges, while drinking as much as was humanly possible. I just didn't want to end up naked, which seemed to be a common outcome, according to Toby.

'She is so gullible. Arts student, so that explains it,' Rachel murmured to me. 'Couldn't fool you though.'

I smiled like it hadn't even been a possibility.

Tears glinting, Kesh slumped into the seat opposite me.

'Rachel,' she whispered. 'You said everyone here would be dressed in red. You told me we had to come down to dinner dressed for tonight.'

'Aww, just a first-year tease,' said Rachel. 'I'm sure someone else will turn up soon.'

'I think you look really *great* in it.' It was a tall long-faced girl from the table behind us, who pushed her chair back until it was almost level with Kesh. Her nostrils flared, almost equine-like, as she drawled out these words, which teetered on the edge of sarcasm. Kesh didn't seem to notice, the ghost of a hopeful smile on her face. Behind the girl, I could see several people sniggering.

'It's a *huge* improvement,' said the girl. Her eyes, wide with mock-innocence, flickered over to Rogan at the end of our table. 'And scarlet ... well it matches your complexion.' There was an explosion of laughter behind us and it dawned on Kesh that this was only more torment. Miserably, she hunched her shoulders and dropped her head, pretending to be engrossed in dinner.

'Get stuffed, Emelia,' said Rachel. 'Why don't you go back to torturing the hired help.'

I realised this must be Emelia Manaway, who was

something of a college celebrity. According to Rachel, Emelia's family had made a lot of money in dry cleaning and she would inherit a million dollars when she turned twenty-one. What was definitely true was that she owned a brand new midnight-blue Honda Prelude which stood out in our college carpark, amongst the handful of beat up Nissan Bluebirds and rusting Toyota Corollas. Rachel claimed that Emelia's next car was going to get upgraded to a BMW.

Rogan got up from the table, his plate empty. 'Meet me in the courtyard with the garbage bin, Toby. I'll get the booze now.' Toby nodded and continued to bulldoze his way through a second helping.

'Is that for the bar crawl, Rogan?' called out Emelia, ignoring Rachel. 'Do you need a hand?'

I watched as she followed him across the room to where the dirty plates were stacked. Rachel noticed.

'You think he's cute, don't you?' she said.

'No,' I answered, and tried to stop my face from telegraphing the truth. 'I was just thinking I've never heard the name Rogan before. That's all.'

'His real name is Joshua,' she said to me. 'I don't know why they call him Rogan.'

'After the curry,' explained Toby. 'Had five helpings of it during the curry-eating competition in Bush Week last year. I don't think he's managed to eat one since.'

46

'What's so impressive about that?' said Rachel.

'Afterwards, they found out it had been made with dog food.'

Those at the table who had chosen the meat option began to look at their plates suspiciously.

'Anyway, he's always got plenty of cash, so Emelia won't be able to bribe him to be her boyfriend,' Rachel continued. 'People think he's gorgeous but there's something a bit weak about the chin, don't you think?'

I didn't. Watching him chatting to a couple of later-year students, I thought he was perfect, but then I realised Rachel was looking at me with a smile on her face. I turned back to my dinner.

'What about . . .' began Kesh, but Rachel interrupted her, hissing, 'Quick, don't make eye contact or she'll come over.'

The entire table immediately looked up and started gazing around the dining hall. There was constant movement around us, like pigeons at a park, but it was obvious who she was referring to. Leiza felt the gaze, turned in our direction and launched herself at us.

'Hello, I think I've met everyone here. If you don't know me, my name is Leiza. You may not have heard but there was another attack on campus last night. A girl from Chifley was hurt. I have a petition here demanding the university increase campus security.' She thrust a piece of paper and a pen at Kesh who, flustered, quickly signed and handed it to me.

Rachel looked at Leiza. 'Is this that Screwdriver Man thing we all got notices about?'

'Yes, I believe that's what they are calling the assailant, but my petition ...'

Rachel interrupted. 'Come on, *Screwdriver Man*? Is that the best we can come up with? Sounds more likely to put up your bookshelves than rape you. DIY not GBH.'

'Call him Jack the Ripper for all I care. That girl needed medical attention and besides, my petition goes much further,' said Leiza firmly. 'Better lighting, more security patrols.'

I looked down at the petition and saw a long list of demands, including 'wimmin's room'.

'Jesus, where do you get this stuff from?' Rachel asked, reading over my shoulder. 'And what does a wimmin's room have to do with security?'

Leiza turned her back towards Rachel and addressed herself in the direction of the nearest 'wimmin', Kesh and myself.

'A wimmin's room would be a refuge from the oppressive male patriarchy that dominates this university ...'

Toby interrupted. 'Leiza, the first attack was on a Marchmain boy. As a gay Asian-Australian, if anyone is going to be oppressed here, it will be me. No one is oppressing you.'

'Can we start?' Then Rachel laughed, pleased with herself.

Kesh, who had been quietly listening, asked, 'How many people have signed so far?'

'Congratulations. You're the first,' and Leiza put her arm on Kesh's shoulder in a show of sisterly support.

Kesh slumped further into her seat.

'Tell you what,' said Toby. 'I'll sign your petition on one condition.' He grabbed the paper off me and began to write.

'Male voices are not part of this discourse,' Leiza said. 'Give it back.' But he fended her off until he signed his name with a flourish. Leiza leant across the table to read what he had written. 'Toby, you are completely sexist.'

He feigned shock. 'You aren't trying to gag a minority voice, are you?' He stood up and, putting his hand on his heart, proclaimed, 'I am only too happy to support your fight for a room for women, as long as you support a men's room as well.'

Leiza was so angry she could barely speak.

'You've convinced me, Toby. I'll sign up,' said Rachel. She passed it down the table. Everyone signed.

'You are making a mockery of a serious issue,' Leiza fumed, as a dark-haired girl from the next table came over and scribbled 'Annabel', surname illegible.

'God, you take these things so seriously,' said Rachel. 'Lighten up a little.'

Leiza narrowed her eyes and gave Rachel a scathing glare but said nothing. Instead, she grabbed the petition and stormed off to another table at the far end of the hall.

'If looks could kill,' said Toby, who picked up his fork to resume eating. 'You better hope she doesn't get you as a target in the Murder Game, Rach.'

Chapter 4

Much later that night, I sat next to Kesh on a grassy bank near the river. At a distance, the river was charming and picturesque, especially as the night was lusciously warm for the tail end of summer. But from where I sat, you could smell rotting vegetation and see tangled litter pushed up against the stones. Upstream from us, a shopping trolley was slowly turning to rust.

The bar crawl had started on the far side of campus and we had spent most of our night stumbling our way back home between drinks, Scullin being the final stop. I had traded some ugly red plastic clip-on earrings for an oversized orange t-shirt which I had tied around my middle. Kesh had borrowed a red-checked flannelette shirt, which she wore as camouflage over the singlet, and had gained a blue headband and one white sock. She had also thrown up two colleges ago and was now pretending to feel much better.

Other people in various hues were taking a breather nearby. Right beside us, a second-year student from our college was lying on the ground next to a paralytically drunk girl dressed predominantly in green. He was wearing a red bandana and a pair of large red ski-gloves. 'Really, my life's ambition is to write a manifesto, you know, like Marx and Engels,' he said, as a glove began to creep up under her dress.

I looked away and caught sight of Michael sitting in the shadows of a large willow tree. Dressed in dark shorts and top, he was the only person without any bright colours attached to him. Instead, he sat on the periphery of it all, watching the world from a distance. A familiar-looking boy, dressed in jeans, a red t-shirt and sporting an electric-blue silk scarf, was talking to him. Michael shook his head, and shrugging, the boy came up to us, and asked if we wanted to score. I tried to make my 'no thanks' relaxed and non-judgmental, but he was indifferent to the rejection and went to ply his trade elsewhere. I knew that I should go and tell Michael I appreciated him rescuing me from Joad, but this late in the night it felt like it was easier to pretend the whole thing had never happened.

'That's Stoner,' Kesh whispered to me, when the boy with the blue scarf was far enough away.

'That can't be his real name,' I said.

'Evan, I think. He's on second-floor Forde with all the druggies.'

Stoner was standing about twenty metres away from us, watching a raggle-taggle group all in white who had appeared on the opposite side of the bank. The river was narrow here, so we could see them clearly. The leader, thickset with blonde curly hair, was dressed in a cream cotton suit and a buttercup yellow cravat. He opened his arms wide, one hand holding a boater hat, the other a champagne bottle with an orange label. He then took a large swig, and shouted over, 'It's heaven with strawberries,' bursting into laughter. But he soon stopped as he stared hard across the river to our side. He pointed something out to his comrades, then yelled, 'Stop, Stoner, I want to talk to you.'

Stoner took no notice of him and began a transaction involving money and quick handshakes with a group further along the bank.

'White is Maggies' colour, isn't it?' said Kesh. 'I thought that was a girl's-only college.'

'Maybe they swapped all their clothes with the friendly inhabitants,' I answered.

There was only one girl I could see amongst the group. She sat down on the river bank, quite separate from the mayhem around her. The boy in the cotton suit gave her a rough kiss on her head. It seemed that some of the boys had decided to swim across to our side and were stripping off. As more flesh was displayed ('Oh my,' said Kesh) the girl seemed quite unperturbed, just looking dreamily at the river. Wearing a white sundress that might have been a nightgown, with straw-coloured long hair parted in the middle, she looked like a virginal sacrifice from a B-grade horror film.

The boy in the cotton suit didn't take any clothes off. Instead, he hopped onto the shoulders of two of the naked boys, who began carrying him into the water, like this was some victory lap. A third boy, grabbing all the discarded clothes, balanced them on top of his head and followed them across. The water must have been cold, judging by their yells. The leader sat there unperturbed, taking sips of his bottle, as they splashed their way across to us. Turning, I noticed Stoner had disappeared into the darkness.

Once they got to our side, the leader slipped onto the bank. He tipped his hat to us. At his arrival, the red bandana boy, who had dispensed with the ski gloves, pulled the slightly less green-clad girl clumsily to standing, and vanished into the shrubs behind us in the search for somewhere more private. The naked boys began to put their clothes back on, as Kesh stared fixedly at a spot in front of her feet.

'Where did that fucker go?' asked one of the boys. 'Can't be too far away,' said another.

The boy in the suit walked up to us. 'Good evening.' He made a low bow.

'Hello,' I said. Kesh was a bit overwhelmed.

'I was wondering if you know Stoner? You were just talking to him.'

'Sure,' I said. 'We're at college with him.'

'Can I ask, and I understand this may be a delicate matter, but was he peddling his wares?'

'He-asked-us-if-we-want-to-score,' said Kesh, in an excitable squeak.

'See, I told you, Nico,' said one now-clothed boy. 'He was selling at the bar during the week. Death Riders' gear.'

'After what they did to Max, we need to send a message,' said the other.

Nico nodded. 'He can't have got far. You start looking for him.' He then walked down to the river and yelled across at the girl who was still sitting on the other side.

'Alice,' he called. 'Are you going to come across?'

Lifting her gaze, she shook her head.

'Walk down to the bridge. I'll meet you there.'

She nodded and he began to run down the path. The rest of the boys headed over the road and up to the oval, on their quest to find Stoner. There were hundreds of people there, dancing between sprinklers shooting a Morse code of silver dashes and dots of water onto the grass. Looking at the crowd, I could see Rachel gesticulating wildly in the middle of them. She hip-and-shouldered the nearest person, who careened into the others, resulting in chaos. Catching sight of us, she came running up.

'So there you are,' she said. 'I've been looking for you everywhere.'

She collapsed on the ground next to me. Her red handkerchief of a dress was stained and ripped along the neckline, exposing a white bra strap.

'How are you?' I asked.

'Oh, average to bad.'

A dark-blue car drove along the road, swerving to miss some drunken revellers, before coming to a stop, letting the occupants chat to a passer-by. It then accelerated off into the distance.

Rachel propped herself up onto her elbows to look.

'Just Emelia making her dramatic exit,' she said. 'You know she threw some punch over me earlier.' Rachel gestured at her dress. 'Didn't matter, because I threw a beer over her. Got her full in the face.'

'Why did she do that?' I asked.

'I was getting her back for teasing Kesh.'

I was amazed at her gall at recasting herself as Kesh's defender.

'What did you say to her?' asked Kesh, who was looking ill again.

'I just told everyone why she's slumming it amongst the plebs at this university. Did you know, last year her mother left her father, after she found him in bed with their cook?' Rachel paused, pushing her hair back off her face. 'Their male cook.'

Kesh gasped. 'Rachel, you didn't.'

'I did. She's lying low and will transfer back home when people forget.'

That kind of story would have the half-life of uranium in my town.

'Everyone's got skeletons. Your secrets are what make you different. What make you interesting. She's just pissed off because it's not a secret any more.'

Flexing a numb foot, I thought that all of it was pretty funny.

Next to me, Kesh put her head in her hands and groaned, 'I don't feel very well.' Ignoring her, Rachel lay back down again, her arms outstretched. A gold disc, engraved with her name, and attached to a chain circling her ankle, caught the moonlight. I watched her warily. There was something feline about her, all purring affection one moment and then clawing the next. It was entertaining as long as you weren't the person getting scratched.

Her right arm was close to where I began to pick at the

grass. Silver bangles had worked their way up to her elbow. I noticed, for the first time, a faint glow in the dark. There were white scars on the inside of her arm, near her wrist, as if someone had underlined something important on an earlier page.

Rachel saw where I was looking and immediately sat up. She turned her arm away, pulling down her bangles all at once. I pretended I hadn't seen anything.

'Truth or Dare,' she said. 'C'mon, let's play.'

'I'm going to be sick,' announced Kesh, running into the nearest bushes.

'Are you all right?' I called after her. She didn't answer. Instead, we heard a gut-wrenching splatter and some loud yells from the bandana boy whose activities she had interrupted.

'She'll be fine,' said Rachel. 'Better out than in.'

'Speak for yourself,' said Toby, wandering up. He was wearing a white singlet, with red sequin shorts, non-matching green and orange socks, and a blue whistle around his neck. He was dragging a large plastic rubbish bin with one hand and holding a stack of paper cups in the other.

'You're missing yellow,' said Rachel.

'Darling, I am the Yellow Peril. Now who fancies a drink? I've stolen what's left of the Scullin punch.'

'What's in it?' I asked.

'A complicated recipe. Loads of red cordial and extremely

cheap vodka. I insist you have some.' He grabbed a ladle from the bottom of the bin, and sloshed liquid the colour of a stop sign into a cup.

'Drink me,' he said, as he handed it over.

I tried not to think about it coming out of a bin.

Sensing my reluctance, Toby said, 'It could be worse. I could have stolen Maggies' punch.'

'Vodka and . . .?' I asked.

'Milk,' Toby answered. 'Known as a Pale Mary.'

My stomach curdled at the thought.

'Scull for Scullin,' Rachel said, as we ceremonially rubbed the waxed cups together. After a night of drinking too much beer, it tasted as though I was gulping down medicine, syrupy sweet with a ferocious after-burn.

'You interrupted us playing a game of Truth or Dare,' said Rachel. 'I'm going first.'

'Good, what do you pick?' said Toby.

'Truth,' she said.

'Lucky for you. I was going to make you go skinny dipping in the river. Those Marchie boys gave me the idea,' said Toby.

'Who are they?' I asked.

'Marchmain Club. Wear white, drink champagne and beat teddy bears with hairbrushes. So of course they take a mountain of drugs. Nico, in particular, is a total mad fucker. He always has the best stuff though.'

'So there's Maggies and Marchies, and tonight they are both wearing white.'

'Yes,' said Toby. 'But tomorrow the Marchies will still be wearing white and open for business. So, back to the matter in hand. What to ask Rachel?'

Shaking my head at the nonsense of it all, I stretched out on the grass and gazed up at the sky. I was managing to stay on the right side of being pleasantly unselfconsciously drunk and the moon seemed to be smiling down on it all.

'I can't be bothered to come up with anything good,' said Toby. 'Tell us the most recent bit of scandal that you've heard.'

'Well, I did hear a bit of juicy gossip about our new Master.'

'About Marcus?' asked Toby. 'Fabulous.'

'It was in his last job, when he was acting Vice Chancellor. This kid was charged with plagiarism or something and Marcus tried to hush it up but instead made everything much worse. There was an investigation into it, and they found that Marcus had previously stopped him from getting kicked out of college for drug use. And then they also found Marcus had been overspending on his expenses account, giving money to the boy. So he was forced to resign before he got the sack and that's how he ended up here. A bit of a step down from his fancy sandstone university.'

Thinking the information over, I asked, 'Was Marcus

having a relationship with him?' It seemed that every male around me suddenly had the potential to be gay.

Instinctively, both Rachel and I turned to Toby.

'Why are you looking at me?' he asked.

'Well, you are the expert in these matters,' said Rachel.

Toby pulled a mock serious face. 'Marcus isn't gay.'

Rachel frowned. 'He must be or that story makes no sense at all. Anyway, Pen's turn next.'

'All right,' said Toby. 'Who do you fancy at college?'

Rachel snorted. 'That's obvious. She was making eyes at Rogan over dinner.'

A denial caught in my throat as I sobered up quickly. I couldn't believe I had been that transparent.

'No, Pen has to tell us the worse thing she has ever done.'

'Hang on,' I said, getting my voice to work. 'I didn't get a chance to pick.'

'Pick truth,' said Rachel. 'You look so innocent but life in a small town is so incestuous and twisted. Lust bubbling under the surface.'

'Dare,' I said firmly.

'Boring,' said Toby.

'I'm sure we can make this fun,' said Rachel. 'You have to kiss the nearest boy . . .'

'Done,' I said, relieved that it wasn't worse and moving towards Toby.

61

'That isn't Tobias,' she finished.

'This is so high school,' said Toby. 'What's next, spin the bottle? Who's the nearest?' He looked about us.

'Well, whoever is in the bushes is otherwise engaged, so that means it's the floor bore, Michael,' said Rachel.

'Shh, Rachel, he'll hear you,' I said. 'Besides, Michael's OK.'

'Have you talked to him? Social skills none. Must be from an all-boys' school.'

'Watch it, lady,' said Toby. 'I went to an all-boys' school.'

'Still, that's the dare,' said Rachel.

'I think I better check on Kesh,' I said.

'No,' said Rachel firmly. 'Toby's her RA. He'll check. You can't be a welsher. Besides, it will probably be the first time Michael has ever been kissed.'

Michael hadn't moved from where he had been sitting in front of the willow tree. He gave no outward sign he had heard any of this, though he clearly was within listening distance.

'Yes,' said Toby. 'Don't be a wet blanket.' He shooed me away.

I got slowly to my feet. My numb foot now had pins and needles. Stumbling, I walked up towards Michael and sat down next to him, deliberately in the shadows, on the far side from Rachel.

'Hello,' I said, feeling uncomfortable. I'd never talked to Michael properly before and didn't really know anything about him, other than he studied Science. 'Having a good night?'

He gave me a look which said he had heard every word of our conversation, 'OK, I guess.'

Voices rang out behind us, and a group of people, all barefoot and flowing dresses, came down from the oval. I watched them walk past. A girl with a wild untangled mane seemed to have something large and white moving in her hair.

'It's a rat,' Michael said, following my gaze. 'She lives at Chifley. I met her earlier tonight.'

'She lives with a rat in her college room?' I asked. 'That's disgusting.'

'Apparently, rats are quite easy to care for. She told me one of her friends had a rabbit, but it nibbled the light cord and was fried. Rats are smarter.'

I couldn't really think of anything to say at this, so I turned back towards Rachel. Kesh had joined them again and was sitting there looking wan. Rachel was peering over at me, an amused look on her face.

'Um, Michael ... I don't suppose you heard what we were saying before. You see, we're playing ...'

'I heard.'

'Oh, good. So you understand that I'm supposed to ...'

'Do what Rachel says.'

'Well ... there's more to it than just doing what Rachel says.'

'Really? She told you to wear that dress tonight, and you did. I heard you talking about it with Toby.'

He had a point.

'About that, thanks for stopping Joad. I should have said that first off. It was kind of you.'

His round glasses reflected in the moonlight. 'I thought university would be different. That you could be yourself here and people would appreciate that. Instead, there are lots of people like Joad and everyone's too busy being fake, pretending to have a good time, pretending to be something they're not, doing what they're told. I don't understand why.'

'That girl with the rat?' I asked, not really sure what he was getting at.

'Yes, her. And those Marchmains. And this whole Rubik's Cube thing. It's all fake.'

A yell from Rachel, 'Tongue included,' and then I heard Toby and her start to chant, 'Why are we waiting? W-h-y ... are ... we ... w-aiting?'

'OK, Michael, I agree.' I was really only listening to Toby and Rachel, desperately hoping their chanting didn't attract a bigger crowd. 'But now what I want to do is kiss you, if that's all right with you.'

'Only if you want to, not because Rachel said.'

'No, I really want to.' And I did, justifying it to myself as the equivalent of a non-verbal thank you. I felt exposed next to Michael, like I was out of the circle and on my own. I wanted to get back to the safety of the pack and watch Rachel demand dares or truths from other people.

So we kissed.

There were loud whoops from the onlookers.

Behind the lens, his pale irises looked as though the colour had been washed out of them.

'You're different, Pen. You don't have to be like the other people here. They're not important.'

'Maybe I'm not that important either,' I said, standing up. 'Thanks though for before. I owe you one.'

As I walked back towards the others, a long rainbow conga line of people came streaming down from the oval. Rachel jumped to the front of it, blowing on a whistle, as if she was leading the army band. It snaked past me, people attaching themselves to it. Kesh, a pale blur in the middle, held out her arm, which I grabbed with the desperation of a drowning person without a backward glance at Michael, and we clumsily shuffled our way along the river bank, across the road and up towards Scullin. As we snaked our way up towards the entrance, I saw someone watching us from one of the rooms on the second floor of Page Tower. It

65

looked like Marcus, but just then Kesh stumbled and I almost fell over. By the time I turned back, the room's light was switched off and the person was gone.

*

Frank is all smiles today, nodding encouragingly. Maybe he didn't think I'd start writing. It's a fortnight since he told me I had to do it. I tried to get an earlier appointment so I can get this over and done with but Ivy, in her usual passive aggressive way, has scheduled me in every second Tuesday morning. It's payback for cheeking her last time.

'How did you feel when he kissed you?' asks Frank.

Already, I am lying to him. As far as Frank knows, a stranger kissed me. Whether he can sense that lie, I don't know. He doesn't come straight out and accuse me of it, but still, for some reason, he keeps returning to it.

'It was just a kiss.'

'But it's not just a kiss, is it? You were the centre of attention for that moment. What emotions did you feel?'

'There was hardly anyone else paying attention. And it was pretty chaste compared to what else was happening.'

'But how did it make you feel? The first thing that went through your mind.' Frank is big on initial reactions and gut instinct.

'It was a dumb kiss. He probably kissed me just because

I was the first person he saw. I wasn't picked out for any-thing special.'

'You're avoiding saying how it made you feel.'

'I don't know.'

'A person might feel flattered with the attention. Some people could have felt a little violated, uncomfortable that their personal space has been invaded. For most people the first few months away at university, separated from family and everyone they know, are an intense experience. People fall in love, become infatuated, are lonely, engage in risky behaviour to be noticed, to make a connection. Perhaps that was what that boy was doing when he kissed you, trying to make a connection. So, I'm exploring how you felt about it.'

'What does it matter?'

'Most of what you have told me about today, meeting Marcus, sitting in the dining hall, you describe it as if you were a spectator, an observer. You notice what's hanging on the wall. The picture of the boy in the office. You describe this kiss as though it's another picture. Something you saw, not something you felt.'

I wonder what he would come up with if I tell him that I did the kissing. I expect he'd twist it around and say, as Michael had, that it was Rachel's decision and not mine, which only proves his hypothesis. You can't win with psy-chiatrists.

'It was just a kiss,' I repeat, fed up. 'Tell me what the answer is and I'll say it.'

'That's not my role here. You know that.'

I want to tell him that his role is to fill out the damn report for my lawyer and make it sound good. But I don't. Instead I glare at a spot of chipped paint behind his head. It is a patch of white about the size of a ten cent piece and if this was my office, I'd have to pick at it until all the light-green paint was pulled off and the whole wall was white again. But maybe Frank's too busy picking at his patients to notice.

'Pen, last time you were in treatment you decided to end it abruptly, against my advice. If we are going to do it properly this time, I need you to commit to what we are trying to do. So, let's continue. How did the kiss make you feel?'

'It was fun. Lighthearted. Just part of the night.'

'Did you ever see this boy again?'

'No, never,' I say. 'Don't even know his name.'

'Well, let's talk about some of the other people you mentioned. Was it easy to make friends at uni?'

And even though I am glad to have got the conversation away from Michael, I find it hard to answer this question.

'I guess so. There were so many people to meet all at once.'

'And yet all the people you talk about in detail seem to be from the same floor as you. Not such a wide group. Friends through geography.'

'They were the people I met first.' I am trying not to

sound defensive but this seems like a pretty hypocritical comment seeing Frank is married to his receptionist. 'Geography probably shapes most friendships. You work with people, go to uni with people, that sort of thing. You do the same things at the same time. Doesn't mean it's not a real relationship.'

'It doesn't guarantee a lasting friendship either. Take you and Tracey,' he says.

Her name is like a punch in the face.

'What?'

'Maybe what you and Tracey had was a school friendship. Maybe given the chance it wouldn't have survived a change in geography. A friendship that ends abruptly can colour our view of it, we mythologise it into something that it wasn't. Then perhaps later we can see that it had a natural end anyway. What we thought was a road would have turned out to be a cul-de-sac.'

I bet he practised that analogy in the mirror this morning. He doesn't understand anything. Tracey is still my friend now despite what he might think. She will always be my friend. For a moment I want to shout this at him, but I bottle it up. I have had to lock away everything to do with Tracey. None of it is up for discussion.

'I think we've made a good start today.' Frank puts on a benevolent face like I'm lucky he has so much insight and wisdom to share with me. 'See you in a fortnight.'

Chapter 5

'But really, I don't understand what is actually sexist about the Murder Game,' said Joyce, known only to his parents as James, as he squirted tomato sauce all over his lunch.

There were more Jameses at college than there were in my whole town. Back home they were called Jimmy, Jimbo or Jamie. Never James. This one was nicknamed Joyce because for the first few weeks he carried a copy of *Ulysses* with him, a bookmark permanently fixed a third of the way in. He was tall with a bad white-man's-afro and a voice that carried across the room.

'I think Leiza was pointing out that, perhaps, some people might argue it trivialises violence against women,' said Kesh, apologetically. She was sitting between Toby and

Rachel. Michael sat at the far end of the table, occasionally looking at people as they spoke, but not joining in the conversation. Rachel was eating toast after having been caught by the cook trying to steal sausages from the bain-marie.

Three weeks into term, the Murder Game, billed as a way of getting to know everyone at college, had begun. You were given a victim who you had to pretend to kill by trapping them alone. For the first few days, the college moved in packs, fearful of attacks and of being waylaid in dark corners. But as the body count grew higher, and more people were eliminated, views began to change from it all being good fun to thinking that it was a childish undergraduate game. Leiza had taken a far harder line and had gone to see Marcus to get it banned altogether.

'Such a killjoy,' said Rachel. 'She's pissed off that her petition has been completely ignored and now just wants to wreck everyone's fun. I mean, she wanted the bar crawl to be cancelled and she complained about the toga party. What would she have us do? Sit round and discuss feminist legal theory?'

Rachel had assassinated four of her targets already and was currently first on the leaders' table.

'Perhaps that would be more deadly,' I joked.

Rachel laughed. 'Still, I managed to kill you.'

'And me,' said Rogan, walking up to us. 'Garrotted with a string of rosary beads. How did you die?' He sat across from me, balancing a plate of food, and gave me a smile. Farmer boy Joad, whom Rachel had christened Toad, moved into the spare seat next to Michael.

It was the first time Rogan had spoken to me and Kesh blushed on my behalf.

'Killed with the tip of a poisoned umbrella.'

Rogan dipped his head with a nod of respect at Rachel and pulled in his chair. Our feet accidentally bumped under the table.

'How is that sexist?' said Joyce. 'It's equal opportunity carnage.'

'I see it more as a metaphor for college relationships,' said Rachel. 'First we get to know each other, second we screw each other and then we kill each other.'

'At least the first two don't sound so bad,' said Rogan.

'What a coincidence. Pen would say the same thing. Maybe you two should get together and go bowling,' said Rachel, giving me a sly sideways sort of glance. A nervous giggle escaped from Kesh and I pretended to be engrossed in my breakfast.

'Can I have one of your sausages?' Rachel asked Toby.

'You certainly may not. I need to fuel myself up before my big weekend,' said Toby. 'There is a whole tray of them over there.'

'That bastard chef is watching me like a hawk. He won't even let me have bacon at breakfast.'

'He's not serving at the moment,' said Rogan. 'I think he's unloading a delivery.'

'I am so desperate for meat,' said Rachel, standing up. 'I might even roast my next victim and eat them.'

'You've got to hand it to her, she gives good game,' said Toby, getting up to make himself more toast. 'If I wasn't going to win the keg of beer for being the most successful serial killer, I'd put money on her.'

Joad rolled his eyes but waited until Toby was out of earshot, before saying, 'First prize is mine. I'm not going to be beaten by any loudmouth bitch or faggot.' He had a distinctive nasal voice that cut through the general rumble. There was a ripple of uncertainty at the table, as people tried to pretend he was being ironic.

'And how do you kill people?' Rogan asked.

'That Screwdriver Man has the right idea,' Joad replied. 'My next victim will have body parts sliced off with a sharp implement while she's still alive and then bleed slowly to death in agonising pain. Here's hoping it's the Not-so-Quiet American.'

Joad spoke with such relish that all conversation at the table disappeared, which was why when I eventually said, 'Maybe Leiza has a point,' quietly to Kesh, it seemed much louder.

'Who asked you, Holly Hobbie?' Joad said. 'Not wearing your pretty dress today, I see.'

It was easy to hate Joad. Not even sitting across from Rogan was worth putting up with him. I got up from the table, my breakfast uneaten.

'You finished?' Toby asked in surprise, as I walked past where he was charcoalling some bread.

'Stuff to do,' I said. Putting my plate in the washing area, I heard, 'Goodbye, Sister Wife,' a parting remark from Joad. As I left the dining room, I thought of all the ways I could kill him.

I was still running through my options when I reached the phones. There was a phone on each floor at college for incoming calls. Two pay phones outside the dining hall were for calling out. Rachel said she never bothered calling her mother in the United States because the queues were a nightmare. But I had to brave them today because it was my mother's birthday.

One of the cubicles had a sticky-taped sign on the door, with 'out of order' scrawled across it. The other phone was being monopolised by a plump second-year girl. I stood in her line of sight, jangling my coins, trying to get her attention, but she ignored me as her conversation became fraught. Remembering Toby's advice, I had brought *The Big Sleep* to reread and settled down on a low-backed vinyl couch that had been placed opposite. I could hear boys playing the pinball machine in the Rec Room further along the corridor, the sounds from the dining hall and the general noise of conversation around college. Far off, someone was practising a violin in one of the music rooms and I began thumbing through the book to find my place.

'Aah, Ms Sheppard.'

I looked up to see Marcus. He stood out amongst the scruffy students, impeccably dressed in a tailored charcoal suit with a subtle pinstripe running through it. It wasn't so much a uniform as armour. No one in my town had ever dressed with such authority.

'How has your first month been? A whirlwind of activities, I expect, as you haven't paid me a visit.'

It had never occurred to me that Marcus would want regular updates on my progress and I gave some stumbled response about assuming he would be too busy.

'I take a keen interest in those I see potential in. Student well-being and all that. How are you coping financially? University can be such a money pit.'

The truth was, my savings were disappearing rapidly but I didn't want to complain to the one person who had already been so generous. I told him that it was all fine.

'Good, good. I live by the credo that one should take care of the luxuries and the necessities will take care of themselves. No doubt, you are more sensible. And here's another of Scullin's rising stars. Good morning, Mr Cohen.'

Coming around the corner from the dining hall was Rogan. He had caught sight of us and was about to turn the opposite way.

'Oh . . . hi,' he said.

'Pen and I were just discussing that necessary evil, money. I understand it can be hard to find part-time work that doesn't interfere with your studies. Perhaps, Joshua, as a later-year student, you could give Pen the benefit of your experience.'

'Sure,' said Rogan, coming closer, though his voice sounded uncertain.

'Delightful. We must all catch up soon ... perhaps afternoon tea? But I must go. Appointment with the Vice-Chancellor and he does hate waiting.'

He walked away, happily nodding to passing students and replying with a ringing 'Good Morning,' to those who greeted him.

Rogan sat down next to me.

'Sorry about that,' I said. 'I'm not really sure what Marcus was going on about.' Rachel had told me Rogan had lots of money. He didn't need to get a job.

'Don't worry about it,' said Rogan.

'What do you mean it's not working?' snuffled the cubicle, loudly, interrupting our conversation. 'Do you want to see other people?'

'You left breakfast quite abruptly,' Rogan said. 'I'm hoping it was Joad and not me.'

'Definitely Joad. He's a complete pig,' I said.

'Perhaps Rachel should roast him.'

I laughed. The girl in the cubicle started to cry.

Emelia and her posse came by on their way to a breakfast of coffee and bitching. She did a showy double take at Rogan talking to me, and they all chorused, 'Hi Rogan' as they cantered past. Emelia turned round and gave him a smile that showed off all her expensive orthodontic work. It looked like she wanted to eat him.

'Want to have breakfast with us, Rogan?' asked Emelia.

'Just finished, actually.' Turning back to me he said, 'So, what are you reading?'

Emelia's face glazed over and the group of them muttered their way up the corridor.

I showed him the book.

'Raymond Chandler?' he said, surprised. 'I was expecting something a little more genteel.'

'Like what?'

'Perhaps something with bonnets.'

'Is that because of Joad?' It came out annoyed even though I didn't mean it to.

He smiled a beautiful smile and stretched out his legs in front of him. I was distracted by how close his limbs were to mine and how easy it would be to put my hand down and brush his jean-covered thigh, so instead I concentrated on his t-shirt, not brave enough to look at him directly in the face.

'Clearly, I got it wrong. More likely to have a pearl-handled pistol than a bonnet.'

'That's right, I'm a femme fatale.'

'Consider me warned. Anyway, what are you doing here?'

I pointed to the phone cubicle where the crying had changed to a kind of choked pleading. He listened.

'That'll be Tess,' he said. 'She was like this all of last year.' He got up and banged his palm firmly on the frame of the wooden door.

'People waiting,' he called out.

There was a sharp intake of breath, then some fierce whispering and then a louder 'Look, I've got to go ... I love you ... ring you tomorrow.' Tess came out, blinking, eyes red. She shot a furious look at me before noticing Rogan standing there.

'Tell me it's not the same guy as last year,' he said.

She gasped slightly, 'Actually, no,' and tears began to leak down her face.

'Oh, right. Long-distance relationships.' He turned and made a comical grimace at me. She gave a watery smile and then left.

'Phone's all yours,' he said, while holding open the door to the cubicle. 'Not a long-distance relationship, I hope.'

'Only if you count mothers,' I said.

'That I can allow.'

We both paused as if neither one quite knew how to finish our conversation.

'Rachel said I should ask you out.'

'Really?' I didn't know if I should feel gratitude or anger towards her. 'Do you always do what Rachel says?' I asked, desperately hoping he did.

'She threatened to garrote me if I didn't. For real this time.'

I smiled. Perhaps I did owe her one. 'Well, we couldn't have that.'

'Glad you agree,' and he grinned back. 'And I think a Raymond Chandler movie is playing at Film Group on Friday night. *Double Indemnity.*'

'Really?' I pretended that Kesh hadn't already asked me to go with her.

A shout came up the corridor. 'Rogan!' It was Stoner. He ambled towards us at faster than his usual pace.

'They phoned,' he said. 'You need to call back.' He handed Rogan a piece of paper.

'You use the phone,' I said. 'I'm not in a rush.'

'No, it's OK. You were the one waiting. Maybe I'll see you at the movie.'

'Maybe you will,' I said with my best wise-cracking dame nonchalance.

I watched him walk the whole way down the corridor, with Stoner talking to him. Then I sashayed into the cubicle and gleefully punched in my home number.

I spent Friday afternoon trying not to fall asleep on the shoulder of a big burly uniformed policeman. Our Contracts lecturer had been sick and the lecture had been rescheduled for the last session of the week in an airless room that had been warmed by an army of bodies throughout the day. I tried to concentrate on what was being said but there was something slippery about the subject matter and I was almost hypnotised by the droning voice. Toby had told me that no one really worried about lectures or tutorials until second semester. Dale, the policeman, didn't seem to know this and sat next to me writing everything down at a furious pace.

'This friend of yours, he's got a law degree?' asked Dale, when I tried explaining Toby's theory of first year to him after the lecture had finished.

'Not exactly.' I stretched out my arms and yawned.

'Any degree?' And in that weird way that yawns are contagious, Dale tried to stifle one. He had an excuse, though. He was on early shift that week and so had already done a full day's work.

'No,' I admitted. 'But he is doing first-year Accounting for the third time.'

Dale laughed and began to pack up his books. 'You can borrow my notes when you decide to start working.'

I followed him out of the room into the corridor. Walking behind Dale, I could see the other students' reaction to him. They ranged from pretending not to stare, to openly gawping, to deliberately avoiding or alternatively, walking past having loud conversations about 'fascism' and 'agents of the state'. It never failed to surprise me that I had swapped from a world where police ran the show to one where they were almost reviled. Perhaps even stranger was that I felt a weird sympathy towards Dale, and I went out of my way to chat or take the always empty chair next to him. After all, I knew what it felt like to be excluded and besides, I figured I would really need his notes come exam time.

In a sense, we were both outsiders from the usual privileged kids who made up most of Law School and that gave us enough in common to become friends. Also, he was different from the police from home. Country coppers. They had barely finished secondary school, let alone had law degrees. Arriving at our door, they refused to give Mum any information about why I was being taken down to the police station. I could guess but Mum had no idea and practically got arrested herself for obstructing the police. They shoved us into an interview room and left us there. But that all changed when my lawyer Bob turned up. He began to order them around, demanding answers, asserting my rights, starting the horse trading. He had power. That night I decided I wanted it too.

'Why are you studying law anyway?' I asked Dale, as we sat down outside in the sunshine. 'You've already got a job.'

'It's because of my job that I'm doing it. Better chance of promotion if you've got a law degree. Do prosecution work. Join the Feds. Get off shift. See my kids more.'

I had noticed the wedding ring on his finger but I hadn't really thought about the possibilities of a Mrs Dale and lots of little Dales.

'You're thinking I'm ancient,' he laughed.

I was but I lied. 'No, I'm thinking how do you fit in study with all that other stuff?'

'You make the most of the time you've got. Take tonight, for example. My wife's taking the kids to her cousin's house so I've got a date with the library. I'll stay there until closing. What are you up to?'

'Going to a movie with friends and then out after that, probably.' Hopefully. My mind was already racing with possibilities of Rogan and me heading out to a nightclub together.

There was a loud throb of an engine and an enormous motorbike drove up the street towards us. It slowed down as it went past, the leather-clad rider, black, squat and square like the bike. Dale's uniform was a magnet and the biker turned his head in our direction, a blank stare from behind a visor as he raised his finger and gave us the bird, before revving his engine until the noise danced off every surface. Certain of our attention, he suddenly accelerated and took off down the street, leaving tyre marks on the road.

Dale watched him go, then turned to me. 'I reckon you borrowed the book he wanted out of short loan.'

I gave a relieved laugh. 'Yeah, he looks just like your average law student.'

'A Death Rider will have had more experience of the law than you've had hot dinners,' said Dale.

In the end, both Kesh and Rachel insisted on coming to Film Group as well, despite my best efforts to put them off, even though Kesh had seen the movie before and Rachel claimed that only misfits gave up their Friday nights to sit in the Physics lecture hall. I decided against telling Rachel that I was meeting Rogan there because I didn't want any more 'help' from her.

It was already dark as we crossed the campus to the Science faculty.

'If this is the same as *Star Wars* last year when the morons behind me quoted every single line of dialogue out loud, even R2D2's, I will punch someone and walk home,' Rachel said, as we pushed our way in the door. The place was about half full, with a steady thrumming of talk and noise, and I started scanning for Rogan. There was no cinematic sexy ambience at Film Group, which took place in a large lecture room with deeply tiered timber seats in front of a roll-down screen. Any hopes of groping in the dark could only have been in the imagination of the desperate, because it would take the dexterity of a squid to get past the wooden edges and metal clamping each seat firmly into place. But it didn't stop me imagining.

'What did I tell you? A whole bunch of freaks. Look, Pen, there's Michael. Kissy, kissy.' Rachel enjoyed pretending there hadn't been any dare and that we harboured a secret passion for each other.

Michael was sitting all by himself in the third row. He looked our way and nodded his head. I stopped to say hello.

'These seats are free,' he said.

'Oh, thanks.' My skin prickled with embarrassment. 'But I said to ... um ... Rogan that I'd watch it with him.'

A girl said, 'Excuse me,' and moved along the row to take a seat, a couple down from Michael. She had long blonde hair and a white top and I recognised her as the Marchmain girl I had seen at the bar crawl the month before.

'Oh, right,' said Michael.

'Another time, maybe.' I took a few steps away.

'Hurry up,' said Rachel, 'or else we will get stuck with Michael.'

'He'll hear you,' Kesh said. But that only made her talk more loudly.

'There are too many boring people that go to Film Group. It's like boring is contagious. You might catch boring just sitting next to Michael.'

We began to climb the stairs to find a seat.

'Maybe all his boringness is a front, a cunning disguise. One of these days I'm going to get into his room for a snoop. Probably find pictures of Pen all over his walls,' Rachel said laughing, but she quickly stopped. 'Half of college is here.'

A few rows up, there was a large group of people making a party of it. Joad and Stoner were passing plastic cups along the row and there was the clinking of glass and metal coming from backpacks. Rogan was at the far edge of the group, drinking a beer, and hadn't noticed me.

'What's going on?' asked Rachel.

Annabel, who lived on the floor above us, straightened up from hunting through the bag in front of her. 'It's the inaugural meeting of the Smoking Aficionados Drinking Group. Didn't you get the notice? Joad leafleted your floor.'

On hearing his name, Joad looked up. Seeing it was us, he sneered and went back to talking to Stoner.

'We didn't get it,' said Rachel.

'It's a Forde Tower bonding exercise. Every time some-one lights a cigarette in the movie, you have to drink beer.'

'There's a lot of smoking in this movie,' said Kesh anxiously.

'That's why we chose it.'

'Sounds fun,' said Rachel. 'Where's my beer?'

Annabel shrugged. 'Everyone had to pool their money to buy the beer. Maybe next time?'

Rachel's face hardened. 'But we didn't know about it because the Toad didn't tell us.'

'Sorry,' said Annabel. 'But it wouldn't be fair ... we needed exact numbers.'

'And Rogan's here,' said Rachel, even louder. 'He's not even in Forde Tower.'

That got Rogan's attention and he gave us a curt nod of his head, as Annabel went back to pulling out bottles and passing them along. Joad made a shoo-shoo gesture of dismissal, smiling evilly. Rachel flounced off and Kesh and I followed her a couple of rows higher, and began clambering over people towards the middle of the room.

'This is all Toby's fault. He's supposed to know about these things,' said Rachel.

'But he's away,' I said, trying to be reasonable.

'Just because he's having a dirty weekend with camp David, doesn't mean he can forget his responsibilities.'

We ended up sitting north of the Smoking Aficionados, and Rogan, who had watched our progress, climbed over the seats to where we were.

'Hello,' he said.

'Hello, yourself,' said Rachel, and pointedly turned away from him and began talking loudly to Kesh about double standards. Rogan sat next to me, the smell of beer and him all mixed up.

'I didn't know about all this until I ran into them on the way over.' He made a gesture back towards the group.

'Oh right,' I said. 'We didn't know about it either.'

Awkward silence. All the conversation topics I had come up with for precisely this situation bubbled up and then slipped out of my head, like small fish jumping out of the fish bowl only to die gasping on the floor.

'So you didn't put money in then,' Rachel said, dropping the pretence that she had been ignoring him.

Rogan looked at her and then, as if deciding it was too much effort, turned back to me. 'I don't know if I'm in the mood for watching movies.'

'Feeling guilty?' said Rachel. 'Drinking beer that doesn't belong to you.'

I spoke over the top of her. 'It's supposed to be good, Raymond Chandler and all.' I couldn't tell whose fault it was that our banter had disappeared, so I settled on Rachel, who was frowning at both of us.

'Maybe we should try another time,' he said, standing up. 'Go see a band. There are a couple of good ones playing after term break, if you're interested. I'll buy the tickets, you being a poor penniless first-year.'

I could feel a smile swelling from deep inside and tried to contain it in order to strike the right balance between enthusiasm and casualness. 'That would be great.'

The lights began to dim, and Rogan nodded his head and went back to his seat, getting slightly tangled up in the process.

'Is he drunk?' said Rachel dismissively. 'The movie hasn't even started yet.'

The room darkened, the projector clicked up to speed and the crowd began adjusting to the classroom dissolving into a cinema. People sniggered at the old Hollywood-style theatrics and there was a cheer from below us as the first cigarette was lit up, less than five minutes in. Eventually, the pull of the story took over, the rustling died and everyone became transfixed. Except me.

I found Rogan's profile in the gloom. I wanted to sit next to him, feel the warmth of his arm, put my head on his shoulder. But then Rachel shifted in her seat and I didn't want her to notice where I was gazing so I turned to the screen. The next time I looked back for him, he was gone.

Kesh made us wait through the credits to see if Raymond Chandler had a cameo appearance in the movie, so by the time we were standing up, the lights were on and the room was a lecture hall again.

'Great movie,' Kesh said, as we shuffled slowly towards the exit, hemmed in by bodies.

'Phyllis's wig was shockingly bad,' said Rachel, turning around to talk to us as she began elbowing her way through the crowd.

'Is that all you can say about it?' Kesh followed her, smiling apologetically at people forced to a standstill.

'It was distracting,' Rachel replied, deciding we needed to walk through a row of seats to the other side of the room, because she was sure that it would be faster. 'The movie was good, except for her fringe.'

'Were you thinking about her fringe when they murdered her husband?' I asked.

Rachel was too busy pushing through the crowd to answer, and we made our way out the doors, running into various members of the Smoking Aficionados lighting up their cigarettes. They were drunkenly debating where to head to next.

'Are you going back to college?' asked Michael.

'*We* are,' said Rachel, in a voice that didn't include him. She crossed over the road.

'Looks that way,' I said. I waited for Michael to say something about allowing Rachel to decide everything but he stayed silent and together, with Kesh, we caught up to

Rachel. She pursed her lips when she saw Michael but said nothing. We took the usual shortcut back to college, around the rear of the Law School where the path skirted the bushland that ran along the edge of campus. With the moon coming out from behind clouds, the shadows had sharp edges while the buildings lurked behind them, insubstantial and ghostly.

'Imagine if Walter had never met Phyllis,' Kesh said. 'He wouldn't have become a murderer.'

'Maybe Phyllis wouldn't have killed if she hadn't met Walter,' said Rachel.

'But she'd already killed the first wife,' said Michael.

Rachel answered dismissively, 'Says who? That idiot daughter? I wouldn't believe a word she says.'

We moved from the edge of the Law School to walk between a narrow corridor of demountable buildings out towards the carpark. There was no one else around.

'Everything could have been different.' Kesh spoke almost in a whisper. 'Poor Walter.'

'You can't blame it all on Phyllis,' said Rachel. The 'Phyllis' echoed back to us from a nearby building. 'She wasn't the one who strangled her husband,' she continued more softly.

'You don't always have to be the murderer to be guilty.' As Kesh spoke, she smiled at me, probably for support, because Rachel was already snorting her disbelief.

'Do you really think that?' I asked.

Kesh was the type of person who didn't like arguments, but here she stuck to her guns. 'Of course.'

She stopped to face me and I opened my mouth to question this, which was why neither of us saw the girl straight away. I imagine she'd been staggering in our direction and heard our voices, but for us she suddenly materialised in the spotlight from the nearest street lamp.

She was a ghostly pale figure, her skin, hair and clothes bleached of colour from the overhead light. But, turning towards us, she began to change. From white to red. Blood was running down her cheek, neck and onto her clothes. She put her hands out and I stared at her face and her clotted blonde hair, glued to the skin. A tight curl of flesh hung limp, below the cut on the side of her head, a hole where her ear should be. The girl looked at us, opened up her mouth and screamed so loudly that when she collapsed, the noise still hung in the air around us.

*

'It was chaos afterwards,' I say to Frank.

'What did you do?' he asks.

I don't tell him that I'd just stood there, transfixed by the blood and thinking another person was going to die in front

91

of me. 'I helped Kesh,' I say. 'She was giving her first aid. I tried to keep Alice warm. That was her name, the girl who got attacked.'

Kesh had knelt next to Alice and kept talking to her, holding one hand against Alice's head, trying to stop the bleeding. The girl was hysterical but Kesh just kept speaking to her calmly as blood poured over her hand. I couldn't take my eyes off it. I didn't move when Kesh told me to take off my jumper and lay it over Alice. Even when she shouted at me to get help, I could only stand there. I don't tell any of this to Frank. And besides, help arrived anyway.

'One moment we were alone, and then in a blink everyone was there. People from Film Group. Students from college. Security guards. Eventually, an ambulance. Even Dale turned up.'

'Who's Dale?'

'A friend of mine from Law School. He's a policeman.'

The poker face disappears, Frank giving me an astonished eyebrow flick. He pretends that he does not judge his patients, but he does in hundreds of little ways. The eyebrow flick. The pressing heavily on his pen as he writes. Sometimes even an escaping sigh when he thinks I've really got things wrong.

I continue as if I haven't noticed. 'He'd been at the library, heard the sirens and came over. Mostly he did crowd control but he insisted on walking the three of us back to college. Didn't leave until we were safely inside.'

'Three?'

'Rachel came back as well.'

'You haven't really mentioned Rachel. What was she doing while you and Kesh were helping Alice?'

'I don't know.'

Sitting in my bedroom, after my appointment with Frank, I'm writing in my diary. I have decided to do this after every session, to try and remember exactly what I say to Frank and what he says to me. Writing down how my lies turn into his truth. Actually, what I told him about Rachel was true on the night. I had barely noticed her or Michael because I was focused on Alice. Rachel eventually turned up after the ambulance had left and Dale was saying it was time to head home. She stood there not saying a word. In fact, she was silent the whole way back across campus and that was what got my attention. When I turned to her there had been a look on her face that I will never forget. She was scared and upset like the rest of us, but it was mixed with something else. Calculating is the only way I can describe it. I didn't understand it then but I worked it out later. Rachel had seen someone in the shadows. Watching. Perhaps there was a flicker of recognition because she had run towards them, chased even as the person turned and fled. It wasn't much and she wasn't certain, not then at least. I think Rachel would have said something if she knew who the attacker was that night. But then again, maybe she wouldn't have. Rachel only revealed secrets when it suited her.

Chapter 6

Sitting on the bus, I stared out at trees which had been green a month ago, when I had first arrived on campus. Now they were changing into the deep orange-reds of autumn. I had changed as well. Arriving knowing no one, I now had a social life and acquaintances were evolving into friends. Friends that occasionally convinced you to do something you would prefer not to. I wasn't sure why we needed to visit Alice in hospital, but Kesh, and to my surprise Rachel, had insisted.

The bus trip to the hospital had been the first time any of us had been off campus since the start of the year and I watched my new home town flit past the window with detached interest. Tall grey buildings, so many pedestrians and large multi-lane roads; everything was bigger than my home town and yet it seemed so colourless compared to my life on campus. University life had become so all-consuming that there was no reason to leave it and explore what surrounded it. We ate on campus, went out on campus, got drunk on campus and even shopped on campus, not that I had much money. Sometimes it was hard to believe there was an actual world outside of the bubble I had created for myself.

I looked over at Kesh, who was studying the directions to the hospital like she was going to be examined on it and worrying aloud that we'd miss our stop. Rachel, sitting next to her, caught my gaze and pulled a face to make me laugh, then went back to staring out the window on the other side of the bus. I turned back to my window so Kesh wouldn't see my smile.

I hadn't been this happy in ages.

The bus stop was right outside the hospital. We stood outside its front doors that hummed back and forth for the continual stream of people coming in and out. Rachel decided to have a cigarette before visiting time began, and joined a huddle of grey-faced people postponing the bad news that waited inside. She got a light from one woman, prematurely wizened like the hospital equivalent of a garden gnome, who was sitting on the bench in her pyjamas, with a mobile drip as an accessory.

'So, tell me,' said Rachel, 'how would you choose to pay your way through university? Become a drug dealer or have a fake marriage to get government assistance?'

'Rach,' said Kesh, glancing at the old lady.

'Don't worry, she'll have heard worse.'

The old lady was too busy hoovering up her cigarette to say one way or the other. Kesh pretended to be distracted by the bunch of limp carnations she had bought for Alice.

'C'mon, Kesh,' said Rachel. 'Play along.'

'Why those two options?' I asked.

'Not all of us are lucky enough to get bursaries,' said Rachel.

'Why can't I just do some waitressing?' I asked.

'Don't be boring,' said Rachel. 'But I guess I can add in another option. Prostitution.'

A hairless man in front of us choked on his own smoke, and Kesh decided that she would go ask the information desk what floor Alice was on.

'What made you even think about this?' I asked.

'Nico, Alice's boyfriend. He's the biggest dealer on campus. The Marchmain Club is just a front. It's not-so-subliminal advertising. A line of white from the guys in white. Mind you, there's a bit more competition this year. Some motorcycle gang's on the scene.'

I tried to remember back to the Marchmains' conversation the night of the bar crawl. 'Death Riders?' I asked.

'That's them,' she said. 'Anyway, answer my question. What would you choose?'

'Seriously?'

'Yeah, seriously.'

I thought for a bit. 'I'd have to choose prostitution, but only if it's legal.'

'Should have guessed. Country girls and their generous ways.'

I tried not to react to her teasing. 'To be admitted as a lawyer, you have to be of good character, so anything illegal would be even more frowned on.' I had read a bit about 'good character' before I decided to study law. I was already pushing the boundaries on that definition, so I had to keep myself out of trouble.

'I would have thought being of bad character would be almost compulsory,' she said, but got distracted by Kesh waving to us from the door.

'Florence Nightingale beckons,' said Rachel. 'We better go tend the sick.'

Alice lay under crisp white sheets in a sterile room that smelt of disinfectant. A friendly nurse had shown us in and then left to find a vase for Kesh's flowers.

We sat there watching Alice's pale face wrapped up in bandages. She was asleep.

'Private room,' said Rachel. 'Parents must be loaded or else this is what our university fees go towards.' She sounded resentful.

'We shouldn't wake her,' whispered Kesh.

Background noises of people moving, machines humming and beeping and the traffic outside filtered into the room. There was the sound of laughter from the corridor and the nurse returned.

'We'll add these to the collection.' She took the flowers from Kesh and put them in the vase. The shelf had several arrangements already, all of them looking more expensive. There was also an enormous white teddy with a hairbrush in its lap. I wondered if that was some sort of Marchmain joke.

'Are you friends of Alice?' she asked, moving to the end of the bed to check something on the chart.

'Um ... no ... not really. It's just we were the ones who found her,' said Kesh. 'How is she going?'

'Not bad, considering. Operation went well yesterday but she'll still be tired.'

'Oh, maybe we should go then,' said Kesh. 'Leave her to rest ...'

But the nurse had moved back towards the bed. 'Alice, Alice dear. Some visitors for you.'

Alice opened her eyes, her vision unfocused.

'Oh good, you're awake,' said the nurse, raising her

voice. 'Look, visitors for you. Here are the girls who found you.'

Nothing close to recognition crossed Alice's face and I started to wish I hadn't come.

'Let's get you sitting up,' said the nurse, and she found the remote, pressed a button and the top of the bed slowly began to rise. Alice's head was a delicate egg leaning back on the pillow. I wondered at the damage under the bandage, the raw skin, the stitches, the hole.

'I'll leave you to chat,' said the nurse.

I deliberately positioned myself behind Rachel. Kesh moved towards the bed and took the spot where the nurse had been.

'Hello, you might not remember us, but we found you ...' Kesh spoke to her slowly and loudly as if English was Alice's second language.

'I remember you,' said Alice. Her voice was low and husky. 'You stayed with me until the ambulance. Held my head.'

'That's right. I'm Kesh,' said Kesh, nodding over-enthusiastically.

Rachel moved to the other side of Alice's bed. 'Do you remember who attacked you?' she asked.

Alice's head didn't move, but her eyes flicked to Rachel. For a moment, I thought she might not have heard the question, but then she said, 'His face was covered.'

'But it was a man?'

Alice's voice began to get fainter. 'Spoke to me.'

Her eyes returned to Kesh as if she didn't want to speak to Rachel any more.

'What did he say?' asked Rachel.

'Rachel, that's enough,' said Kesh, gently. 'Remember what the nurse said, Alice is tired.'

'I don't know, all right.' Alice sounded tearful.

'What did his voice sound like then?' Rachel was so insistent that she sat down on the bed, trying to lean across to get in Alice's line of sight. Alice grimaced in pain at the movement.

'Rachel, get off the bed,' I said. 'And stop badgering her.'

Rachel stood up but when she looked at me, she was annoyed. 'The police will have asked her the same questions.'

'But you're not the police,' said a voice in the doorway. 'So, what's it to you?'

There was a large outline in the door. I only recognised him when he moved into the light, a bald Nico dressed like us in jeans and a t-shirt, holding an enormous bunch of flowers. There was no boater hat or bottle of champagne today.

'Excuse me,' he said, forcing Rachel to move away from the bed to let him in.

He kissed Alice on the forehead.

'Your hair,' she murmured. A small hand reached out, a

bandage on the back keeping the drip in. She touched his shaven head.

'It's so we match. Our hair will grow back together.' He put his hand on hers, and I noticed his was shaking. He held on to her hand for a moment, then brought it down gently and placed it on the cover. He showed her the bouquet.

'More flowers. Nico,' she sighed.

He put them down on the ledge next to the bed. Then he turned to us, arms folded, and he looked more like her bodyguard than her boyfriend.

'Who are you and what do you want?' It was clear he didn't recognise us from the bar crawl.

Alice gave a feeble half protest at this, and Kesh quickly began to explain. Nico's hostility eased but only slightly. He pulled up a chair, sat down next to the bed, and stared hard at Rachel through bloodshot eyes. His body jangled as though a mild electric current was running through it.

'Why are you asking so many questions?'

Rachel shrugged. 'Interested.' She moved away from him and walked over next to me.

'I'm sure Rachel just wants whoever did this to be caught. I mean, that's what we all want,' said Kesh.

Nico nodded, which Rachel took as an opening to keep asking questions. 'So does Alice remember what the Screwdriver Man said, or not?'

But this seemed to have flicked a switch in Nico.

'You checking up? Someone sent you, didn't they? That maniac in the balaclava, he sent you?'

He stood up, his face contorted.

'You came to see how well he carved up Alice? She's got to have another operation. Her hearing is permanently damaged.'

Alice tried to tug at his sleeve to get him to sit down. 'Nico, Nico, stop,' she pleaded, but he ignored her.

'Wanna know what we've said to the police? Tell them from me, I'm no dog but you screw with me and I'll screw with you. Leave Alice out of this.'

Exhausted, Alice's hand dropped back to her bed and she lay there, pain on her face.

'All right, we've got the message. We're leaving,' said Rachel.

Kesh got up, upset. 'We just wanted to make sure Alice was OK. That's all we wanted to do.'

'Just get out of here.' Nico was spitting with rage. 'I'll kill anyone who comes near Alice again.'

Chapter 7

After my appointment with Frank, I go to the library and write about the hospital visit until closing time. I decide to take the long way home, past the saleyards and around the cemetery. I avoid the centre of town. I walk along the road that leads up to The Hill. You can see The Hill from almost anywhere in our town. I used to go up there all the time with Tracey. We would sit at the top and plan how we would escape from here. I always knew I wanted to go to university but Tracey wasn't sure. Her father wouldn't pay for her, we both knew that. The one time she had argued with him about it, she came to school with welts on her legs from where he had beaten her with his belt. *'He says you're a bad influence,'* she told me. That was funny because my mother said the same thing about her.

I turn off The Hill road and take the underpass under the highway rather than using the bridge. I want to see if the graffiti is still there and it is, red against the grey. It hasn't faded much and I wonder if it is refreshed regularly, like flowers on a grave. Gone but not forgotten.

P.S. IS A MURDERER.

I stand there remembering the first time I had seen those bright dripping letters, except then the initials read T. C. You can still make out Tracey's initials under mine and when I put my finger up and touch the cold concrete, it is her letters that I trace over again and again. It is dark before I head home.

'Where have you been?' asks Mum, accusingly. She is wearing her best getup, tight, sparkly with everything on display. 'You knew Terry was coming for dinner.'

'You didn't have to wait,' I say.

'I wanted us to all sit down together.'

Mum is someone who still believes in fairytales. If Terry wasn't here, Mum would be in her dressing gown and slippers and we would eat packet noodles or tinned soup in front of the television. But Terry is always here now.

The three of us sit in our small kitchen that smells of

burnt onion and spice, surrounded by dirty dishes and sticky surfaces, eating a meal so awful that even Rachel would have happily chosen chilli con carne in preference. Terry keeps pushing his spoon down into the sludge trying to smooth out the lumps, but the spoon never goes near his mouth.

'Got the recipe from the new girl at work. Vegetarian but eats chicken still. Not an inch of fat on her,' Mum says, trying to cover up the silences. 'Had to go to the health food shop for some of the ingredients and they charge like wounded bulls there.'

'Mmm,' Terry says. 'Might get some chips down at the pub.' That's the thing about Terry, he's only a hippy sometimes.

Disappointed, Mum turns to me.

'You like it, don't you? You told me how you ate all that vegetarian food at college.'

I don't bother to pick up my fork. Terry pushes back his chair with both hands on the table. He's too tall for our kitchen. Long hairy arms and legs. The rickety table wobbles and my bowl is in danger of spilling. I could have given it a surreptitious shove and been able to blame it on him. But there is no point. A saucepan full of the stuff is sitting on the stove.

He gazes around the kitchen, mentally cataloguing our possessions. But there is nothing expensive or shiny to capture his attention for long. This house and everything in it belonged to my grandparents. In fact, technically still belongs to my grandfather, even though he's been in the nursing home for years.

'Saw that university fella of yours yesterday, on the television. Back in court,' Terry says.

'Where did you see that?' Mum is surprised, because Terry pretends to hate television. He calls it the idiot box. Takes one to know one. Mum unplugs ours and covers it with an old sheet before he comes over.

'Mick's got one in his caravan. He had it on while we had our lunch,' he says. 'Back in court,' he repeats, in case I missed it the first time. 'Off to jail soon.'

I say nothing because I'd already read the newspaper report about it at the library. There was a large photograph of Marcus being bundled into the back of a taxi, arm flung up, shielding his face from the camera. He had been all alone. No friends or family with him, not even his lawyer was in the picture. There was something shrunken about him, as if he had already been found guilty.

'It's only the committal hearing,' says Mum. 'Then it's the trial. Different standards. Beyond reasonable doubt for a trial. Mind you, shouldn't be hard seeing he's as guilty as sin.' She pulls off a diamante earring and massages her red lobe.

Terry looks surprised at Mum's grasp of the legal system.

He opens his mouth to question it, but I get in first and ask him how the Taj Mahal is going. Mum gives me an encouraging smile. Most of the time I ignore Terry because he is a waste of space. The only reason he is in town is to help build some dropout's mud-brick house. At the start, he pretended to Mum he owned it and she was dumb enough to believe him, but it really belongs to his friend Mick. He calls it his job, but the amount of time it's taking, it barely qualifies as a hobby.

'A couple of weeks and Mick'll be in. Sooner the better. Gonna be a wet spring.'

Mum clips the earring back into place and checks her reflection in the oven glass. She frowns, patting her hair. The hairdresser talked her into having a perm, and she isn't convinced.

'Another washed-out Blossom Festival Parade, no doubt,' she says. Mum pretends to dislike the Festival but really she would love to have been crowned Cherry Blossom Princess and I kind of ruined that for her. Not too many single mothers become royalty in this town.

Terry sniffs and I wonder how long he's planning to hang around. He has talked about visiting friends up the coast once the house is finished and then heading further north to pick fruit, but I suspect he will be reluctant to give up his newly found meal ticket. Still, a few more home-cooked vegetarian meals and he might leave of his own accord.

'So you'll be heading off soon,' I continue.

Mum tenses and gets up quickly. 'Reckon it could do with some salt.'

Terry stretches out and cups her backside as she walks past. 'Your mum's asked me to move in.'

Mum had told me this dinner was important to her. Now I understand why. We are going to be a happy family.

'Yeah, and I'm going to do a bit of work on your house,' Terry continues.

I look over to my mother, amazed that she can fall for this again.

'Terry thinks we could pull down the back verandah and make it into a sunroom,' Mum tells the cupboard full of crockery, refusing to look at me.

'A sunroom,' I say. 'Wouldn't a pool room be nicer? You could put a bar in.'

I think it was Shane, who only talked about guns and hunting, who came up with that one. He never started because Mum couldn't afford the equipment he said he needed. He left after six months when he got a job mining, taking all my grandmother's jewellery with him, as payment for services not rendered.

My mother sticks her head out of the cupboard and shoots me a behave-yourself look. Holding the salt in a glazed clay pot marked sugar, she comes back to the table.

'Doesn't have to be a sunroom,' Terry says. 'Lots we can

do to fix this old place up. Keep me busy for ages.' His face wears a lazy, satisfied look.

I play the innocent and even pick up my fork. Mum senses my scepticism and tries to change the subject. 'Now, eat up,' she says. 'Don't want it to get cold.'

Terry chokes down a mouthful. 'Definitely needs salt.' He begins to sprinkle it on liberally. 'Why aren't you eating?' he asks her.

'You know how when you cook something, the smell of it fills you up.'

'All this sounds expensive. Where's the money coming from, Mum?' I want to see if she has learnt anything from Shane.

Terry jumps in quickly. 'It won't cost that much because . . .' but Mum gives the game away.

'Terry says I could get a power of attorney for Dad and then take a mortgage out on this place.' She looks so happy I haven't got the heart to rain on her own personal Blossom Festival Parade so I deliberately keep my face blank. Still, now I know nicking the electrical goods isn't enough for Terry. He wants real money.

'But,' says Mum, 'if Bob gets you a good settlement against that university, we might not need to get a mortgage. He bloody should too. I mean, the amount of money he charged us last time. When he put in that fancy swimming pool, I said he should call it the Shirley Sheppard

Memorial, seeing all my savings went to pay for it.'

'Why did you need a lawyer?' asks Terry. He must be the only person in town who doesn't know and I wonder how long before he will. If I thought it would make him leave, I'd tell him myself.

'You know, just the usual,' Mum says, too quickly. 'Charge you for anything and everything.' She grabs her handbag which is sitting under the table, and hunts through it, pulling out a lipstick.

'Has Bob said when they're going to make you an offer?' she asks. Terry pretends to be engrossed in his dinner, but he is listening hard.

I shrug. 'He's waiting on Frank's report.' My face stays neutral as I start to lie. 'He thinks the university is going to fight, so he said not to get my hopes up unless we can afford to litigate.'

Mum's mouth drawstrings in disapproval.

'Where are we going to get that sort of money? You could have been killed. They can't get away with that.' She frowns and then pats Terry's hand. 'Excuse me, while I nip to the little girls' room.' Really, she wants a sneaky cigarette. She started again when I was in hospital. Terry doesn't hold with smoking.

She walks out, leaving us alone in the kitchen. I refuse to make eye contact because this is usually the moment when Mum's boyfriend says something to mark out his territory as the new man of the house. The nice ones say something about not being my dad but perhaps we can be friends, but that's not Terry.

'Aren't you gonna eat that?' he asks, pointing to my untouched bowl. His leg brushes up against mine under the table.

'I've had enough.' I swing my legs out of his reach and, as I start standing up, he grabs my arm.

His smile is wide and wet with a meaty tongue and sharp yellowed teeth. 'Think you're so much better than the rest of us with your lawyer and your shrink. Writing about us in that blue book of yours, full of all your secrets. Maybe I should read it one day.' He makes a panting kind of laugh.

I can't tell if this is supposed to be a threat or a come-on. Keeping my voice even, I say, 'Let go of me.' His hand slowly tightens as he tries to drag me towards him. I force myself to look straight into his eyes, dark and unreadable, and say, 'The last person who tried something like this is dead.'

He loosens his grip and I pull my hand away. Pretending I am fine, I stand up, grab my bowl and scrape it out into the bin then place it in the sink. The sound fills the kitchen as he sits there, saying nothing. My scalp prickles from his eyes watching me. As I leave the kitchen, Mum comes bustling back in, smelling suspiciously of mint, and says it's my turn for the washing up.

Chapter 8

'Look at all these hypocrites,' said Rachel. 'If Salman Rushdie popped through those doors for a chat, this lot would head for the hills.'

It was the first Academic Night of the year and our dining hall had been turned into an auditorium with serious people in glasses trying to say smart things while waiting for the talk about Rushdie's fatwa to begin. Kesh, Rachel and I, dressed in white shirts and black skirts, had been commandeered to serve at the food and drinks table.

Kesh was wearing a tight-fitting blouse that she had borrowed from Annabel. The material gaped as the buttons strained to keep it together.

'You don't think this is too revealing?' she asked, doing up the third button which had popped again.

'Kesh, your boobs are the most appetising items on display,' Rachel said, hitching her black skirt higher. She had a point. In front of us was a trestle table with sweaty cubes of anonymous cheese sitting next to toothpicks of cocktail onions and processed meat. Rows of thimble-sized glasses were filled with what the Sub-Dean had described to us as 'perfectly adequate sherry'.

'This stuff should come with a health warning,' I said. 'It looks worse than our dinners.'

'They should have put Stoner in charge of refreshments,' replied Rachel. 'That would get the party started.'

'Or the Marchmain Club,' said Kesh, trying to keep up with the conversation.

Rachel frowned. 'I don't know. I hear they might be disbanding, Nico's gone to pieces with the attack on Alice.' She was interrupted by the Sub-Dean bounding towards us.

'More trays are coming up from the kitchen now, but remember, no serving of food or drinks until after the talk.' He began moving the plates of cheese to one side. 'And girls,' he smeared a smile across his face, 'for the duration of the evening, as we are being convivial, you may refer to me as Bryan.' He hurried away again to direct Rogan, who was coming out of the kitchen area, balancing two trays of vol-au-vents, towards us.

Rachel scoffed, Kesh giggled and whispered 'Bryan' to herself, but I just watched Rogan.

'All yours,' he said, handing me one tray and then the other.

I put them down next to the sherries. 'What are they?'

Rachel bent over to take a closer look. 'Road kill, I expect,' she said.

Rogan turned to me. 'I heard you went and visited that girl in hospital last week. The one that got attacked.'

I nodded. 'Kesh has been twice.'

'How's she going?'

'She's supposed to get discharged in a couple of days,' Kesh said, distracted by the button popping again. 'She's got to have another operation but that won't happen for a while. Her parents are taking her home to recover over Easter but I don't know if she'll be back after term break.'

'Did she see who attacked her?' asked Rogan. He was looking tired and pale and I wondered if he had caught the cold that had been travelling around college.

Kesh shook her head but Rachel butted in. 'She told us she didn't, but I reckon she knew more than she was saying.' There was a mischievous look on her face.

'Nico definitely knew more about it,' I said, thinking about his rant.

Kesh leant forward, putting increased pressure on the buttons, and spoke in a low voice. 'I shouldn't say this, but

I wouldn't be surprised if he was violent. He's really scary. The way he thought we knew the Screwdriver Man and screamed at us. I think it's good Alice is leaving to get away from him.'

'Four students huddled together. Must be a conspiracy.' Marcus appeared, dressed in a high-collared lightweight black linen suit. It was the second week of April but the nights were already winter cold and college heating had been turned up so high that inside was a tropical hothouse.

Rachel explained.

'Aah, that poor girl,' said Marcus. 'A bad business, all that. Most unfortunate.' He frowned, shook his head but then brightened. 'Now, you must tell me your views on Rushdie's predicament. An excellent topic for our first Academic Night. You know, I've met Salman,' he continued in an off-hand sort of way. 'London, a few years ago. He was most urbane. Though I have to admit his appearance ...' He waved his hand across his own face. 'The droopy eyelids, pointed beard and eyebrows. It was all a little satanic really.'

I wondered if he had deliberately chosen tonight's topic merely to name-drop.

'As though I was supping with the Devil,' Marcus went on. 'Though one must say,' he looked at the food in front of us, 'Lucifer would provide better catering than this.'

'Have you read it?' I asked, pointing to the copy of *The Satanic Verses* he had tucked under his arm.

116

Marcus murmured something about perhaps over the break before saying, 'Aah, the Guest of Honour,' and moving towards a short, round man wearing a three-piece suit that bulged like upholstery. He was nearly beaten by the Sub-Dean, who almost ran across the room, pushing the less important guests out of the way. The atmosphere immediately changed as huddled groups launched themselves into the Chancellor's gravitational pull. Marcus, taking the man's sausage-shaped arm, began to navigate the room, introducing him to people, while effectively edging out the Sub-Dean, who followed in their wake.

'Is that the Chancellor?' asked Kesh. 'He's so old.'

'Otherwise known as the Octopus, so you better watch out wearing that top,' said Rachel. 'He's the type who pretends he's a hugger, and then gropes you. At Chifley's Ball last year he put his hand up a girl's skirt.'

'Did she make a complaint?' I asked.

'Better than that, she got revenge. Slipped a mickey into that fat fuck's drink, and he ended up passed out in the toilets with his fly undone. They took pictures.'

Kesh was horrified. 'They could have got into a lot of trouble over that.'

'He deserved it,' said Rachel, unrepentant. 'Besides, you ain't anyone unless you've been mickeyed.'

Rogan, who had been scanning the crowd, turned back to us. 'One ancient mollusc heading your way. I'll make myself scarce.' He reached out and put his arm around my shoulders. 'Sit with me for the talk, Pen. I'll try and keep my hands to myself.'

I thought how disappointing that would be if he was serious, and watched him disappear into the crowd.

The Chancellor made steady progress over to where we stood, the Sub-Dean hovering behind him. Marcus had been caught up in conversation with a man wearing leather patches on his cardigan's elbows.

Red-faced from the heating, the Chancellor demanded a drink of Kesh's breasts.

'I'm sorry,' began Kesh, 'but we aren't meant to serve any drinks until after . . .'

'Don't be ridiculous,' snapped the Sub-Dean. 'Get some sherry for the Chancellor at once.'

At this, some parched academics came up looking hopeful, but were shooed away by the Sub-Dean, who grabbed a glass of sherry from the table and presented it with something of a half bow. The Chancellor looked coldly at the Sub-Dean and icily at the glass.

'Didn't realise we were on rations,' he said. 'Marcus . . . Marcus,' he called. Marcus, who had been loudly recounting his Salman Rushdie anecdote, came over.

'Bryan, being overzealous again? Don't worry, Leonard, I have some very good whisky in my office. Let's get this talk started and I'll revive you with it at the end.'

He gestured to Rachel, handed over a set of keys, and gave her whispered instructions. She immediately left the room.

I found Rogan and sat down next to him. We hadn't really spoken much since the Film Group night, but when he discovered I had been one of the people to find Alice, he had been really concerned. I took that as a hopeful sign. He asked more questions about my hospital visit to Alice, and, grateful for a topic of conversation that interested us both, I told him more about Nico, whom Rogan knew from a tutorial last year. We talked until Marcus stepped up to the microphone and introduced the lecturer, a visiting American academic.

Dr McKillen had a soft Southern accent that gently blurred the end of sentences, belying her rousing message of a call to arms. While she sounded nothing like Rachel, she seemed to share her view that most of those who said they supported Rushdie and his freedom of speech were not doing enough. People's commitment to the cause was tested when she started to read some of the controversial passages from the book. You could feel a ripple of anxiety move through the audience as if militants would storm the building, and I could see the Sub-Dean glancing at his watch so often that it seemed like a nervous tic. When she finally finished her speech, exhorting us to stand up for what was right, Marcus quickly confiscated the microphone and said that instead of going into the advertised question time, perhaps people should debate the issue amongst themselves while sampling from the 'selection of delights cooked up by the Scullin kitchens'. This was embraced enthusiastically by the audience who hadn't yet seen what was on offer.

Rogan stretched his legs out.

'What did you think of that?' I asked.

'Easy to say in theory. I feel bad for the innocent people getting threatened. You know, the booksellers or publishing employees. Rushdie is being guarded twenty-four hours a day. Who's looking after them? Sometimes, other people pay the price for you trying to do the right thing.'

I nodded, not sure of what to say.

He shrugged his shoulders. 'Anyway, how's your term going? You enjoying Law?'

'It's all right,' I answered. 'Duller than I expected. Lectures especially. Weird sitting in a class with more people than in my year-level at school. Tutorials are OK.' Outside of Dale, I hadn't really bothered to meet many people in my course and tended to stay close to college rather than hang around Law School.

'Did they do the whole "look to the left, look to the right, only one of you three will make it through this course" thing?'

'That's a joke, right?' I asked.

'Must just be an Accounting first-year tradition. Anyway,

I've got to help Toby stock the beer fridge. He's expecting a rush to the college bar when people see what Bryan has in store for them.'

Kesh was already behind the food table when I got there.

'Rachel hasn't come back with the whisky,' she said, looking anxious. 'You don't think she's off drinking it some-where? And here's the Chancellor now.'

The Chancellor had set a determined course back to our table, ignoring Bryan, who was trying to introduce him to Dr McKillen. Marcus was walking with him, nodding to people as they went past.

'I think we can declare our first Academic Night a suc-cess,' Marcus announced.

The Chancellor snorted. It wasn't clear if he was agreeing or deriding.

As they reached us, Rachel slipped into the room holding a bottle and a couple of glasses.

'Perhaps you could have a pastry while we pour you a whisky, Chancellor,' I said, offering them the tray. Marcus, out of loyalty, picked one and took a large bite.

'What are they? Fish?' asked the Chancellor.

Marcus was making hard work out of swallowing it. 'Fowl would be a more accurate description,' and he directed a wink in our direction. 'Stick to the whisky, Leonard.' He waved a hand at Rachel.

'Yes, you wouldn't want a man to die of thirst,' said the

Chancellor, who on close inspection looked like he'd been hitting the bottle hard before he arrived. 'Might cut down on the conversation.'

By this stage, the Sub-Dean, abandoning Dr McKillen to well-wishers, had weaselled his way next to the Chancellor, pressing more food onto him as a way to get his attention. But the Chancellor was too busy leering at Rachel's short skirt to notice.

'A ministering angel, Marcus. I am beginning to see the attraction of being more hands-on with the students.' He laughed loudly at his own joke. 'Now, young lady, where do you come from?'

Rachel didn't answer, concentrating instead on pouring the drinks, so Kesh piped up.

'Rachel's mum is an ambassador so Rach has lived everywhere.'

Rachel shot Kesh a dirty look, but the Chancellor was captivated, and as Rachel passed him his whisky said, 'Is that so? Where is her current posting?'

Again, Rachel seemed reluctant to answer but was saved by Leiza, who pushed into the group, carrying a ream of paper.

'Excuse me, Chancellor, in light of the recent attacks on campus, I want to present a petition to you demanding better security ...' The rest of her message was swamped by the Sub-Dean who seemed to think she presented a threat to the Chancellor and jumped in front of him, waving his arms. This achieved nothing other than knocking the whisky bottle out of Rachel's hands. It smashed onto the floor. A nearby academic, already a little unnerved by the talk or perhaps the catering, screamed.

'Bryan, look what you've done,' I heard Rachel say, delightedly.

The Sub-Dean coloured but tried to pretend it had nothing to do with him. Marcus took charge, neatly taking the petition from Leiza, saying he would ensure the Chancellor would receive it at an appropriate time. He then escorted the Chancellor away with promises of cognac in his office. Rachel, who had been splashed by the whisky, used that as an excuse to leave Kesh and me to finish the cleaning up, directed by a furious Sub-Dean.

It was at least another hour before we got to the Rec Room. This was where students usually hung out if they were staying in college for the night. Sparsely furnished with a handful of rickety tables, its main attractions were the TV perched high on one wall, and on the other side of the room, past the pinball machines, the small college shop which sold lollies and stamps and, after 6 p.m., beer. Rachel, back in jeans and a t-shirt, was perched up next to the counter, chatting to Toby who was on shop duty tonight.

She was rolling cigarettes, tendrils of tobacco peeping from a bright yellow plastic pouch on the seat beside her, her tongue darting out to lick the edge of each tobacco paper.

'All in all, a very interesting night,' she said.

'Not if you had to actually work,' I answered.

'I've been working hard as well, just more cerebrally than you minions. Look what I still have.' She shook a set of keys at me.

'Do they belong to Marcus?'

She nodded. 'Think of where I could get into with these beauties. Every room in the college.'

This didn't concern me too much as Rachel waltzed into my bedroom whenever she wanted to anyway.

'I already had a snoop around Marcus's office. Checked out a few student files in Carol's filing cabinet. Very interesting. Do you know Michael's mother died when he was ten? I expect it was of disappointment in having produced something so weird.'

'She died of cancer,' said Toby, sharply. 'And if you say one more word about what you read, I'm taking those keys back to Marcus and telling him what you did. You could be expelled, you know.'

Rachel poked out her tongue, and then picked up her cigarette, which she started smoking with impatient gasps. Ignoring her, I looked around the room for Rogan. Small groups of people sat at tables chatting to each other. A tight knot of boys gathered around the pinball machine. In the middle of them was Joad. Michael was sitting on a chair at the edge of the group. The boys began to laugh, and I heard Joad say. 'You're on, mate. I accept.'

'Rogan here?' I asked Toby.

Toby shook his head. 'Got some urgent message and headed off.' He pulled a couple of beers out of the fridge for us. 'Here you go, on the house.'

'That's very generous,' said Kesh.

'Well, when I say on the house, I'll put them on Rachel's tab. Least she can do. One for Michael as well.' He frowned at Rachel, as if daring her to argue with him. But she was too busy tucking the keys away in her bag and looking as though she was about to leave. 'And here's the party pooper.' Leiza stalked across the room towards us. A smattering of applause broke out from the handful of girls in the corner, but it quickly died away.

Toby stared at her. 'Leiza, not one single thirsty academic have we had in here tonight. We were going to make a killing, but instead, thanks to your one-woman protest, they have all hightailed it out of here.'

Leiza was even more annoyed. 'Don't you start. It took ages getting all those signatures and I bet Marcus doesn't even give him the petition. They think it will all be forgotten by the start of next term and they won't have to do a thing. Get me a drink and give me a break.'

'Let me buy it for you,' said Joad, who came up to us, carrying empty bottles. 'A beer?'

Leiza narrowed her eyes, obviously wondering what the catch was, but nodded her head all the same.

'I thought that was courageous of you standing up to the Chancellor. To quote Dr McKillen: "Be brave, take action".' He smiled at Leiza. 'I admire you doing that.'

'Me too,' said Kesh.

Leiza shrugged. 'Don't know if the Sub-Dean will see it that way. He called it a career-limiting move, but then I think he was referring to his own. Apparently, we will be having a meeting tonight to discuss it.'

'Talk of the devil,' said Toby quietly, for standing in the doorway was the Sub-Dean. 'I'll keep your beer cold for you.'

The Sub-Dean blinked belligerently at us. 'Ms Parnell, a word.'

Joad actually walked Leiza to the door, patting her on her arm as she left the room. Snorts of laughter came from Joad's table of friends.

Toby waved at Michael and pointed to the beer. Michael looked blank but came up to us and I passed it over to him.

'For you,' I said.

Michael studied the beer, while I turned back and looked at Joad, who was still standing at the door, seeming pleased with himself.

'What's he up to?'

'It's for a bet,' Michael said. 'I heard them before.'

Before I could ask any questions, Kesh continued talking.

'What happened to Alice was dreadful. We should all be campaigning for better security cameras and more patrols.'

Toby shrugged. 'I don't know, Kesh. Would it really make a difference? You can't put cameras everywhere. There's always going to be some danger. Don't people just have to be sensible?'

'Are you saying it's OK women can't walk around campus by themselves?' asked Rachel. She was still annoyed at Toby. 'Alice has been disfigured for life. I'm not saying Leiza isn't a pain in the ass, but this time she's right.'

'I know the solution,' said Joad, who had swaggered over and rejoined the group. He signalled Toby for another drink.

'What?' said Rachel.

'Just say yes. There'd be no rape if you chicks put out more. That Marchmain pricktease got what she deserved.'

For one moment, the only sound was a series of descending pings from the pinball machine. Then Rachel walked straight up to Joad and smacked him as hard as she could. His head snapped back with the force of the blow. Fingermarks appeared on his face. He gaped at Rachel and then raised a closed fist to punch her, but Toby had already jumped the counter to get between them and Stoner stepped forward and grabbed his arm.

'C'mon man,' said Stoner. 'You don't want to do that.'

Joad swore as Toby told him he should leave. Some of the boys who were with him beforehand came up looking sheepish, and helped hustle Joad out of the room.

'You need ice on your hand, slugger,' said Toby, heading back to the right side of the counter. He scooped up some ice from the freezer, put it in a tea-towel and gave it to Rachel.

She made a fist and then flexed her hand. Her palm was bright red. 'Should have got in another one.'

'You could be in a whole lot of trouble,' I said. 'Maybe you'd better go to bed.'

Rachel pressed the ice into her hand. 'Hark at you, Little Miss Bursary. Of course you'd never do anything that would get you into strife.' She gave me a knowing look before saying loudly, 'You all know Joad had it coming to him.'

'Here's hoping the Sub-Dean agrees,' Toby said. 'C'mon, Rach, Pen is right. Head to bed.'

'Are you kidding me? The night is but young.' Before anyone could stop her, she picked up her bag and walked out of the room.

*

Frank puts down his notepad. 'I sense that you are not fully engaged with this process, Pen.'

'What do you mean?' I slam the diary shut. The pages

make a muffled slap. 'That's what we agreed. I write what happened and you write my report.'

'Do you view it like a bargain?' he asks. 'A direct exchange?'

'Yes, and I'm keeping up my end.'

Frank looks at me carefully. 'You could think that. Tell yourself that you've arrived on time to our sessions and have mostly answered my questions. But still, I get the impression you are not engaging in the process because you don't believe you belong here. That you really don't need treatment.'

There is no answer to that because it is exactly what I am thinking. I guess a broken clock gets to be right twice a day.

'Why did you choose to tell me about the Academic Night?'

I shrug my shoulders.

'I think you did it because it allows you to blend into the background and instead gives me all these other people to think about and analyse. A maze of human behaviours to get lost in. I am getting a picture of everyone else but you. But what you need to realise is that you are my patient, not the others. I am treating *you*. So next time, I don't want to hear about what you did in term break, or the Sub-Dean's pettiness, or how you wrote an essay or attended lectures. Next appointment I want you to start with the Friday after term break. That's your real end of the bargain.'

Reluctantly, I nod.

'Good. No more distractions then.'

But that's not right. What I read out wasn't a distraction.

Things don't go wrong in an instant. There isn't one single moment when the world suddenly splits in two. Rather, it begins with a minute crack, and then another and another, until they join together, getting bigger and wider and all the time you keep fooling yourself that this can still be fixed. That you can fill them in and everything will return to normal.

The Academic Night was the beginning. A hairline fracture, a fissure too small for Frank to notice. But I can hardly blame him; at the time I didn't see it either.

Chapter 9

It was the Friday afternoon after term break and Rachel stopped talking the moment I knocked on Kesh's open door. She was lying cat-like across Kesh's bed, ash falling from her cigarette onto the faded pink ruffled cover that Kesh had owned since primary school. There was an ash-tray on the table above her head that was solely reserved for her use. Kesh, who suffered from asthma, didn't smoke and wasn't supposed to be on our floor at all. An administrative error had meant that her non-smoking floor request had been overlooked but she didn't want to complain about it.

'A gun?' asked Kesh, who had her back to me and was standing on a chair, tying a piece of string to a hook.

Rachel caught sight of me and her mouth curved into a thin-lipped smile.

Uncertain, I rapped my knuckles against the wood. Kesh turned and beamed. Her face was the equivalent of a polygraph, unable to hide her thoughts or emotions.

'Let me guess, the Murder Game?' I asked.

'Well, no, not that Murder Game anyway,' answered Rachel.

'Rach wants to know if I have ever used a gun. Have a look through my make-up, while I get this washing hung out.'

Kesh moved the chair across the room and clambered up, threading the string around a hook on the wall and then pulling it taut.

'What are you doing here?' Rachel asked me. There was a barbed tone to her voice which I ignored. Ever since she had come back from term break there had been an amplification of her sharpness, as if just touching her could give you an electric shock.

'Tonight's the big date,' explained Kesh. 'I'm doing Pen's make-up.'

'What date? Not with Rogan?' asked Rachel.

I said nothing, and walked over to Kesh's dresser. Kesh had spent a small fortune trying to get boys to focus on her face instead of her chest. She owned an impressive array of make-up pots, tubes and brushes. I concentrated on finding a lipstick I liked.

'You're not really going?' Rachel asked.

'Didn't you tell him to ask me out?' I replied.

'Oh that. Well, now I know you better, I don't think it's a good idea.'

'Maybe you don't know me that well, because I'm going,' I said, starting to get annoyed. 'He bought tickets to see a band at the bar.'

Rachel snorted, dismissively. 'The whole college is going to the bar tonight. That's not a date, that's a class outing.'

I shrugged in an offhand kind of way but there was a bit of a 'fuck you' thrown in for good measure.

Kesh, sensing danger, tried to change the subject. 'Pen, have you used a gun?'

I grabbed a handful of lipsticks and sat down on the floor, my back against the cupboard.

'A country girl, course she has,' said Rachel. Her voice was a pretend sweet sing-song but I could hear the malice. 'But then you don't seem to like the country much. Didn't go home for the holidays like the rest of us.'

I refused to answer her. Staying for term break had allowed me to catch up on my studies and write an essay. I had even tried to visit Marcus to find out if there was any paid work I could do during the holidays, but Carol told me he was away and the Sub-Dean was in charge. I didn't bother asking him. If I was careful, I could eke out my money until next semester. After that I'd have to look for waitressing work.

'I'm from the country and I haven't,' said Kesh, stepping over my legs. She began pegging out wispy bits of bright material, lacy bras, lace undies, all belonging to Rachel, along the clothes line that cut the room in two.

'Hippy communes don't count,' said Rachel. 'So, Pen, have you?'

'Sure,' I said, beginning to draw lipstick lines on the back of my hand and rubbing them in.

'When?' Rachel pulled herself upright and, grabbing a pillow, placed it between her head and the lip of the window, positioning herself so she could see me clearly through a frame of a pink camisole and bright green French knickers.

'One of my mum's boyfriends was a gun nut and I've been rabbiting on a friend's farm.'

'Is that all?' There was something insistent about the way she spoke that made me more wary.

'Why are you asking?'

'Nothing important,' she said, and although her tone was casual, her eyes never left me. 'Just, in the holidays I found this old newspaper article about a policeman who was shot with his own gun a few years ago by a teenage girl, and it got me wondering how many teenage girls know how to shoot guns, that's all. I mean, pretty embarrassing to be shot by your own gun.'

I stared down at the red on my hand. It was too much

like blood, and I fumbled in my pocket for something to wipe it away.

'Actually, I remember that case. The policeman died, didn't he?' asked Kesh.

'They said if he had got help straight away, after the first shot, he might have lived,' said Rachel.

I wondered who 'they' were and how 'they' could have possibly known that.

Kesh clicked her tongue. 'The ambulance guy told me that could have happened to Alice if I hadn't stopped the bleeding.'

'There was this other girl who saw the whole thing but didn't go for help. Instead, they both just let him die,' Rachel said.

'Awful,' said Kesh. 'How can people be like that?'

'I don't know,' said Rachel. 'Maybe they had their reasons. I'd like to know what they were though.'

She scrutinised me as if I was a specimen under observation and I felt pinned by her gaze.

'Wouldn't you like to see the article, Pen? For some reason I thought of you when I read it.'

For one moment, I couldn't breathe. The word 'why' stuck in my throat, but Rachel guessed at my response.

'Must be because you're a law student. I've got it somewhere in my room, unless that dickhead's taken it.' She rolled onto her side. An elbow collided with the edge of the table, knocking the contents of the ashtray over the bed. Kesh stopped hanging out the washing, and began brushing the ash off, before it marked the cover. Rachel rubbed her elbow and looked crossly at her. I wanted to go over to her and shake the truth out of her. Ask her what she thought she was doing. But I didn't trust myself and kept to where I was sitting.

'What do you mean, someone's taken it?' I said.

'Just the latest thing the Toad is doing.'

There had been a brittle peace on our floor since Rachel had hit Joad, but it had the potential to fracture at any moment. Both of them had been reprimanded by the Sub-Dean and Rachel had been told that if she got in any more trouble she would be asked to leave, which she refused to take seriously. 'They can't get rid of me,' she told us. 'I know too much.'

A series of minor but nasty incidents had occurred in the week since term had started. Taxis and pizzas, not ordered by Rachel, but in her name, had turned up at college. Her mail had been found in a reception bin by an apologetic Carol. And the latest, her wet underwear had been taken from a washing machine and trampled on the laundry floor, the same washing that Kesh had probably rewashed and was now pegging out in her room.

'Joad comes into my room when I'm not there.'

'How do you know?' I asked.

'He moves stuff around.'

I had never spent much time in Rachel's room. To be honest, neither did Rachel. She enjoyed commandeering other people's rooms and public areas. Her own she used as a train station, from which she was always arriving or departing.

'Remember Wednesday?' she asked. 'How it rained really hard in the afternoon. I came back from Language Lab and my window had been opened and my bed was sopping wet. Then two nights ago, I was fast asleep and suddenly, at three a.m., my alarm went off. Volume was up full bore. I just about had a heart attack.'

'You should report him,' said Kesh. 'That's really creepy.'

Rachel rolled a cigarette, holding it in her nicotine-stained fingers for us all to admire, her fingernails bitten down low, exposing the deep pink-red underneath.

'But how do you know it's Joad?' I asked.

'How do you know that it isn't?' she snapped back. She lit the cigarette. The needling that was always part of Rachel was dialling itself into something more menacing. But we were rescued from our conversation by a man in the doorway, with a gun in his hand, or rather Toby, brandishing a water pistol.

'What's going on here? A meeting of the coven and I didn't get an invite.' He bounded into the room, all excited.

'What's with the firearm?' asked Rachel.

'I'm going to commit a murder and I'm going to enjoy it. Kesh, I've got to ledge out of your window to Joad's room.'

While every room was able to be securely locked and bolted by the door, it was easy to break in through the window, provided you didn't have an issue with heights. All you had to do was crawl along the common window ledge that stretched the length of the building and sneak in through the window. It was forbidden to do so, of course, after a girl had fallen from the second floor of Page Tower and broken her leg the year before.

'You're killing him with a water pistol? That is so lame,' said Rachel.

'What do you want, a red-hot poker? I've been stalking that bastard all week but he is hardly ever alone. He's usually hanging out with Stoner, but Stoner's playing the pinnies. He's not answering the door, but I know he is in there. I can hear music.'

Kesh bit her lip. 'It's against the rules.'

'Screw that,' said Rachel. There were only a handful of people left in the Murder Game and she was sensing victory. That morning, she had been vocal about who she would invite to share the winning keg with her.

'Why not wait outside the room till he comes out,' Kesh suggested.

'There's someone in college trying to kill me, remember.

I'll be a sitting duck. And I found out that Joad was the one who started the rumour that I had AIDS.'

'Toby could go from my room,' said Rachel. 'But then it's further, which would only make it more dangerous.'

Defeated by the joint attack, Kesh said, 'All right. But if anyone asks, you crawled from Rachel's.'

Toby stood on her bed and slid the window back. He carefully prised the fly screen off, handed it to Rachel and hoisted himself up onto the ledge. Turning back to face us, he saluted. 'If I should fall and die, I leave all my CDs to Kesh. Rachel, you get my collection of used sex toys and Pen . . .'

'The stereo,' I said.

'My best pair of sequin disco hotpants, in memory of the good times.'

'Can I trade that for your stereo?' I asked.

'Philistine.' Toby hoisted himself through the gap and climbed out onto the ledge. Pretending to overbalance, much to Kesh's horror, he blew a goodbye kiss and started crawling, the water pistol stuck into the waist of his jeans.

'Excellent,' said Rachel. 'I had no idea Joad was still in.'

Kesh peered out of the window, her forehead creased. 'He's crawling . . . he's there, I think . . . he's stopped, grabbing his pistol . . . this ledge is so narrow.' She leant out further, sticking her head through the window. 'He's looking in ... no, hang on ... he's crawling back already. Thank goodness, that was quick.'

She jumped down and Toby's feet came into sight and then the rest of him, like a film on rewind. He reversed past the window, diving head first through it and lay laughing on the bed, his water pistol clutched in his hand.

'Did you kill the fucker?' asked Rachel.

Toby was laughing so hard, it took a while before he could get out, 'No.'

'Why not?' Rachel shoved his feet off the bed, and sat down next to him.

'He wasn't alone. Shall we say, he had his hands full.' Toby made a suggestive grab in the air and thrust his pelvis back and forth. He then put his hands to his cheeks and gave a silent scream.

'Did he see you?' I asked at the same time as Rachel said, 'He was having sex? Who with?'

'You will never guess in a million years.'

Kesh began waving her arms. 'Don't tell us. It isn't our business. I shouldn't have let you.' But no one paid her the slightest attention. She picked the fly screen off the desk and began hooking it back into place.

'Tell me,' Rachel demanded, pushing Toby. He squirted the water pistol in her face, and then dropped it beside them. He seemed torn between wanting to drag out the anticipation and blurting out the answer.

'It was ... Leiza.'

'No,' said Rachel, absolutely delighted, and I could see her eyes gleaming at all the possibilities this information could open up.

'Scout's honour. Dyb, dyb, dyb, or in this case, dob, dob, dob,' said Toby.

'But he hates her,' said Rachel.

'No he doesn't,' said Kesh. 'He's been helping organise her rally. You know, the one protesting the Screwdriver Man attacks and the lack of security on campus. Ever since Alice got hurt it has been all systems go. I saw Joad photocopying flyers the other day in the office.'

Toby sat up, looking sceptical. 'Joad, a closet feminist? Next you'll be telling me you believe in Santa Claus, Kesh.'

Rachel looked as if all her Christmases had come at once. 'No one is going to believe this. Where's your camera, Kesh?'

'Michael mentioned something about Joad having a bet about Leiza,' I said.

Rachel chortled as she stood up on the bed. 'It must be to have sex with her. This just gets better and better. I've got to see it for myself.'

Kesh flared. 'No one else is going out that window. If you do, I am going straight to the Sub-Dean.' For once, she looked as if she'd stand up to Rachel, and after a moment's hesitation, Rachel decided not to push it.

'Fine.' She slouched off the bed. 'But you can't stop me sitting outside his door until they surface. Then I can tell Leiza about the bet and watch the fireworks start. She might murder Joad for you, Toby.'

'As long as it goes on my tally,' said Toby. 'Anyway, I've got better things to do than wait around for them. Residential assistants can't be seen as condoning such behaviour.' He walked out of the door, sniggering to himself.

Rachel noticed that he had left his water pistol behind. 'Hey, Tobs, wait up,' she called and quickly followed him. There was a muffled exchange and then we heard Toby yell, 'Bitch' at her. Rachel came back, looking even more satisfied.

'Joad is my next target 'cause I just killed Toby with his own gun.' She punched the air, and then turned to face me. 'Just like what happened to that poor policeman.'

True to her word, Rachel sat in front of Joad's door and didn't move the entire time I was in Kesh's room getting my make-up done. I barely spoke to Kesh, who fussed around wondering aloud whether to use a glossy or matte lipstick. I sat there, silent, my mind churning.

'All done. Don't you look beautiful,' she cooed. 'I'm sure you'll have a great time tonight.'

Thanking Kesh, I left, only to find Rachel was sitting in the breakout area, right outside Joad's door. She was fishing out noodles from a mug with a fork, a couple of beer bottles next to her. Michael came wandering up the corridor. He didn't stop until he had reached his door, which was a couple up from my room. I could hear his key turning in the lock.

'Why don't you just knock on the door and get it over and done with,' I said.

'Why would I do that? The anticipation is the best bit,' Rachel answered. 'I love to keep people dangling on a line.' She curled her feet up next to her. 'Stay with me and we can have a chat. I'll make it worth your while. Look, beer.' She pulled a six-pack out from under her chair.

'I thought your allowance hadn't come through.'

Rachel waved a hand dismissively. 'This term I've got other income sources. But don't change the subject. I always knew you were hiding something. Getting caught up in a murder case was a bit more serious than I expected, but maybe the newspaper article was inaccurate.'

It was a shot straight across the bow.

'How did you find out about it?'

'Read your bursary application in Marcus's office last term.'

'You did what?'

'I was curious, that's all. Saw that you were a witness in

a case. It rang a bell. Did a bit of research in the holidays. But you weren't just a witness. You started off being charged with it and you were found guilty of being an accessory, whatever that means. Sounds like I should wear you on my wrist.' She rattled her bangles and smirked up at me.

'Why are you doing this? I thought we were friends.' I was trying to whisper as I didn't want anyone to overhear, but mixed with anger at her betrayal it came out as a hiss.

She put her head to one side, watching me closely. She was enjoying this. 'Friends tell each other things, Pen. I just want to know the truth. Tell me what happened and I'll give you back the article. Scout's honour.' She held up three fingers and smirked at me.

'So you still have it?'

'It will be in my room somewhere, I'm sure. I can find it for you now.'

'I've got to meet Rogan.'

Rachel's two perfectly plucked eyebrows became slanting accents. 'If you really wanted it, you would stay here with me.'

Just then, Joad's door opened and his ruffled head stuck out of it. When he saw us, he glowered, went back inside and quickly shut the door.

'About time,' said Rachel, suddenly distracted from me. 'OK, not now. I'll meet you over at the bar.'

'Rachel, you're not going to tell people, are you? You're not going to tell Rogan?'

She smiled. 'Why would I do that? Remember, I was the one who told him to ask you out. But as it happens, there's something I need to talk to Rogan about anyway.'

'What?' This came out sharper than I meant it to, and Rachel laughed.

'Guilty conscience, Pen?'

She had me exactly where she wanted me, but I wasn't going to be as easily caught as that. Rachel wasn't the only one who could call the shots.

'Fine,' I said. 'Come to the bar. If you kill Joad, I'll buy you a celebratory drink.'

Rachel looked at me, surprised. 'Sounds good. I'll see you there.'

Leaving her curled up in a chair, positioned squarely in front of Joad's door, I made a detour back to my room before heading down the stairs.

Chapter 10

With a fluid movement, the guy on the door held my wrist, inked it and put it under the ultra-violet light to check. Even allowing for the lamp's luminescent glow, his skin had the pallor of someone who didn't often see the sun. Food obviously wasn't a high priority either, as his combat boots looked like ballast for his scrawny body.

'Mr Cohen,' he said, noticing Rogan standing behind me. He shook Rogan's hand and then, in a complicated twist, flipped it over to stamp. 'Business or pleasure?'

'Always a pleasure to see you, Pete.' Rogan nodded his head at the two bouncers who stood either side of the table. Wearing Death Rider black motorcycle jackets with large red crosses emblazoned on them, they ignored him as if customer relations were not in their job description. Turning back to Pete, he said, 'Should be a good gig.'

'For you, maybe,' Pete complained. 'I've locked all the windows. Got extra security. We're trying out a new ultra-violet ink and I still reckon we've got hundreds more people in here than what we've sold tickets for. I don't know how the buggers do it.'

'Students, what do you expect? You'll make your money back on alcohol.'

'You're one to talk. We're only licensed for just under two thousand people. If we get busted for overcrowding and are shut down, none of us will be happy then.'

Rogan laughed. 'You're paranoid, mate. No one checks anything here.'

'Am I now?' Pete said. 'Or is everyone out to get me?' He grimaced before grabbing the wrist of the next person.

There was a yell behind us, some drunken swearing. Suddenly, the bouncers were roused, their capacity for violence awakened. Turning back, I saw a stubbled head, the face obscured by the enormous arm of a third bouncer. The boy was in a headlock, yelling while being dragged away into the shadows.

'You're banned, Nico,' Pete shouted. 'Piss off. Don't come back if you know what's good for you.'

Rogan and I stood there, until Pete said, 'Keep moving,

folks, nothing to see here.' Rogan gave me a nudge and I moved past the desk and into the building.

The bar was at the sunken end of the split-level Union Building. The upper half, where we entered, housed the campus shops. The box-like bakery, mini-supermarket, optometrist and news agency were all closed now with locked roller doors keeping them safe from the drunken hordes. We walked past them down the large steps that led into the dark underworld of music and noise.

The stage was straight in front of us and the support band was already playing. Around the corner, beer and spirits were served in plastic cups, and past that were the pool tables, toilets and a handful of chairs. The decor was grubby black and you had to gently peel yourself off each surface touched.

Standing there, I could make out voices but not words floating above crashing guitars. Bodies were crowded between us and the stage. Boys, uncoordinated individually, moshed as one, moving towards us like the tide. I hung back, mindful of getting swamped. Rogan, sensing my reluctance, grabbed my hand. At his touch, my skin sparked. He plunged in and pulled me after him.

The air was salty with the sweat of strangers. The darkness smelt of cigarettes and alcohol. Jostled by the crowd, Rogan moved behind me, keeping his arms around my body as a protective barrier. He set a course past the mixing desk, and soon we were at the far edge of the crowd where there was room to stand side by side. Rogan let go. I felt a hiccup of disappointment and wondered if I could take his hand as casually as he had taken mine.

Standing there, I didn't listen to the music, or watch the band. Instead, I focused on him. Should I take a small step and kiss him on the mouth? Nestle into him accidentally on purpose? People around us were doing exactly that. Next to us were a lip-locked pair clutching at each other with the desperation of people who still lived at home and needed to make the most of any darkened room. Elsewhere, intertwined couples were more relaxed. Some of them had been together so long they were starting to resemble each other, like dogs and owners.

Rogan turned his head and I smiled, hoping that maybe he wanted to take that small step towards me. But he wasn't looking my way. He scanned the audience. With a sudden burst of drums and a crash of guitars, the song ended. The crowd cheered enthusiastically as the lead singer shouted goodbye and the band left the stage.

A couple of fluorescents flickered on, turning the room from pitch-black to murky, and a roadie clambered across the stage, moving bits of equipment. The PA squawked and began pumping out recorded music. Rogan jogged my shoulder and mimed getting a drink, as the people around us began moving in all directions, but mostly towards where the alcohol was sold. I was left next to a neglected juke box as he went to stand in line. Sticky-taped to the top of it was a piece of lined paper, scrawled capitals running perpendicular across it saying, 'Choose Smoke on the Water, get evicted, signed Your Friendly Bar Staff.'

'I dare you to play it,' whispered Rachel in my ear. She stood there in her red dress, with a small leather handbag slung across her body, the strap as thin as a whip. The dress didn't fit as well now. Frayed at the edges from past nights, her hipbones and ribs were ridges under the material. My stomach turned to stone at the sight of her.

'You got Joad?' I asked.

'Fucking awesome. Joad and Leiza came out together and I asked Joad if it was true he had made a bet about bonking her. The look on her face. They had such a massive screaming match, I was tempted to get my Walkman to record it. Eventually, she stormed off and when he tried to follow her, I stopped him, took out the water gun and splat, killed him.'

'What did he do?'

'Went completely berserk. I thought he was going to punch me for sure. But people had heard the yelling and came out. Even Michael took time away from whatever weird shit he does in his room, and when Joad saw all of them, he left. But anyway, I've killed the Toad.' She began to look around us. 'So, where's Rogan and where's my drink?'

'He's buying drinks now.'

'So, this really is a date,' she said, looking surprised. 'Hope he's not doing it for a bet as well.'

'What?' I asked, a wave of doubt crashing into my brain.

'And speak of the devil, perfect timing.' Rachel turned towards Rogan, who weaved his way through the crowd, carrying two beers.

'Rachel,' he said, and although his face was neutral, I could hear the frown in his voice.

'Thank you, kind sir,' said Rachel, and grabbed the first beer. Rogan looked annoyed as he handed me the other.

'Now, Rogan, you are just the person I needed to see.' Rachel kept her eyes directly on him, taking a swig of the beer. 'Pen, I really must borrow your date. But don't worry, I'll bring him back in one piece.' She grabbed his hand and pulled him away. I thought he would protest, refuse to budge, tell her to stop being stupid, but he allowed himself to be dragged to just out of earshot. As I watched them, I began to feel something like hatred towards Rachel.

Rogan had his back to me, so it was her face I focused on. I could see her mouth moving and felt stabs of anger at what she must be telling him. I wanted to stop her and Rachel had given me the perfect idea. I even imagined the words I would say to her: 'You ain't anyone unless you've been mickeyed', as if she herself had given me permission. I fumbled in my bag for my sleeping tablets, a relic from the past. All I had to do was to dissolve them in my beer and get Rachel to drink it, and when she started to become drowsy, I'd find someone like Kesh or Toby to take her home. Tomorrow, I'd work out some story about the court case to satisfy her curiosity and convince her not to tell other people.

But before I had even got them out of my bag, Rogan was back. I tried to smile as if I had been having a great time standing next to a juke box, worried that somehow this date was all a joke.

'I've got to go do something,' he said.

I tried to read on his face what Rachel had been saying.

'What was that about?'

'Nothing important.'

'I could come too.'

'No. You stay here. You don't want to miss the band.' He leant forward and his mouth brushed my cheek, a kiss that five minutes ago would have meant everything. Now the timing was off and I wondered if I was being played. All I could think of was how angry I was at Rachel.

Rogan pushed through the crowd. I tried to follow his progress and then caught sight of Rachel waiting for him at the top of the stairs. Where she stood was well lit. The light splashed across her face, turning her skin a skeletal white. Rogan jumped up the steps three at a time to meet her. They didn't leave by the front door as I expected, instead walking past it and towards the metal-box row of shops. I didn't understand what they could be doing there. Everything was shut up. But Rogan moved in between the bakery and the optometrist and opened a door. Rachel went through it and then, looking around furtively, he followed her. I began to move past people, trying to see where they had gone. I climbed the steps. To my right, at the entrance, a girl in a low top and tiny skirt was arguing with the two bouncers that her ticket had been stolen and she should be let in. They stood watching her, almost licking their lips. I quickly darted behind their backs and made it to the door.

It was the type of door you'd walk past every day and never notice. There was nothing on it to give a clue where it might lead to. No 'Private' or 'Keep Out', no exit sign above, just a door. Mimicking Rogan's look around, I checked there was no one watching and opened it. Inside was a dimly lit corridor with rooms leading off it. Probably offices, I thought. There was no sign of Rogan or Rachel and, feeling uncertain about going any further, I turned to retrace my steps, only to run straight into solid muscle.

I was facing a chest that blocked the doorway and the light outside. He wasn't one of the bouncers but he looked as if hurting people was a professional objective. He was enormous.

'What are you doing?'

'My friends,' I stammered. 'They came in here. I just wanted to . . .'

There was a greedy smile, a metal tooth in the middle of it. A red cross was tattooed on his neck. He placed a hand on my back. It was large enough to span my shoulder blades. 'Let's look for them then.'

'Maybe I made a mistake.' I tried to turn towards the door but his fingers moved from my back to my front, stopping at my chest, before forcing me back along the corridor.

A light clicked on ahead of us. A skinny figure in combat boots appeared. The ticket guy Rogan had spoken to.

'Tommy,' said Pete. 'Who's that with you?'

The hand on my back lifted momentarily and I ducked under the arm and ran for the door. Behind me, I could hear Pete speaking and Tommy laughing. I ran back down the stairs, into the crowd. Hiding behind a group of girls, I turned to see if either of them had followed me, but they hadn't. I decided there was safety in numbers and headed towards the pool tables to get as far away from them as possible.

Even in the middle of the day, sunlight struggled to break through the eternal night of the pool tables area. Black walls, black roof, weak light illuminated only the tables themselves and the haze from cigarettes.

Goths were clustered around the first table. A girl in a purple dress was watching two boys playing. At her neck, I saw eyes gleaming red in the dark, peering through her hair. That rat had a better social life than most students. People from college were playing on the next two tables. Emelia was taking the shot, her tongue poking out as she concentrated. She had stopped me at lunch and asked me if Rogan and I were 'an item'. I had given her a non-committal response that nevertheless implied that the answer was yes, so she was the last person I wanted to know that Rogan had interrupted our date to do something secret with Rachel. I took the furthest route away from her and noticed Toby playing nearby. His aim went wild and, swearing, he passed the cue on.

'What's up?' he said. 'You OK?'

I was beginning to feel a bit stupid for following Rachel and Rogan in the first place, so all I said was, 'You got in,' because I knew Toby didn't have a ticket.

'Of course, I'm an expert in back passages,' he said in a mock-camp voice. He pointed to a low, blacked-out window next to the table. People were sitting in a group in front of it, but looking closely I saw an additional head slowly emerging, until an extra body joined them. I recognised the white sheep-fleece hair. It was Joyce, for once without a book. He sat there chatting casually for a minute or so, then, picking up the mostly empty glass that had been placed in front of him, he finished the drink and strolled over to the bar to order the next round.

'Make mine a triple,' Toby told him, as he walked past us.

'I thought they locked the windows,' I said.

'Screwdrivers aren't just for cutting up defenceless women,' Toby answered. 'You seen Rachel?'

I shook my head.

'I've just been telling everyone how I could kill that bitch. You know, she got me this afternoon with my own pistol. The cheek. Mind you, she better watch out. Joad's outside and he might just murder her good and proper. But I forgot, where's the rugged Rogan?'

'I don't know.'

Toby handed me a glass of what looked like water.

'Trouble in paradise? Young love in peril? Tell your Uncle Toby all about it.'

I shook my head, shrugged off his embrace and downed the glass. It was gaspingly hot.

'Always more fish in the sea, which doesn't mean you need to drink like one,' Toby said. 'Now let's see if there is anyone's shoulder suitable for you to cry on. Joad's here, of course, if you prefer a human pig. We could ask Leiza if he has a corkscrew penis. Or if you prefer butch with a moustache, and really who doesn't, there's a guy over there who could be an undercover cop. Then of course, there's Michael, if you want to take pity on the socially awkward.'

I looked up to see Michael at the far side of the table, standing with, and yet still separate from, the group. Someone opened a door nearby, and the light from outside the room glinted off his glasses, making his eyes metallic, as though he was a computer, taking in data and not giving anything in return.

'Toby, it's your turn,' Annabel yelled out from behind us. Someone started saying 'One-Two, One-Two,' into a microphone.

'Wait there until I finish hustling,' he said.

But I didn't, because I wasn't going to spend the night with people asking me where Rogan was or talking about Rachel, and I had caught sight of the man with the moustache whom Toby had described. It was Dale.

'I'll be right back,' I called to Toby.

After winding my way through two more pool tables, Dale noticed me and smiled.

'What are you doing here? Shouldn't you be reading your case-law, revising notes?' I joked. 'Don't tell me you're slacking off.' Behind us, I could see Stoner, who had been openly plying his trade around the pool tables, was now staring at Dale in shock.

'Guilty as charged. Thought I'd come and see the band. My cousin's the bass player. Wife's away with the kids. Don't like being home in an empty house.'

There was something in the way he spoke that made me wonder if everything was OK at home, but I felt too uncomfortable to ask.

We watched the empty stage. Rows of people stood in front of us, waiting in anticipation.

'You know, people think you're undercover,' I said.

Dale laughed. 'I thought I was being discreet, standing in the corner.' There was nothing discreet about him. People were giving him a wide berth because he looked exactly like a policeman, from his button-down shirt, neatly pressed trousers, to the way he stood alertly with his weight evenly distributed on both legs.

'A young lady with a rat told me I should be off doing something useful. She suggested arresting the Screwdriver Man.'

'Is that why there's extra security?'

Dale's face turned grim. 'Death Riders are not my idea of security. Stay well away from them.'

I thought about telling him what had happened before, but then I saw Rachel cut through the crowd and push to the front of the queue at the bar. I couldn't see Rogan around. Now was a good time to confront her, so I said goodbye to Dale. She bought a beer and left it on a ledge before heading into the toilets. I stood outside for a few minutes. There was a loud roar as the drummer came out and sat behind his kit. People began to move towards the stage. Girls came flooding out of the toilets but no Rachel. I pushed open the door.

Black-penned graffiti covered the roughly painted walls: 'Ally's a bitch', 'Jo was 'ere', 'Shazza 4 EVA'. New Uni-Safe posters warning women about the Screwdriver Man covered older Uni-Safe posters warning women about someone else. No one was at the sinks and only one cubicle door was closed. As I walked in, a toilet flushed, and Rachel came out of it, rubbing her nose. She went over to the sink and washed her hands before she caught sight of me in the mirror's reflection.

'Hey,' she said. She threw her arms around me, but misjudged where I was and stumbled. 'Isn't this the best night?' She tried hugging me again.

'Where's Rogan?' I asked.

Rachel shot me a blurred version of her unrepentant look. 'Who cares about Rogan? You shouldn't.' She turned back to the mirror, her make-up smudged across her face. She sniffed several times and ran her hand under her nose. 'You know, after all that's happened, you shouldn't be messing around with Rogan.'

'What do you mean?'

'Didn't you say you need to be of good character to be a lawyer? The way I look at it you're already pushing the boundary on that one. I mean, uni is a lot better than what happened to your friend. You know the one . . .' She cocked two fingers in a gun shape and shot me. 'Assuming she was your friend, which could be wrong, because I'm guessing you weren't friends by the end of it.' Giggling, she turned her finger gun on herself.

A white hot heat began to throb behind my eyes.

She turned to look in the cracked mirror, playing with the strands of hair that hung down over her face. I wanted to walk over to her and grab a handful of them and pull hard.

'What did you do with Rogan?' I asked. 'What did you tell him?'

Her eyes were almost closed to slits. 'You know, Rogan made me swear not to say anything.' Clumsily putting her hand up to her mouth, she mimicked zipping her lips shut. I watched her in the mirror and felt rage. I didn't have the words to express how much. I just knew I didn't want to talk to her and I didn't want Rachel to keep talking to me. I turned to leave.

'Don't do anything I wouldn't do,' she called out.

Walking out the door, I noticed Rachel's beer was still sitting on the ledge.

So I did it. There would be a full reckoning the next day, of course. I knew that but I just didn't care. I wouldn't find anyone to take her home. Let one of the bouncers look after her. As far as I was concerned this punishment didn't even seem like enough, but it was all I could think of. I pulled the tablets out of my bag, crumbled a couple into her drink and waited for Rachel to come out.

'You still here?' she asked.

'Joad's out the front. Thought you should know. Your beer?'

She nodded and I handed it to her. I smiled.

'Down the hatch,' she said, and drained it in one. 'And if the Toad's out there, I'll go the back way to have a ciggie. Need some fresh air.'

I watched her push the fire door near us that had been propped open with a paint tin full of sand and cigarette butts. She swaggered through.

Chapter 11

There was still no sign of Rogan as I moved towards the music. I attempted to shove a path through, but the crowd was resistant to latecomers and I got shunted to the far edge of the speaker stack, with half the stage obscured. I couldn't see much through the people in front of me, other than the lead singer, a thin girl in the middle of the stage, wearing a black singlet, jeans and enormous hooped earrings.

The guitars and drums were dialled up to eleven and next to the speakers, the bass line became my heart beat. The girl was playing her guitar, dancing in a sideways shrug. As she came up to the microphone, her face hidden behind her fringe, her voice smacked into me.

She was strong and sexy and I doubted if any guy had

ever abandoned her during a first date. I watched her as she whispered, screamed and scowled her way through the songs. Sometimes, when the crowd shouted out the chorus, her voice was swamped but she sang on and didn't care.

Still angry after my run-in with Rachel, I pushed forward again and made it to the moshpit by the time that emotion was jostled out of me. After several songs that I felt in my bones, my ears were ringing and slam-dancing giants seemed to be circling me, completely shutting out the world. I moved further back. That was when I caught sight of Rogan sitting at the bar. Stoner was perched alongside him, talking in his ear. It was hard to work out Rogan's expression, but it was clear he wasn't looking for me. I moved further into the crowd, but every few minutes I would catch myself looking in his direction and even though Stoner disappeared after the next song, he sat there not moving.

The encore finished, the lights turned on at full strength revealing a grimy floor, and I was standing like an idiot amongst blinking couples who had been making out in the anonymous darkness. I turned away from where Rogan was sitting, trying to see if there was anyone I knew, to look as if I had been having a great night with friends. Through the crowd, I saw Michael coming towards me. He waved an arm to catch my attention, but being with him would be even worse than being alone, so I pretended I didn't see him and began to move towards the pool tables in search of Toby.

A hand reached out and caught me around the waist. 'There you are,' said Rogan. 'I've been looking for you everywhere.' He pulled me close to him.

I was too conscious of the warmth of his arm, the length of his body against me, to convincingly play it cool. He leant forward and kissed me on the mouth. Any recriminations vanished.

'Had a good night?' he asked.

'Had its moments,' I answered, a little breathlessly. 'You?'

'To be truthful, I'd have to say right now is definitely the highlight.' He smiled. 'Still, I thought the band sounded good.'

'Yeah,' I said, my world suddenly exploding with possibilities. 'Their singer is great.'

Rogan ordered beers and found us a couple of seats near the wall.

'Sorry about before,' he said. 'I just wanted this night to be easy. See the band, have some drinks. Fun, you know. But Rachel. Look, I know she's your friend . . .'

I thought back to her in the bathroom. 'She's not my friend. Just has the room next to me.'

'Oh, good,' said Rogan. He put his arm around my shoulders. 'I don't like saying this about anyone but she is full of it. The stories she tells, I wouldn't believe a word of them.'

'Toby warned me about that at the start of the year,' I said, relief washing over me.

'Maybe we should head into town after this?'

I nodded enthusiastically. For Rogan I'd leave the confines of university.

People were finishing their drinks, making plans for the rest of the night and beginning to leave. We sat and watched. Dale was waiting for those in front of him to move. He gave me a nod. As I went to wave goodbye, Rogan grabbed my arm.

'Do you know him?'

'Sure, I was talking to him earlier. He's a cop. Toby thinks he could be working undercover.' I said this as a joke but Rogan stood up quickly.

'I've got to head back to college. You coming?'

Not waiting for an answer, he grabbed my hand. And with none of the electricity from earlier, he pulled me through the crowd, towards the fire exit.

He kicked the paint tin propping the door open out of the way. It lurched sideways, cigarette butts and sand spilling on the ground. The door slammed behind us and the noise was instantly cut off, as if it had been strangled. Standing in a small courtyard surrounded by a timber fence and a gate, I could smell fermenting beer and rotting food. Two large industrial bins were next to us. Far away, I could hear sounds of people leaving, laughing, talking and singing, but out here there was no one.

'You coming back to Scullin?' Rogan asked, dropping my hand.

'How about town?' I asked. 'Go to a club?'

He shook his head. 'I've got to get back.'

Unsure what had gone wrong, I stood there confused. He opened the gate and began walking. The wind picked up and I could feel goose bumps forming. My clothes were still warm, damp with the sweat from the bar. I followed, pulling the gate shut behind me, giving it a shove to make sure the catch had clicked into place. Tracey always said you could tell a country kid by their compulsive need to close all gates.

'Always finish what you have started,' she'd say, imitating her dad's English accent. *'Take responsibility. No excuses.'*

He was quick with the clichés but even quicker with his belt.

The path we were walking along, more a worn dirt strip, was the quickest route between the bar and the sporting fields on the other side of the river, but only if you were prepared to get wet. A full moon, partially covered by clouds, gave the ground a faint glow. Trying to catch up to Rogan, I tripped on an uneven patch of ground, a tree root lying just under the earth. At my stumble, Rogan turned back. He stood there, tense, waiting for me.

'C'mon, it's freezing,' was all he said. He started moving ahead in long strides.

This part of the river was wide. Clumps of ferns and sprawling bushes covered the banks. As the path ran parallel to the water, I looked across to the far side. Scrubby poplars stood to attention, guarding the playing fields behind. But as I watched, a smaller shadow moved amongst the trees. I stopped to look again but the wind pushed clouds across the moon, the light dimmed and I lost sight of it.

'What are you doing?' Rogan asked, less impatient now. He looked back in the direction I had been staring.

'Thought I saw something,' I said. He gazed out into the darkness. The clouds shifted and the river turned from black to scum-flecked grey in the moonlight.

'In the river?'

'No, over in the trees.' But the direction of his gaze didn't change.

'What's that?' he asked, not pointing across the bank, but down into the water. It was a larger patch of darkness, rotating on the river's flow, stuck amongst the reeds on the far side.

'Just some rubbish,' I said. But Rogan frowned, pushed past branches and slapping leaves, and clambered down the embankment.

'It's definitely something large.' His voice moved from

curious to anxious. 'It kind of looks ...' but without finishing, he pulled off his socks and shoes.

'What are you doing?' I said, scrambling down the loosened dirt and pebbles to stand next to him. 'It'll be junk.' But at the water's edge, it was more solid than that.

Rogan ignored me and put a foot in. Swearing under his breath at its coldness, he began to wade out.

'How deep's the water?' I called. 'You can swim, right?'

A sudden drop in depth took him from knees to waist. His arms windmilled and he almost overbalanced. The water got deeper still as Rogan neared the shape and he began to swim. The churn from his splashing freed whatever it was from its moorings and it began to float along the river, as though this was a game and it was trying to evade him. Rogan stretched out his hand and grabbed. It lifted before flopping backwards with a sucking slap, submerged, and then bobbed back up. Now it was longer, blossoming in the river.

'Too deep to stand ... can't get it out of the water on my own.' His teeth were chattering and I could hear his fear. I began to take off my shoes, slipping my heels out, peeling off my socks, hoping that someone else would turn up, take charge and we could leave. But there was no one.

As Rogan came nearer, pulling the thing behind him, I stepped in. Sharp stones cut at my feet, so kicking my legs behind me, I swam out to him, clothes weighing me down, my breath snap-frozen in my lungs. Even as I got to Rogan, a matter of metres, I was shivering, but it wasn't the temperature. The shape had become a body. An arm stretched out towards me in the water.

'We need to flip it over,' Rogan said. He counted, as if we were going to lift an awkward piece of furniture. I stood in the chest-high water, my heart sinking down into the slimy silt, not wanting to touch the skin. Both of us grappled with the wet clothes around the torso, and like a monstrous puppet, it staggered upward, turned and fell.

Rogan recoiled and I could hear shock catching in his throat. But I already knew who it was, the scars glistening on her wrists, the golden anklet and the handbag, twined around her like a hangman's rope.

We dragged her over the rocks, until she lay on the riverbank. Panting, I knelt on the ground next to her, Rogan on the other side. I stared at her face, expecting her eyes to pop open, to hear her laugh and say 'got you'. But Rachel's skin was blue in the moonlight, naked without her makeup, and she didn't move at all. The bangles she always wore were missing.

'Fuck,' said Rogan, his breath shallow. He felt her wrist for a pulse. All I could hear was my own heart beating in my chest. He moved to her face, covered her mouth with his, and began pumping in air, feeling her ribs, positioning his hands, hesitantly at first and then becoming firmer, pushing down on her chest. But it was like handling a slab of meat.

'Go get help,' he said. 'I'll keep trying.'

Much later that night, I was taken back to the river. People talked in hushed tones, huddled behind official tape. I looked for Rogan and saw him in the distance, wrapped in a blanket as I was, talking to a policeman. Uniforms were moving around a plastic cocoon, strapped to a gurney. A tall man slid it gently into the ambulance as if he might wake her up. They drove away.

No sirens. No flashing lights.

People talked to me but it felt as if I was the person underwater. I could see heads nodding and mouths moving but I caught few words. When I tried to listen, the ambulance officer talked of stitches and a tetanus shot. The problem was their questions only had one answer. All of this was my fault. I just kept shaking my head until they gave up.

The Sub-Dean took me to his car to drive me back to college. He winced as I sat down on the passenger seat which he had already covered with a towel. Looking down at myself, I saw my dress was ripped and wet, covered with mud. He kept talking at me but I looked out of the window and watched the campus floating past, a different place at night, hiding its secrets as I had tried to hide mine. When he turned into the car park, I told him I was going to take a shower. He said something about finding Toby to take care of me but at the front door, I told him I just wanted to be alone and limped up the stairs straight to the bathroom.

The hot water burnt needles into my flesh. As my body began to thaw, pain returned. Turning the tap to maximum strength, I crouched, huddled in the cubicle. The bandage on my right foot where the rocks had cut deepest began to peel off, so I unwound it. The heat burnt the raw flesh. My leaking foot turned the water pink. I watched it splash on the white tiles. Blood, dirt, river, shower, this night, everything disappeared down the drain. I wanted to be washed away.

I turned off the shower and wrapped myself in the blanket again. Unlocking the door, for one moment I thought I saw someone standing in the bathroom, but it was only my reflection in the mirror. Rachel would often be in there, brushing her teeth, putting on make-up or plucking her eyebrows, saying how the light in the bathroom was better than in her room, when really what she wanted was an audience. My last picture of her was the face in the toilets, looking at me in triumph, as if she had held all the cards. That was when I felt the hard pebble inside of me. A tiny piece of flint that said at least my secret was safe.

As I left the bathroom, I walked past the chair where Rachel had been eating noodles, the cup and spoon still lying on the floor. I passed Joad's door, Kesh's door, until I got to Rachel's. All was quieter than I ever remembered it

171

being. Everyone must be asleep or still out. I looked back down the corridor. Only one door had a light shining under it, Michael's, but there was no noise coming from inside.

Opening my own door, I felt a breeze from the window and noticed a piece of folded paper had fallen to the floor. A newspaper article. The one Rachel claimed was missing. The date was from three years ago. A stark two-word headline: ARRESTS MADE. She had scribbled my name at the top of the page. Had she slipped it under my door, giving it back to me as she had promised? That thought was almost too much to cope with. Feeling lightheaded, I stared down at the article. An enormous picture of a solitary wreath stuck to a wire fence. *Two fifteen-year-old girls were taken into custody late last night and charges are expected to be laid this morning*, it began. No names mentioned in the article of course. We were minors after all. But what was there was enough. The whole town knew it was Tracey and me.

I ripped it up viciously until all that was left were wisps of paper that meant nothing.

*

Frank is being quiet today. There are often long silences in our sessions. Anxious silences, bored silences, angry silences and sometimes we are both playing chicken, attempting to force the other to speak.

But this is an odd silence because I can't quite grasp the nature of it. I don't know what he is thinking and I need to.

All good liars tell the truth most of the time. Today, I am lying the easiest way of all. I am telling the truth selectively. I make my excisions razor-sharp. I only tell him how we found Rachel in the river, just like Frank had asked me to. Nothing about what happened at the bar beforehand. Nothing about college afterwards. This is one of the advantages in telling the story, you choose where it starts and finishes.

Frank looks out the window while I speak. I have asked him why he does this and he says that some patients get self-conscious and more guarded if he looks at them directly. They find it confronting. He says he will look at me if that's what I prefer, but I tell him no because it's easier to skip pages if he isn't watching.

Sometimes he takes notes as I read but the rule is he isn't allowed to interrupt. He has to wait until I have finished the part for today before he can ask questions. That was my prerequisite before agreeing to do this.

Once I finish speaking, I carefully close my diary so he can't see I have written lots more than I am reading out. Ivy has been keeping to a strict fortnightly schedule, so there has been plenty of time for writing. But Frank doesn't notice. He is too busy looking out the window, leaning back on his chair, hands clasped. Thinking.

The man who owns the gift shop is out the front today, sweeping the verandah and brushing away the dust from between the railings. They are a glistening black, topped with arrowhead tips. You could pick them up and hurl them like spears. He shines them every day but only so he doesn't have to stay inside to talk to his mother. Even though she's retired, she's often there with a vinegar look etched into her face.

If I didn't hate him, I'd almost feel sorry for him. I hate his mother more though.

'I've sent the report to Bob,' says Frank.

I stop looking outside. 'So, that's it then. The end of our sessions?'

His voice is measured. 'That's up to you, of course. But the purpose of these sessions was for me to write a report for your legal case. I've done that.'

I sit there, almost bewildered, not quite knowing what to do. Shake his hand? Head for the door?

'Can I read it?' I ask.

'Of course,' he says. 'I can print a copy for you now, but I imagine Bob will send you one, in any case.'

I imagine he would as well. That way he can charge for it.

'I'll get it from him, then.'

We sit there for a bit longer.

'You seem surprised,' says Frank.

'I hadn't realised it would be finished so quickly. You said it would take a while.'

'One of my main recommendations is that you should continue in therapy,' Frank says. 'Particularly, after what you read out today. The death of a friend is a traumatic thing to have to deal with, as you know. I've already spoken to Bob and he's certain that the university will pay for more counselling. But it's up to you, Pen.'

I pretend to be weighing up my options. I thought I would be running out of here the moment I could, but now it has come to it I'm reluctant to go. There is something seductive about the attention, about being the centre of the universe if only for fifty minutes at a time.

Frank senses my hesitation and continues. 'If you do consider staying on, I want to broaden out the diary idea.'

'What do you mean?' I ask, instantly suspicious.

'Revisiting traumatic events like Rachel dying could open up wounds that you consider closed. Events we never got a chance to discuss properly last time.'

I can tell he is trying to avoid saying Tracey's name.

'You should allow yourself to explore that territory in your diary as a starting point,' he says.

'No,' I say, because there is nothing I want to talk to him about regarding that. Nothing at all. I bite the inside of my mouth to stop myself from saying any more.

'Pen,' he says, with almost a pitying look on his face. 'People think there are set stages to grief and that as long as you tick the boxes, a magical closure will occur, but life is a lot messier than that. Facing that grief is important. I understand you are reluctant but you will carry the burden of it until you do. The grief you feel – maybe it's even guilt about what happened – is distorting the way you view the world.'

That he says 'guilt' is a shock and I bite harder. The iron taste of blood is in my mouth but I force myself to smile and say, 'That isn't necessary.'

'OK, OK.' He holds up his hands as if he is surrendering. 'I'm happy to wait until you want to discuss it in our sessions.'

'All right,' I say and keep the forced smile on my face, until I realise that he has neatly manoeuvered me into continuing with the counselling.

Chapter 12

I slowly wound the spare bandage around my foot, pulling it tight. The red gash was covered by layers and layers of white until it disappeared completely. No one knows how big the hole is if they can't see it. Gives you time to knit it back together.

There was a knock on the door and I thought it might be Toby sent by the Sub-Dean to check on me, but it was Rogan, looking exhausted. He'd showered and changed into a clean pair of jeans and a top. We stood there staring at each other.

There was nothing I could think to say. If I began to speak, everything might have slipped out, that Rachel's death was all my fault, that I had spiked her drink with my sleeping tablets. Already, the reason why that had seemed necessary was slipping through my fingers, crumbling like sand.

He had no words either. Instead, he kissed me roughly and I could taste toothpaste on his icy lips. The smells of the night, the sweat, beer and cigarettes, had been washed away.

The warmth from my lips began transferring to his, as if I was the one resuscitating, and slowly he pulsed into life. His stubble bristled against my face. An arm shifted, pushing past my dressing gown until his fingers made contact with my bare skin. Cupping his hand around my breast, he pinched my nipple, feeling it swell and harden. The sensation of his cold hand sparked a rush of warmth. There was the sound of a door opening along the corridor and he pushed me back into the room.

Turning off the light left us criss-crossed with moonlight and shadows. He peeled away my clothes so that I was completely naked. Pressing close, I felt the coarseness of his jeans, the fabric of his t-shirt and the cold metal of the belt buckle digging into my flesh. He kissed me, roughly exploring my mouth with his tongue, before pushing me away and pulling the t-shirt over his head. Tight curls began at his collarbone, lightly covering his chest before tapering down to his waist. I traced my fingers down their path until I found the buckle, pulling the leather belt free.

Unbuttoned his jeans. As I slipped onto the bed, I watched him finish getting undressed. He was so beautiful that momentarily everything outside was pushed away and any thoughts of what this had cost disappeared. When he lay on my bed, I wanted to hold his face in my hands and gaze at him forever, but too soon he produced a condom and was inside me. The bed moved underneath us, until that moment of stillness, and then he groaned and collapsed beside me. I lay there, burrowed down between his body and the wall.

'Rachel was just an accident, a terrible stupid accident,' was the first thing he said. His voice was fierce. 'That's what we tell the police tomorrow.'

'Police?'

'I spoke to them tonight, but they'll want to interview both of us. A formality.'

I lay there, feeling every cut and bruise. I wanted to say that talking to the police is never a formality and ask him for every detail of what he had said and what he had been told.

'Come here.' He turned on his side and put his arm out. I lifted my head and he snaked it underneath me, holding me close. I nestled against his chest.

'It's just because we found her. I mean, we barely saw Rachel last night and it was all an accident, nothing to do with us.'

179

I only heard his words through one ear. In the other was his heartbeat, and yet I could tell that he did not believe that, any more than I did.

It was still dark when I woke. A noise outside. Rogan stirred as I went to get some water from the sink.

The noise again. A motorbike starting up.

Looking out the window, I saw the ruby-red of its tail light as it accelerated away, but then I was distracted by a movement outside my window. A shadow was walking towards our building. It stood under the street light for only an instant but I recognised who it was. Marcus headed towards the back door and out of sight.

A murmur from behind me and my attention quickly moved back into the room. I watched Rogan turn and settle down in the bed, not missing me. Pulling the dressing gown back on, I sat at my desk, studying the shape of his body. Rogan didn't need to know what I had done. No one did. I would take this terrible thing and tuck it away deep inside me where I kept all the other terrible things. Locked away for good. My own personal vault.

There would be a funeral, of course, but then it might not even be here. Her parents could fly in and take Rachel to be buried far away. Even if it was here, I could cope with that. I had coped with worse. The policeman's funeral had been held in my town's church, all sandstone and stained glass. People had crammed into it, including Tracey and her family. Her dad was standing in the council elections and had a good chance at becoming mayor. He had been in Rotary with the policeman. Hundreds more stood in the park outside, including Mum and me, and listened to a crackling Police Minister vow that 'no stone would be left unturned to bring the perpetrators to justice', on the temporary PA that had been rigged up. Mum snorted when she heard that. 'Take them out the back and beat them to death, more like it.' We waited on the main street behind the line of blue uniforms that made up a guard of honour. It stretched past the church, along the park and reached the court house. The hearse drove past slowly, following the drones from a lone bagpiper. 'Wouldn't want your house to get robbed today,' said Mum, as the black car turned the corner. 'Not a copper working west of the mountains. They're all bloody here.'

Rogan stirred again, and as I turned to look at him, Mum, the hearse, the bagpipes, all vanished. Rogan in my bed was more than I'd hoped for. There had been a high price but already I was telling myself that it was too late for regrets. Rogan and I could outlive what happened to Rachel. It would be a tragedy with a happy ending, I thought, mesmerised by the way his hair fell across his forehead, the hollow of his collarbone, his face relaxed with all of the anger and tension from the night gone. I wondered if this was what it felt like to be in love.

There was the gunning of an engine, a screech of tyres, and laughter spilled from the dark. Peering out of the window, I could see Emelia's car had pulled into the car park. She killed the engine and more people than seemed possible to fit in began getting out. They were coming home from the nightclubs in town. I wondered how far she would go to get Rogan into her bed. Not as far as I had.

'I should leave,' said Rogan.

He turned to face me, his head resting on his arm.

'You don't need to.'

'You're not sleeping.'

I moved from the window, back to the bed. 'That's not your fault.'

But he was already getting dressed, reclaiming his clothes from a couple of hours before. His fingers fumbled on zips and buckles. There was something furtive about the way he was doing this, like he was trying to escape.

'I need another shower anyway.' His voice was deep, not quite awake yet.

'All right.' I was not well acquainted with after-sex etiquette. My limited experiences had been fumbled encounters in looking for affection with boys who wanted to screw the 'bad' girl in town and then would pretend not to know me when I saw them next.

'Marcus said his office at ten. Remember, we hardly saw her.'

I didn't look at him but stared up at the ceiling. The bed held a residue of his warmth.

'How's the foot?' he asked, grabbing one of his shoes.

I tried to flex it, stiff from bandages, and felt a gasping streak of pain.

'Guess I'll see you tomorrow,' he said, not waiting for my answer.

'Guess so.'

He turned and reached for the door and as it opened, I could feel the outside world come rushing in. Alone in my room, I fell back on the bed with guilt pressing down on me, sitting on my chest, clutching at my throat. I lay there a long time, paralysed, on sheets that smelt sour.

Chapter 13

Limping badly down the stairs, arching my foot so I didn't put pressure on my cut, I steeled myself for hearing Rachel's name and pockets of silence when people saw me. But I passed discussions comparing hangovers, plans for the rest of the weekend and the general whir of college life. It seemed unbelievable, in a place where minor rumours travelled at warp speed, that somehow people didn't yet know. But as long as they didn't, I could cling to the last moments of normality.

I almost made it to the dining hall when I heard Kesh calling out my name.

'Wait up,' she said, apologising her way through people who had finished breakfast.

I tried to look like I was in a hurry and couldn't stop but I was walking at a snail's pace.

'I've been looking for you but you weren't at breakfast. Did you have a good time last night? I heard you were kissing Rogan at the bar.' She gave a squeal and luckily seemed to think this was answer enough to her question. 'Anyway, have you seen Rachel? I've knocked and knocked on her door but no answer. She probably had a big night as well but it's just her clothes are all dry and she wanted them back.'

Right then I envied Kesh more than I could believe possible. If only clothes could be my biggest problem this morning. It was tempting to shrug my shoulders, say I didn't have a clue. Don't ask me, I know nothing about it. But I knew I couldn't do that.

Pulling Kesh out of the line of human traffic, my mind clicked through the euphemisms on offer. All inadequate. 'Are you all right?' she asked, confused.

'Rachel's dead.'

She blinked slowly with surprise but then began to laugh.

'You're kidding? She must be furious. She had her heart set on winning, especially after she killed Joad. Maybe I'll leave her alone for a bit 'til she's calmed down.' Her smile disappeared when she noticed the bandaging on my foot. 'That looks nasty.'

I nearly left it there. I could tell her it was just an accident, hobble away and let someone else explain to her what I meant. But as I looked back down the corridor I saw the Sub-Dean walking towards us with two solid shapes behind him.

'No, she really is dead. It happened last night.'

My words were too loud as the corridor suddenly silenced on seeing the police. Heads turned our way and then back to them.

'What do you mean?' Tears began to roll down her cheeks and I felt conspicuously dry-eyed, detached from the reaction which was beginning to swell around me.

'I can't explain now. The police are here.'

I couldn't keep looking at her and I began to walk away. She grabbed my arm to stop me. 'Tell me what happened.'

I pulled away and my hand accidentally hit her. 'Not now, Kesh.'

The Sub-Dean, wearing an ugly brown suit, bobbed like a cork as he worked his way through the throng. I watched students do a double take as they saw who was walking behind him. Some slunk away, clearly unnerved, probably disappearing to dispose of any evidence of their own petty law-breaking. Kesh's arm fell to her side. The Sub-Dean passed us, saying curtly, 'Ms Sheppard, this way.'

I waited until after the police walked by, a man and a

woman. Kesh shrunk back, making room to let them through. But I felt a flicker of hope at the sight of their uniforms, the crisp light-blue shirts and dark-blue pants. They were not detectives. This was not a homicide investigation. Rogan was right. Maybe this could be a formality. Something inside me shifted and I realised that it wasn't just guilt that I had felt. It was also fear.

I walked down the corridor, leaving Kesh quietly sobbing behind me. Rogan was already sitting outside Marcus's office. His face was beautiful with his hair slicked back. There was a nick on the underside of his chin where he had cut himself shaving. Carol, wearing a black suit as if in mourning, was sitting at her desk, her eyes solemn. 'Go straight in,' she told us.

Marcus was standing by the French windows, contemplating the garden, a dark-blue suit on today, but no tie. A chink in the armour or a nod to the weekend, I wasn't sure. He turned towards us.

'Sit down. The Sub-Dean is organising coffees for the police.' Marcus gestured to a row of wooden chairs perched opposite his table. They had been placed in a u-shape formation. He sat down and frowned at us.

'This has been a most unfortunate accident but we mustn't allow things to get out of hand. It is important that I do the talking here. You are not to volunteer anything. Only answer if they ask a direct question. If it starts to get difficult I will halt proceedings and state we want a lawyer present. Do you understand?'

Rogan nodded and I did the same. This was how you dealt with the police. I felt instinctively grateful that Marcus was protecting me.

A knock on the door and the Sub-Dean ushered in the police. The man was balancing a fine china cup and saucer. Carol was hovering in the background.

'Thank you, Bryan,' said Marcus. 'No need for you to stay.'

The Sub-Dean rocked back and forth on his heels at this dismissal, but then after an audible exhale of disapproval said, 'Very well.'

The police sat down, perched on chairs in front of Marcus. It was as if he was conducting the interview, not the other way around. A subtle power play.

He introduced us and them, Sergeant Durham and Constable Morriset.

Sitting across from blue uniforms brought up old memories and my stomach clenched at the thought of them. My hands trembled, so I laid them in my lap, pressing hard against my legs. Rogan was staring straight ahead, his foot tapping the floor. Trying to keep calm, I remembered what Bob had told me to do in the witness box. Listen. Focus. Breathe. I kept saying to myself that this was not three years ago. This was different.

I shuffled around with my chair but really I was looking at the woman, the constable. She sat nearest to me with the sergeant on the far side of her. Mid-twenties, I thought, though the uniform gave her an ageless quality. Strong swimmer shoulders and hair scraped back in a perfect bun under her cap. She was looking around the room, taking in the floor-to-ceiling books, the photographs with politicians, the shiny emblem from his last university. She frowned when she caught sight of the picture of the boy hanging behind the desk. Her steady brown eyes swung back to Marcus, her face changing from neutral to disapproving. The man with her was older, dark hair, greying temples, a stomach beginning to bulge over his belt. Her superior. You could tell because she was the one with the notebook out. He had the type of face that had seen too many night shifts and motor accidents. At the moment he seemed more interested in Marcus's desk than the artwork, his hand gently running along it, large square fingers tracing the grain.

'Nice table,' he said. 'Lovely bit of wood.'

Marcus sat back in his chair, looking agreeable. 'Yes, isn't it, Sergeant Durham.'

The sergeant nodded, impressed. 'Cost a bit.' He held his coffee cup above it. 'Got a coaster?' Marcus nodded and Carol scurried off to the sideboard and then left.

I began to relax. It was going to be OK. This was all for a file that would end up in some cabinet, forgotten about.

Sergeant Durham put his cup down and sighed. 'Best get started.'

Marcus cleared his throat. 'First, let me say, that whatever we can do to assist, will be done. I understand Joshua already spoke to the police last night.'

Rogan nodded his head as if he was a windup toy. Sergeant Durham said that there would be a few questions and Rogan leant forward on his seat. Marcus picked up a file on his desk and, putting on a pair of half-moon glasses, began to leaf through it, as if he was only present as a formality and this didn't require his full attention.

'Did you see Rachel Brough at the university bar last night?'

Rogan jumped in, talking too quickly. We had seen a lot of people from college and had chatted to Rachel early in the night but she had left before the band started and we didn't see her after that. His answer sounded rehearsed.

'She left alone?'

'Yes,' said Rogan. He was definite.

Constable Morriset put down her pen and spoke for the first time, her voice friendly and informal. 'Wasn't she worried walking around campus at night? What with the attacks?'

Marcus looked up distracted, as if he couldn't quite follow the reasoning. 'Surely, Ms Brough's death was accidental?'

The constable gave the sort of look which said she was the one asking questions.

Rogan shrugged. 'She didn't seem worried.'

'Other people told us that they saw her with you, Joshua,' she continued, ignoring Marcus, focusing on Rogan.

Rogan refused to budge, which was a mistake. He didn't realise that the police listen to lies all the time. They know the sound of them, can see them in your face, eyes, the shape of your body. The sergeant sat next to her, arms folded, not so interested in the table now.

'Had she taken any drugs?' he asked.

Rogan went all wide-eyed and shook his head, as if we didn't do that sort of thing at Scullin. Both of the police openly smirked at this. Rachel had taken drugs and an autopsy would only confirm it. Constable Morriset turned to me. 'How about you, Penelope? Did you see her later on?'

'Yes,' I said, choosing my words carefully. 'Rogan ... I mean Joshua didn't know.' I turned to him and tried to look apologetic, as if I had only just this moment remembered it. 'It was in the girls' toilets. She was fine.'

All the time I was speaking, Marcus watched me. His eyebrows disapproved. I was talking too much.

'Did Rachel regularly take drugs?' the constable asked me.

I started saying that she didn't but Marcus interrupted

again. 'I was under the impression that Ms Brough drowned in the river.'

'Drugs are believed to be involved,' said the sergeant.

His words hit me sideways. I had told myself I was responsible but hearing it out loud was still a shock. Bile rose and for a second I thought I would be sick. Next to me, Rogan shifted uncomfortably in his seat.

'But still an accident,' Marcus insisted. 'An unfortunate accident.'

'We need to know where she got the drugs from. She was carrying a substantial amount in her bag. More than you would expect for personal use alone.'

Marcus pursed his lips, pushed back his chair and stood up. He moved towards the window, looking out towards the garden once more. Everything was ordered, clipped and neat, but the colours had gone, the rose bushes reduced to grey, spindly sticks. Marcus inspected this, before turning back. He made an elaborate show of his reluctance.

'I had hoped this was unnecessary, but perhaps it is for the best. Ms Brough has been warned twice this year already for drug use at college.' He picked up the folder that had been sitting on his desk. It looked brand new.

'Minor matters,' he continued, 'but I take these issues very seriously. Try to nip things in the bud. Counselling offered, but refused. Ms Brough in fact denied involvement, despite all indications being to the contrary.'

'You didn't think to inform the police?' the constable asked, her cool stare moving from Rogan onto Marcus.

'Too minor, I assure you.' Marcus gave his answer to the sergeant as if they could sort this out amongst themselves. 'But Ms Brough was told that if any other evidence came forward of her drug taking or related activities, I would have no other course open to me but to put these matters in the hands of the authorities and expel her. I personally warned her of this.'

The policewoman wrote something in her notebook. 'Do you believe she was selling drugs?'

There was the slightest flick of an eyebrow from Marcus, echoed in a tilt of the head from Rogan.

'Unfortunately, yes,' he said, not even looking at the constable. 'One did hear rumours. Nothing substantial and certainly no evidence presented, but rumours, yes.'

Rogan nodded his head in agreement, but he refused to look anyone in the eye and stared at his feet.

'An unfortunate end to a rather unhappy young woman,' Marcus continued. He sat on his chair again, put down the file and took off his glasses. 'I won't go through all the details,' he went on. 'But there had been several violent altercations with fellow students, one at the end of our Academic Night and even last night, another, I understand. Is that not so, Ms Sheppard?'

Surprised to hear my name, I could only look at him

dumbly and slowly nod my head, feeling as though I was participating in someone else's cover-up. But at the same time I had to marvel at how he was doing this. This was how you lied. Tell enough of the truth until it all binds together and becomes too difficult to pull apart. Spinning straw into gold.

'Considerable mental health issues in her past. I think I can best sum her up as troubled. Indeed, when I heard of this accident, my initial thought was that perhaps, knowing that there would have to be further sanctions because of her behaviour, that she might have . . .'

Marcus didn't finish his sentence but merely let it float there. Then, to distance himself from his own suggestion, he looked down and flicked through another couple of pages on the file.

'You think this was suicide?' the constable asked, her eyes narrowed.

Marcus gestured dismissively. 'Forget I mentioned it. I'm sure it was purely an accident.'

'Do you have the details of any doctor treating her?' asked the sergeant. Unlike the constable, he didn't seem too concerned. 'We'll need that for our report to the coroner.'

'I'm expecting her parents shortly. I can ask them for you.'

'That's fine. We'll have to talk to them as well,' the constable said.

Marcus shook his head. 'Spoke to them early this morning. Shocked, as you would expect. Only child. They live about four hours west of here. Small country town. Said they'd drive here straight away.'

At the thought of her parents I felt a wave of guilt so strong that it swept away comprehension of what was being said.

'Just one last question, Joshua,' the constable said. 'Why were you down by the river? That's not the quickest way back to college.'

I hadn't expected this and blankly turned to Rogan. He was surprised as well. 'We just left by the back way. More privacy, I guess.' He gave a forced smile and put his arm around my shoulder, gripping too tight.

'So sorry you should have been troubled by this sad event.' Marcus stood up. 'I know you must be very busy.'

'Over-worked and under-paid,' said the sergeant. 'But I think that's everything. We're unlikely to need to trouble you again.'

As Marcus shook hands with the sergeant, the constable stopped at my chair and handed me a piece of paper. 'That's my number in case you remember anything. I really am sorry about your friend.'

It was her genuine concern that nearly got me. I almost told her everything. She hesitated, as if knowing I had something more to say, but all I stammered was, 'I'm really sorry too.' The most truthful thing that had been said in this room.

The sergeant signalled to her and she moved away, both following Marcus out. As the door shut, Rogan took a couple of deep breaths.

'Why do you think she gave you her phone number? Do you think she believed us?' He looked at me as if it was my fault. 'I mean, he did, I'm just not sure about her. Still, I'm glad that's over.' His voice wobbled. 'Never had to talk to police before. Kinda freaked me out.'

Straightening, he stood up and stretched, walked over to the window and pretended to look outside. Starting to relax, he began turning back into the handsome stranger I had watched from across the room at the start of the year. He looked so relieved I was tempted to let everything be, but I just couldn't. Talking in a low voice to make sure we couldn't be overheard, I asked, 'What was that all about?'

'What do you mean?' He made an exaggeratedly puzzled look, mouth pulled down, shoulders raised.

'Rachel didn't deal drugs. She didn't receive warnings about drugs.' I almost started laughing, partly in relief that the interview was over, but also because it was ridiculous.

'What would you know about anything?' His voice hardened.

'I know ... I mean, I knew Rachel.'

'Really? How well? Did you know that she grew up in

196

some rural backwater or were you under the impression that she spent most of her time living in New York? That her diplomat mother is actually a part-time cleaner? Marcus made quite a few discoveries when he spoke to them this morning. She was a mental case. You said it yourself, a liar. That phoney American accent she put on. Smacking Joad. What about those scars on her wrists? Fucking crazy.'

He turned away from me, furious now. I tried to mentally unravel what he was saying. I might have called Rachel a liar but it was the truth that I had been worried about.

'You heard what the police said. A walking pharmacy. She overdosed. She died. End of story. Pretty simple. No need for anyone to make it more complicated.'

He had moved across the room, until quite by accident, he was standing between me and the picture. The sun threw up strange shadows, and for one moment, I had the sensation that the boy who had been lying down, was now standing there alive and menacing. Maybe I had been wrong about the boy. Maybe he was someone to be scared of.

Rogan looked at his watch. 'I'm getting out of here. Going away for the weekend. Away from this fucking place.'

He left me standing there as abruptly as he had the night before at the bar. Except this time there was no jukebox and he wasn't with Rachel.

Chapter 14

Everywhere I look, thoroughbreds are lunging for lines, noses out, tails flying, muscles rippling in their flanks. One horse has all four hooves off the ground, the jockey on his back about to vault over the head. Another is a tightly cropped headshot, showing a luxurious mane, long narrowed face and a pair of enormous flared nostrils. It reminds me of Emelia. I am surrounded by winners, which is the way Bob likes it, even if most of the pictures, faded and sun-damaged, are of races held before I was born.

Sitting here in my lawyer's reception area, I realise that my life is a purgatory of waiting rooms and file notes. There's Frank's file, police files, my student file and now Bob's one, buried somewhere in his office, a combination of scribbled words on coffee-cup-ringed paper and the official sort, demanding money. If I disappeared tomorrow all these files would still exist, purporting to be a record of me. Another reason to write my own version. The true account. While I think about this, I stare up at Bob's favourite photograph, which has pride of place behind the desk of his secretary, Jan.

'Smooth Criminal edging out Ruffian and Copperfield in a photo finish.' Bob wanders in. 'Who says crime doesn't pay?' He strides off. 'Well, hurry up,' he calls over his shoulder, 'we've had a response.' Bob is full of short bursts of small-man aggression.

'Robert J. Cochrane – Barrister & Solicitor' is painted in old-fashioned gold lettering on the door, but everyone calls him Bob. His office is on the first floor, above the stock feed agents in the main street. Bob was a day boy at the posh boarding school on the outskirts of town. Today he is wearing his old school tie.

I follow his billiard-ball head down a corridor of post-mortem grey into a room covered in an avalanche of beige files and lever arch folders. The only splash of colour is an advertisement for the upcoming Cherry Blossom Races – *Get Your Backside Trackside* – with a picture of a jockey whipping his horse so hard the hand blurs.

Bob looks as if he wants a whip because he can't find my file and begins barking for Jan. He sounds like the terrier on Tracey's farm. Nipper had no fear and would take on mongrels twice his size. Then he started on the sheep. Tracey loved that dog but she was a country kid, she knew the score. *'Chained up all day, that's no life for anyone. Better to be dead,'* she told me when I asked her about what happened. I didn't find out until much later that her father had made her shoot Nipper. *'Your dog, your responsibility,'* he told her.

A taste for blood is bad in a dog, but it makes for a good lawyer.

Jan sticks her head round the door, waving the file in her hand. 'You left it on my desk this morning.'

Jan makes up for the corpse-like colour scheme by wearing lime-green pedal-pushers and bright dangling earrings in the shape of parrots. She has been Bob's secretary for years. 'Saw Mum at the hairdresser's,' she says to me. 'How's the perm going?'

'She hates it.'

'Dries your hair out something shockin'. I said, Shirl, lover boy will leave town and you'll be left looking like you stuck your finger in the electricity socket.' Jan gives a gum-showing grin. Efficient and precise about her work, she paddles her make-up on thick. Late on summer afternoons, her face resembles melted wax.

'Out you go, Janice,' Bob interjects. 'Important business to discuss.'

'Hair's important too, for those of us that have it,' is her parting shot before closing the door.

Bob laughs like a car back-firing and then begins reading the letter to me. It is full of careful words; 'not accepting liability,' and, 'money given as a goodwill gesture.'

'They've made an offer,' says Bob.

'That's good. How much?'

'Piss-off money. I've already rejected it.'

I start protesting but he keeps on talking. 'They've already given money for the shrink, which implies you've incurred pain and suffering for which they are responsible or they wouldn't have paid for it.' He throws the file on top of a tower of paper which threatens to topple. 'Rule One of being a lawyer: find the weakness, apply the pressure. I've already sent them Frank's report.'

I've probably heard about five different Rule Ones in the time I've known Bob. The first one was three years ago when I was arrested, sitting in a police interview room because they didn't want to put a minor in a holding cell. I knew Tracey was in the room next to me, because I could hear her father's voice through the wall. Shouting at the police or at her, I couldn't tell. When Bob strutted through the door, ready for a fight, he told my mother that Rule One was 'never take on a client who can't pay', and he pocketed her pay packet right there in the room as his retainer. I tried to talk to him, to tell him what had happened but he held up his hand. 'Rule Two,' he went on, 'is to know when to shut up and listen to your lawyer. A policeman has been murdered. You're lucky to be in here and not strung up from the nearest tree. They will stop at nothing to get a conviction. No sob story is going to make the slightest difference, especially one with no corroborating evidence. Tracey's fingerprints and DNA are all over the car. No matter what you say, she is going down for it. You were with her that night, but we can still save you, though only if you listen to me.'

I blink away the memory.

Bob is talking about the responses he has had from all the parties we are suing but I don't pay close attention. I'm a digger looking for a lucky strike. I don't really care who pays up as long as someone does.

'Now we've got the report from Frank saying you are a basket case due to their negligence, we'll see a proper offer,' says Bob. 'But their own quack wants to assess you.'

That must have been in the letter.

Frowning, I say, 'I'm not even sure I want to keep seeing Frank now that we've got the report.'

'It adds to the overall picture,' says Bob. 'You don't have to see him every day. Just make the odd appearance so we can say you remain in treatment. You'll have to look the part as well. Scar's impressive. Make sure you wear your hair off your forehead so the doctor can get a good look. No make-up covering it either. And your clothes, none of this rubbish.' He returns the frown, looking at my Doc Martens. 'How about that lovely frock you wore last time? Made you look like Little Miss Muffet. They'll want to see how you'll present in court. Not that we will get that far.'

'Doesn't fit me.' I wasn't going to wear that dress ever again.

'Well, you're going to get a new one. Everyone needs a keep-out-of-jail outfit. I'll tell Ros to give it to you on account.'

Ros is Bob's wife. She owns a clothing shop, or rather a 'boutique', the most expensive one in town. She looks down her nose at all of Bob's clients but she's quite happy to clothe them for a fee. She chose the dress last time. Bob tries to keep as much of the money as possible in the family.

I went through this process three years ago and I never want to do it again. Crossing my arms, I stare at the poster, doing my best impression of immovability.

'You want to get back to university, don't you?' Bob leans back in his chair, chin disappearing into folds of skin. 'Then you will do what needs to be done, which includes looking the part. I'll get the other side to pay for it. Put it down as disbursements on the bill. Photocopying.'

'Can't I buy a suit this time?' I ask. 'People take you more seriously in a suit.'

'We don't want a professional ball breaker. We need you looking innocent and traumatised, something that only a very big cheque is going to fix. I'd dress you in a school uniform if I thought I'd get away with it.'

It's almost lunchtime and Bob is losing interest. Scrabbling around in his in-tray, he extricates a form guide. There's the usual bulge of betting slips in his top pocket.

'Now, Jan tells me your mother wants an appointment. What's that about?'

'Power of attorney for my grandfather.'

Bob looks up. His eyes are red-rimmed and I can see the broken capillaries around his nose. 'Trying to get her hands on the house again. Jan says there's some layabout sniffing around.'

I nod.

'And Grandpa? Compos mentis?'

I haven't visited him in a long time. 'Depends on the day,' I guess.

Bob hunts around for a pen to start circling today's top tips.

'Powers of attorney take some work. Might have to petition the court. Busy this time of year. Reckon you've got three months. Enough time to get rid of the parasite?'

I think about Terry's self-satisfied smirk. 'Don't know.'

'A girl of your abilities,' and he waves me out of his office.

As I walk past Jan talking on the phone, she gestures for me to wait.

'Only appointment available is Friday. No, not this week. The following ... Yep ... you want morning. He's no good to anyone after lunch on a Friday ... See you then.' Putting down the phone, she points towards the window. 'Shirley's here to pick you up. Waiting outside.'

I look down and see our car parked nose to the footpath. Mum is supposed to be at work.

'Bob talked to you about her?' Jan asks.

'Thanks for telling him about Terry.'

Jan sniffs as though it was nothing. 'Saw him down at the pub on the weekend. Seemed very pally with the girls on Julie Cuttmore's hen night. He was talking to her for a long time and all. Cuddling up to that Kim Stephens, though he must be twice her age. I reckon they left together.'

I think of dumpy Kim enjoying her night out, forgetting about having two kids, trying to find someone to replace Lee.

'Have you said anything to Mum?'

Jan squawks, her earrings flapping. 'Do I look stupid?'

Guess it is down to me to break the bad news.

I find Mum chatting to the red-faced stock agent in a striped shirt, standing in the doorway of his empty shop.

'Hi, Mum. Hi, Mr Phillamey.'

'Here's my girl,' she says. 'Finished at last. Hop in. I'll give you a lift home before my lunch-break's over.'

'Take care, Shirley,' says Mr Phillamey. 'Sorry to hear

about what happened to you, Pen.' But he doesn't look sorry. Another person who thinks I had it coming to me.

'Thanks, Bruce,' Mum says. 'It's been a hard couple of months, but what can you do?'

When the car doors are shut, she mutters out of the corner of her mouth, 'He gossips worse than an old woman.'

I look back at him, standing in his doorway. He keeps a steady gaze as if escorting us from the premises. We reverse into the street.

'Rabbiting on about those foreign-currency farm loans going bad. Doesn't mention he was the one spruiking them a few years back.' Mum changes gears and accelerates up the main street. 'Apparently the Cuttmores are in strife. He made a special point of telling me that.' She turns her head and gives me a significant look.

I slump back on the seat. The Cuttmores took out that loan to pay for Tracey's defence. They went with flash city lawyers who promised to do the impossible, but instead disappeared with their money.

'How did it go with Bob? Have they made an offer?'

'No.' I keep my face turned away from her. 'Letter said they consider the matter finalised.'

Mum swears, banging her hand against the steering wheel, and swears again. Then she is quiet but only for a block. 'Terry's depressed, sitting around doing nothing. He won't go anywhere with me, not even down to the pub. Spends more and more time out at Mick's. We just need cash for tools and material and Jan's saying Bob can't even see me for another two weeks. Stupid racing carnival.'

I wonder if I should mention Kim now, but decide against it.

She stops at the lights. 'Grab my handbag.'

'Do you want your cigarettes?' I ask.

'I've given up, remember,' she lies. 'Just pass it to me.'

I pull her battered brown bag out from behind my seat, one handle broken. Mum fishes through it and passes a magazine to me.

'Girl from work found it at the dentist's yesterday. Shoved it up her jumper so she could show me. Page seven.'

Dog-eared and ripped, it has Princess Diana on the cover. I don't bother turning the pages. I've seen the article before. Marcus had shown it to me a couple of days before he was arrested.

The light changes from red to green. Mum guns the car through the intersection, turning left in front of the oncoming traffic she is supposed to give way to.

'They'd have got good money for that.' She jabs her finger down on top of SUPER JEWELLERY GIVE-AWAY in large white letters, but right next to it is the smaller yellow of EXCLUSIVE: A MOTHER'S GRIEF. The car begins to climb the hill towards the highway that cuts our town in two. 'Not that they needed it. Go on, have a look.'

I leave it in my lap. I don't want to see the grainy pictures of Mrs Parnell looking distraught, being shown where her daughter's body was found. But even more than that I don't want to see what the family was like before it happened. A mother smiling at her daughter, who was going to university to conquer the world.

'Is this why you came to pick me up?'

'The girls at work say they get proper make-up artists and hair stylists. Sometimes you get to keep the clothes. You could do that. Tell your side of the story.'

A long silence this time. We pass the real estate agent, the video store, and the place where the old Cook-a-Chook used to be. It burnt down a year ago, an insurance job according to Mum, and hasn't been occupied since. She waits until the used car-yards that mark the end of the shops and the start of the houses.

'So . . .?'

'No.'

'Everyone else is making money from it.' Her mouth is taut with irritation.

'Blood money.'

'All very well to be high and mighty about it. Don't see you getting a job to pay the bills.'

'Her daughter is dead. Would you have preferred that

happened to me so you can get a free shirt?' I hurl the magazine into the back so that it hits the seat with a smack.

Mum slams on the brakes and there is an angry beep behind us. She pulls to the side of the road.

'How can you say that? Have you got any idea what it was like for me when they called me up saying you had been rushed to hospital? Driving all that way with no idea what had happened to you?'

I sit there and say nothing, because the truth is I hadn't thought about that.

She pulls out and heads to the highway, full of people passing through our town, not bothering to stop. Waiting for a break in the traffic, she says, 'It's not just the money. For once people would be on our side. After all we've been through.'

'I don't want to talk about this any more.'

'You spend all day writing about it. You talk about it with Frank. Why don't you want to talk about it with me? I know more from reading the papers than I do from my own daughter. Just talk to me. That's all that I'm asking. Is that so hard?'

I look out the window and say nothing but she doesn't stop trying until we reach home. I get out of the car, refusing to say goodbye, and she accelerates up the street as though she can't leave me quickly enough.

I walk around the side of the house, to come in by the back door. Through the gate, down the footpath, I stop at my bedroom window. Terry is in there hunting through my clothes drawers. I stand back, peeping around the frame. He is searching for something, rummaging amongst my bras and undies, pulling out the next drawer, looking at my t-shirts. I make my way to the back door, slipping through it, walking silently up the hall until I am standing there, watching him kneeling on the floor.

'What are you doing?'

He jumps, but recovers himself. He pushes in the last drawer like he has every right to be here. 'You're home early.'

'What are you doing in my room?'

He gets to his feet. 'Saw a mouse this morning. Your mother asked me to lay down some traps.'

Fucking trap you, I think, anger pouring out of me. 'Get out.'

'No need to be unpleasant.' He smiles with his hungry mouth and steps towards me.

'Just get out or else.'

'Or else what . . .' He lunges so quickly that I don't have time to move, grabbing a fistful of my hair, pinning my arms, pushing me face down on the bed. He lies on top of me, pulling my head back so he can see my face. I have been too stupid and too slow to realise just how dangerous he is.

210

'You're too soft,' Tracey had said.

'Been talking to Julie Cuttmore about you.' He breathes a mist of beer onto my skin. 'Blames you, she does, for what happened to her sister. Reckons you should be in jail. Asked me to help her. I could do anything to you, and no one in this town would lift a finger, give me a medal more like.' When I flinch, he runs his long red tongue along the side of my face and laughs. His groin presses down hard into the small of my back. I lie there immobilised. His weight shifts, and I tense, waiting for hard fingers pulling down my jeans or pushing up my top. I can't move my head, but my eyes try to see what might be in arm's reach. Something hard to crack his skull open.

But instead he gets off me. Confused, I try to stand, but he kicks my legs out from under me, and I fall, hitting my head on the bed frame.

'Clumsy, clumsy.'

I scramble away on hands and knees until I am in the corner and can't retreat further. I turn to watch him, ready to scratch his eyes or kick his balls if he moves closer. He stays well out of my reach.

'I'm not going anywhere. If you don't like that you can leave,' he says, and he walks away, out of the room. His footsteps go down the hall but I don't move until I hear the tap being turned on in the kitchen. I run to my door, close and lock it. My legs buckle out from under me, my body shaking.

I crawl over to the closet, holding the door carefully so it doesn't make a tell-tale squeak, pulling it open. A pale ghost stares back at me from the mirror, a scar running across her forehead. I wipe his spit from my face and put my fingers to where I fell. Tender. But the bruise won't be bad enough for Mum to believe me. There is a limit to how many fairytales she is prepared for me to ruin. I'll get him back all the same.

The closet is full of suitcases, boxes of lecture notes and shoes. I pull them out and place them on my bed, making as little noise as possible, so anyone standing at the door can't hear what I am doing.

This is my hiding place.

Even the police missed it when they searched the entire house three years ago. It is a section of floorboard that runs along the wall, sitting in the groove, not nailed down. A minuscule crack hidden near the closet frame. Slowly, I lift the broken board, pull the pillowcase out. I brush away the grime and open it up. My book is still inside.

Safe.

'Leave the gun in here,' Tracey had whispered, the two of us huddled together, looking into the hole. I placed the tea-towel covered bundle in there and put the floorboard back over it, like the lid of a coffin.

'What will we do?' I whispered back.

'Don't worry. I'll take it with me tomorrow.'

'You'll get rid it?'

'I'll take care of it. It's my responsibility.'

And in a strange way she did. By the time the police found that gun, it was too late.

Chapter 15

It was a typical late autumn afternoon: small groups sitting in patchy sunshine that was about to disappear; boys kicking a football; students pretending to do some work before dinner but actually gossiping about how Emelia had written off her car on Saturday. She didn't even break a nail. Joyce had abandoned *Ulysses* and was pretending to read another fat book with a serious black cover. *Crime and Punishment*. I didn't know whether to laugh or cry when I saw the title. Leiza was arguing about paint colours with a group of girls who were looking mutinously at a large bundle of white sheets.

To an outsider it would be a normal college scene. Yet to me, sitting at the far end of the courtyard, on a bench outside the laundry block, the change was obvious. None of the usual laughing or shouting, no one playing loud music. There was a feeling of unease, as if the college had collectively woken up from the party. Officially, nothing had been said about Rachel's death, as if it was an embarrassing lapse of taste that could be ignored. Notices had gone up on each floor saying that the Murder Game was cancelled. Rachel was not mentioned but the connection was easy to make.

It had been three days since Rachel's death and I had spent each one listening hard to what people were saying around me, and even harder to what they weren't. All the time trying to act normal, whatever that meant in the circumstances. Today, I had decided, normal people did washing.

Toby was on one side of me, smoking a cigarette, and Kesh sat on the other.

'Time?' said Toby. He was in a tetchy mood.

I looked at my watch. 'Still got twenty minutes.' I gingerly stretched out my legs in front of me. My foot had been stitched carefully by the university doctor. 'Nasty cut, but will heal,' she said. I hoped the prognosis could be applied to the rest of me.

Stoner ambled towards us across the courtyard, carrying a large material bag with dark clothes poking out the top. He was wearing a faded black t-shirt with 'Megadeth' written on it in Nazi-style Gothic. I wondered if this was a deliberate choice given the mood or perhaps the only thing he owned that didn't need washing.

'Any machines free?' he asked.

'One's broken, we've got four, Michael has the last one,' said Toby.

Stoner looked at us as though this was too much information to absorb and then said, 'But there's only three of you.'

'I separate my whites from my colours,' Toby snapped. 'Is that a problem?'

Stoner blinked and then almost smiled. 'Don't own any whites.' As Stoner only ever seemed to be wearing black, I supposed there wasn't much variety in the way of colours either.

'I could put yours in after I'm finished.' Toby became brisk and business-like. 'But it'll cost you.' He mimicked smoking a joint.

Stoner shook his head. 'No can do. Don't have any.'

'What the fuck, Stoner? First, the Marchies are supposedly out of the business and now you. I heard those bikers supply you and they are supposed to be awash with the stuff.'

'Stop freaking out,' said Stoner, who was doing a good job of beginning to look freaked himself. 'It's just a temporary hitch in the supply chain. I can do an IOU.'

'Redeemable when?'

Stoner shrugged. 'It's complicated, you know.'

'No hashee, no washee,' said Toby. There was a hesitation before Stoner began laughing, as if his brain was on time delay and he had only just got the joke. But Toby wasn't joking.

'OK, OK. It's cool. I'll come back later then.' Stoner picked up his bag, balanced it on his head, and strode away.

'What was that about?' I asked Toby, who dropped his cigarette and ground it viciously into the dirt.

'Who knows? Stoner has been raking in the money from selling. What's the bet he didn't want to hand over a freebie, the tight bastard.'

The sun dropped behind the building and the wind picked up, pushing grey clouds overhead. The footballers nearly kicked a ball right on top of Leiza's partly painted protest banner and her angry voice echoed around the courtyard. Looking sheepish, they decided to head to the oval. The girls tried to go inside because of the weather but Leiza wouldn't let them and started collecting rocks to hold down the material.

I got up and walked around the brick laundry. My foot felt bruised with moments of sharp pain, but anything was better than just sitting there. I needed to keep busy.

'Going to rain soon,' I said, walking back. 'Supposed to rain all week. What time are you leaving, Kesh?'

Rachel's funeral was scheduled for Friday but I didn't

have the guts to attend and had used an essay that was due as an excuse. Toby had also refused to go, convinced that the small town wouldn't welcome him for being Asian, gay or a future accountant. He didn't say which. That had left Kesh travelling by herself with the Sub-Dean.

'The Sub-Dean thinks if we leave at six a.m., we'll be there in plenty of time.' Her voice was hoarse.

'Didn't want to fork out for accommodation, the cheap-skate,' said Toby.

The hum of dryers, the thuds and gushes from the washing machines covered up the lack of conversation.

Eventually Kesh turned to us, puffy-eyed from crying. 'You don't think Stoner gave those drugs to Rachel?'

'Who knows?' said Toby. 'Remember how much stuff she was carrying. The Sub-Dean went through it yesterday in the RA meeting. There was LSD, amphetamines, coke, even some heroin. That's serious shit. We're not just talking a couple of Es and some dope. That would be like Stoner's entire kit and then some.'

'What if it was Stoner's and that's why he doesn't have any now?' asked Kesh.

'How would Rachel have ended up with Stoner's stash?' Toby asked. 'You think she nicked it?' There was a pause where none of us said what we were thinking – that it sounded exactly like something Rachel would have done.

'Do you think she was supplying, like Marcus said?' I asked. I had been so sure he had made that up.

Toby looked uncertain. 'She was talking a lot about drugs, saying there was a drug war happening right under our noses.'

'War on drugs?' Kesh asked, confused.

'War for drugs, the way she told it,' Toby said. 'The Marchmains versus those bikers who supply Stoner. Like some commerce case study, all about market share and monopolies. Think about it, it would be worth heaps. Biggest single site for dealing in the city by a long shot. Anyway, it's over now. Once the Marchies lost Nico they fell apart and now those bikers are in charge.'

'But what has that got to do with Rachel?' asked Kesh.

Toby pushed his sunglasses up onto his head and I could see black circles under his eyes. 'I don't know. But she didn't get warnings for drugs. We all knew when she got in trouble over smacking Joad but I never heard about any others. RAs are supposed to be told about that sort of stuff.'

'You think Marcus was lying?' I asked, thankful for someone else to be raising questions that had been bothering me.

'Maybe he just doesn't want to look clueless in front of the police.'

'So many people are lying,' said Kesh.

I tried to pretend that I wasn't, and made a pathetic attempt at deflecting my guilt. 'Including Rachel herself, I guess.'

Kesh took the bait. 'I just don't understand that. I mean, we were her friends, weren't we? You tell your friends the truth.' An unconscious echo of what Rachel had said to me that night.

The dead get summarised like an epitaph on a headstone. Hero. Victim. Murderer. And according to most college people, Rachel's would have been Liar. People had been angry when they found out the truth about her background, and pretended the two were connected. That if she hadn't lied about who she was, she wouldn't be dead. It was all her fault. While the hypocrisy of Rachel hiding her own background while trying to discover mine wasn't lost on me, I didn't have the energy to get angry about it. What did any of us really know about each other? I was busy reinventing myself at university. Most other people were as well, I guessed. All of us trying to present varnished versions of ourselves to the world. Rachel had gone a step further and reinvented her past.

'Fuck it, Kesh, we all lie,' Toby said, watching the movement in the courtyard. 'When I go home, I take out my earring and put away the sparkly shorts. And when Mum asks me if I've met a nice girl yet, I smile and say "one day".'

'Did you know about Rachel's background?' I asked him.

When he turned to look at me, his eyes were liquid. 'Maybe at some level I didn't buy the international jet-setter life, but really I just didn't care. She was a laugh. I mean, I know she lied, but you know she never belonged in some country shithole, not really.' He pushed the sunglasses back down over his eyes but not quickly enough to cover the tear that had slipped out.

Guilt stuck in my throat like a fishbone. I had to find something else to do, something small and practical to get through this. I glanced at my watch, saying, 'Washing nearly finished,' then sat back down, grabbing Toby's cigarettes and lighter. 'You mind?' He looked up, puzzled, but nodded all the same. I pulled one out, stuck it in my mouth, focusing on holding my hands around the lighter.

It had been years since I had smoked a cigarette. Taking a drag, I was hit by memories more than by the nicotine. Tracey and I used to steal them from my mother and smoke them up around the back of the town swimming pool. My stomach lurched.

I was rescued by Leiza marching towards us. An arm-swinging sergeant major. Behind her, the girls on painting duty were beginning to pack up. 'Have you got the buckets out of storage yet?' she asked Toby.

'What buckets?' replied Toby, making a quick retreat into his shell of who-gives-a-fuck. He scowled up at Leiza.

'The glue for the protest posters. All RAs agreed to help. You're plastering the Science block.'

'Says who?'

'It's for the march. It was discussed at the RA meeting you missed. I thought as a friend of Rachel's you would want to be involved. We need to demand that her death be investigated properly, that this screwdriver lunatic be caught, plus more security patrols around the bar at night and better lighting.'

'I'll help,' said Kesh.

Leiza gave her the sort of look a crocodile gives a chicken. 'Excellent. You can make the glue. Just go with Toby now and he'll get the buckets for you. We're heading out around midnight. Arts could do with an extra person putting posters up. Then I need someone to hand out flyers this week.'

Toby held up a hand to stop the flow. 'Fine, fine, I'll do it if you stop talking. C'mon Kesh, before she enslaves you for life. Pen, put our clothes into the dryer. I don't want to come back and find them all over the floor.'

Holding the cigarette in my hand, I nodded, waiting to stub it out the moment his back was turned.

As Toby and Kesh headed inside, Leiza took the seat next to me. 'Christ, I could do with one of those.' She pointed at the cigarette.

I gestured mine at her. 'Barely been used.'

She shook her head. 'This whole thing is a nightmare. That girl Alice is maimed and Rachel's dead but still no one wants to do the work to protest that women's lives are important. I waste all this time checking people are actually doing what they said they would do. They never are. Then I have the Sub-Dean questioning the appropriateness of the rally – "How will I ensure crowd safety? Surely there are better ways, Ms Parnell, of making your point than organising a rabble. I hope your studies aren't suffering from this extra-curricular distraction."' Leiza screwed up her mouth to mimic the Sub-Dean's peevishness.

I stubbed the cigarette out on the seat next to us. 'Why do it then?'

'Because it's even more important now. The university wants to forget about the attack on Alice, sweep Rachel's death under the carpet so that it doesn't put off prospective students and their parents. I was no fan of Rachel but she doesn't deserve that. You're going to be at the rally, right?'

'I guess.'

'No, really. It's crucial we get as many people at it as we can, or else nothing will change.'

'OK.'

She nodded. 'Now, there's something I've been wanting to talk to you about.'

I waited for her to tell me about the lack of women's representation at the student council or how far off women were from achieving equal pay, but instead she said, 'The night Rachel died ...'

Immediately, I could hear my heart beating.

Rogan had left college the morning afterwards and still hadn't returned so I was the only person available for the handful of ghoulish ambulance-chasers who wanted to know all the details, but even they had stopped when I just stared them down and refused to answer. Most people had left me alone. Out of embarrassment, kindness or perhaps even a lack of interest, it was hard to say.

'What about it?'

'Look, if it was me, I'd want to know. You see, I saw her.' Leiza pushed back her hair, hooking it behind her ear, and looked straight at me in her disconcertingly forthright way.

'Rachel told me about that,' I said, speaking quickly with relief. 'When you came out of Joad's room.'

'Not then,' said Leiza, and she looked embarrassed, which I thought was impossible for her. 'She told you about the bet?'

I nodded my head. 'Joad's a pig.'

'And then people told me what he said on the Academic Night about rape and Alice's attack. Disgusting. He thinks he can get away with that, but I'll show him.' She shook her head. 'Anyway, that wasn't what I meant. I saw Rachel later on that night.'

'How much later?'

'I was going into town. She was about to head into the bar when she saw me. I think she wanted to find you.'

'So before ...,' I began, trying to work out how worried I should start feeling.

'Yeah, before she took whatever she is meant to have taken ... I mean, she was a little drunk perhaps, but she was fine. Came right up to me and made a few cracks about Joad but then she mentioned you.'

'Me?'

'I wasn't really listening to her because I was still so angry. But I'm certain she said something along the lines that if you knew what she was going to do that night, you'd be even madder at her than I was. And this is the bit I remember clearly, "Pen would kill me."'

'Kill her?' My voice sounded shrill, even to me. 'Are you sure? What else did she say?'

Leiza nodded. 'That was it. It was because I wanted to kill her that I remembered it. I said something like, "Pen and me both," and walked off. I just thought it was a bit ... odd ... in light of what happened. Look, she didn't seem scared or anything. More that it was a joke. You know, typical Rachel.'

There was a movement behind us, and I sprang up too quickly. My foot spasmed in pain. Michael stood in the doorway, with a plastic basket of freshly washed clothes.

Leiza looked at him and then at me. 'Oh, hello, Michael,' she said in her official welcoming kind of tone.

He looked at us and nodded his head.

'Just packed our banners up. We'll have to finish painting them inside. Are you coming to the rally?' she asked.

'I intend to,' he said. 'I think it's important.'

'Good, that's good,' said Leiza, trying not to be surprised. Michael usually avoided group activities. She smiled and then paused to allow him to move on. Instead, he sat down on the bench opposite, watching us as if our conversation was a designated spectator sport.

Leiza frowned, then, lowering her voice, turned to me. 'I'll talk to you about this another time,' she said.

I shrugged as if there wasn't really anything to discuss. 'I better go put the clothes in the dryer. Toby will . . .' I had to stop myself from saying 'kill me' and Leiza looked as though she guessed what I was going to say, but then one of the girls who had been painting the banners waved at her from the doorway and yelled something about a spelling mistake. Immediately distracted, she hurried off across the courtyard.

I stood there, trying to prevent myself from getting rattled by what Leiza had just said and wishing Michael would stop looking at me.

'How did Rachel know?' he said.

'Know what?' I asked.

'That you wanted to kill her?'

I felt queasy from the cigarette, my foot ached and I was

exhausted. I didn't have the patience for one of Michael's discussions.

'It was just a dumb joke, Michael. People make them, believe it or not.' I turned to leave.

'But you did want to kill her,' he said, his eyes owlish behind his glasses. 'You spiked her drink.'

I could hear an odd high-pitched hum cutting through the periodic streaming of water and the constant rumble and thrum of the percussion of the washing machines. It seemed to be getting louder, until I realised it was in my head. I sat back down because I was worried I might fall.

Waiting until the noise receded, I took my time before looking up at Michael.

'That's not true and none of this is your business. Now, excuse me but I've got to put Toby's clothes in the dryer.'

'I didn't understand it at the time when I saw you pulling something out of the bag, crushing it over the beer. But when I saw your face, I could see you wanted her dead.'

He had put it together, an equation solved, ripping a hole right through the heart of all my lies. It was over. I was found out.

'You're wrong,' I began, and my voice was pitiful, weak, and pleading. 'I didn't . . . an accident.'

But Michael didn't seem to care. I kept talking, blustering, making excuses, outright lying. It was pathetic and he stood there, patiently waiting for me to stop. He wasn't looking for confirmation nor was he prepared to believe a denial. 'It's all right,' he said when I came spluttering to a standstill. 'I hated Rachel too.' Behind us, one of the machines finished and began to beep.

'What happens now?' I asked, shakily. I couldn't believe we were having this conversation, let alone that he knew what I had done and didn't seem to be that bothered by it.

'You don't need to worry about me. Really.' He smiled at me and it was the first time I had ever seen him smile. There was something so fragile about it that I wanted to cry. I was beholden to Michael and the thought terrified me.

'You're worth protecting. I told you that you were different from the others. I wanted to tell you that night at the bar,' he began, but I couldn't cope with anything else. I was almost light-headed with shock and panic and just wanted to get away.

'Please, please, I can't talk about that night. I have to go put the clothes in the dryer.'

He nodded. 'When you are ready then.'

I walked back inside the room and closed the door. Through the window I watched Michael carry his laundry across the square and then I headed straight to my room. I needed to get rid of my Rohypnol. I had been so stupid not to do that the night Rachel died.

Racing upstairs, along the corridor, I ran into my room, making sure that the door was locked behind me. I grabbed my bag, more of a leather pouch on a string, that I had taken to the bar that night. I dumped out the contents on my bed. Wedged into the bottom corner, covered in fluff, were two tablets. I pulled them out, holding them in the palm of my hand. Standing over the sink, I crushed the tablets to a powder, turned on the water and washed them down the drain. Evidence destroyed.

Crouching on the floor, I opened the cupboard below, reaching my hand back behind the water pipe to where I kept the rest of the packet away from prying eyes. Not there. I peered in, too small a space to get my head right inside. It was the place where useless forgotten things lived until enough time passed and I decided to throw them out. Hunting through it, there was a half-full box of tissues, some dishwashing liquid, crusty sponges the texture of dried old bread, never-used shoe polish and my faded Rubik's red t-shirt. But no tablets. Even when I frantically pulled everything out of the cupboard, they still weren't there.

I ripped the sheets off my bed. Lifted up the mattress. Pulled the books out of the bookcase. Dumped all my clothes on the floor. Checked every pocket. I kept telling myself not to be paranoid, that they had to be here some-where. I thought back to the last time I saw the packet. Rachel was in the common area, sitting on the old squeaky chair, her legs curled up next to her, a cat ready to pounce.

She hadn't even been looking at me, instead staring at Joad's door, determined not to blink in case she missed a moment. It had been too easy to retrace my steps and walk back along the corridor. Quietly unlock the door so as not to get her attention. Stealing into my own room. Bringing the bottle could have led to awkward questions if anyone saw it, so instead, I had put a few tablets into my bag and then raced off to meet Rogan. I left the rest sitting out on my desk, on top of a pile of photocopying I still hadn't read. I never saw them after that.

In the end, I had to accept they weren't in my room. Someone had taken them.

Chapter 16

For the days that followed I stayed at Law School, leaving college early and returning late to avoid as many people as possible. I waited for someone to confront me with my own pills and make the accusation that I was a murderer, but nobody did. When anyone did try to talk to me, I pretended that I was mourning instead of hiding. Whether this nuance was appreciated I have no idea.

Marcus had called me a survivor, and after some shaky moments I pulled myself together and decided to be one. Having once owned some sleeping tablets meant nothing. My real issue was needing to keep Michael onside. He was the only person who knew for sure what I had done. He said he wouldn't tell anyone, and I believed him. I knew he liked me and that made him vulnerable, able to be manipulated. I understood that only too well.

A side effect of spending so much time away from college was that I didn't realise Rogan had returned until I opened my door to a soft late-night knock.

'Nice,' he said, grinning, as he took in my mismatched flannelette pyjamas. 'Fetching.'

'What?' I was curt to cover up my embarrassment.

'Haven't seen you around and thought I'd check up on you.' He was trying to pretend that I was the one who had disappeared from college, who had run home and had left a whole bunch of unanswered questions. I had played the scene over and over in my mind of what I would say to Rogan about the way he was making a habit of abandoning me, but with him standing there and smiling, all the caustic comments vanished without being spoken aloud. I needed the potential for something to be good in my life.

'Can we talk?'

'Here?' I said, uncertain. I looked behind me but all I could see was my bed, and I could feel my face flush with desire.

He looked a bit uncertain as well. 'No, I've got somewhere better.'

'Dressed like this?'

'Absolutely,' he said, and laughed.

College had adapted to Rachel's death in that weird way you do when you don't have a choice. Conversations were brittle, but the sharpness of grief, or in my case guilt, had already begun to dull into a bruise. Still, it had felt like a long time since I had heard someone laugh like that.

I followed him down the corridor. There was a curious space between us as if he didn't want to let other people know we were going somewhere together, but I thought maybe I was being overly sensitive. When I saw Michael sitting on the chair outside Joad's room as I walked past, I slowed down and put even more distance between us and felt grateful for it.

'Hi, Pen,' Michael said. There was something puppyish about the way he said it, breathless and happy all at once.

I nodded my head in the way you do to be friendly but you just can't stop to talk right now because you really are much too busy.

Rogan chose to climb the stairs, rather than head downstairs as I had expected. On the next floor up, the top floor of the tower, he walked all the way along the corridor until he stopped at a door. On my floor, this was where the vacuum cleaner, mops and cleaning products were kept. But this was different – a room, not a cupboard, with a concrete floor and roughly painted white walls. It was bare except for a plastic chair, a bench running along one wall and a large bath.

'Only bath in the Tower,' he said. 'I don't think it's ever been used. Last year Stoner set up his hydroponics in here.' He balanced the chair on top of the bench, looked up at the ceiling and then back to me. 'You might be a bit too short. I'll go first.'

He climbed onto the chair and reached up towards a manhole that I hadn't noticed. Breathing hard as he pushed the cover aside, his head and shoulders disappeared into the dark space. Bracing his arms against the edges of the square, I was left staring at his bottom half, the belt I had once helped undo. He stretched upward, his t-shirt moved and I saw a flash of skin. His stomach muscles tensed and, with a fluid movement, he pulled himself into the hole.

I could hear scuffling overhead and a bright light shone down. 'Found the torch,' he said, his face reappearing. 'Your turn.' I was already on the chair, and probably could have managed to drag myself up, but instead I grabbed his wrist, and was hauled into the roof space.

Moving from my knees to standing, I fell against Rogan, a crack of nose on bone. We apologised at the same time. The musty cavity stretched away from us in all directions, beyond the torch's beam. Dust was everywhere, so thick I could feel it settle on my skin.

'How did you know about this?' My words disappeared into the gloom, absorbed by the dark.

'Stoner told me. Somewhere to hide his stash if he needed to.' I thought back to Kesh's speculation at the laundry and wondered if Stoner actually had that much of a stash at the moment. 'But we're not there yet.' He held the torch under his chin, which lit up his face with sinister shadows. 'Scared?'

'It's an improvement.' I laughed then, and all the pent-up fear and frustration inside dissolved in the snug blackness.

'Be careful where you stand,' he said. 'Keep to the beams.'

'Would you fall through?'

'Do you want to be the first person to find out?'

He walked along the one nearest to us, stopping every few steps to shine the torch and put his hand on the next truss. I walked after him, arms outstretched, almost giddy. The roof began to slope down and we had to crouch so as not to bang our heads.

'Easier to find in daylight,' he said, when we were almost doubled over. He pointed the torch at a spot directly in front of us. Peering, I could see the inside of the roof and the shape of a bolt. Handing me the torch, Rogan pulled at it. The metal made the kind of noise that you can feel in your teeth. Then he pushed with both hands outstretched and a square of the roof hinged forward, clanging open.

We stuck our heads through. Heaving ourselves out of the damp heat, we balanced on the edge of the opening. A strange feeling of euphoria washed over me with the night air. I felt free, marooned on a private island, cut off from the rest of college and my problems.

'Careful,' he said. 'Some of the tiles are loose.' He shuffled forward until he was sitting with his legs angled out in front. I passed him the torch. There was a neat stack of tiles next to us and I thought perhaps once they covered the hatch and wondered why one had been built in the roof and how Rogan had discovered it. But there was something so magical about being here I didn't want to ask questions. That was what had got me into trouble with him last time.

As high as we were, the trees were higher. One was close enough that its branches brushed the side of the gutter. I could hear the swish of the leaves rubbing against the edge. I wanted to tiptoe across the branch and climb the trunk, right up to the sky. Gaining my bearings, I worked out that if we scrambled up and over the ridge to the far side, we would be overlooking the courtyard.

'How many times have you been up here?'

'A couple. If we'd been here earlier we could have seen the sunset,' Rogan said, lying back on the tiles. 'Still, no clouds tonight.'

The moon hadn't risen yet. Stars scattered across the sky, not as bright as the ones at home. Tracey and I would bunk out and climb The Hill to look at them and plan our escape. I thought of Rachel. Where she lived, even further west than me, there would have been limited artificial light to compete with the stars. There they would have been the boldest. I wondered if she had looked at them as she perfected her American accent and dreamt up a whole new life.

I moved next to him, feeling so small and unimportant

that for a moment I could forget that I had done such big and terrible things.

'Beautiful,' I said, and shivered, the night settling on my skin. We lay there side by side.

He cleared his throat and hesitated, before asking, 'Did the police come back?'

And I realised this was the reason he hadn't been at college since Rachel's death and why I was up here on the roof. The question he wanted to ask without any witnesses. No one to hear the concern in his voice. This was the extent of the talk.

'No,' I said, and I stared at the stars so hard that my vision blurred.

'So, I guess that's the end of it,' he said.

But I didn't want it to be the end. So I asked him if he would go to Leiza's rally with me the next day. It wasn't an ideal second date but I could sense that if I didn't ask him then there might not be one. There was no answer. Instead, he leant across and kissed me. Perhaps he just wanted me to stop talking, but I kissed him back all the same. He clambered over to lie on top of me, not an easy thing to do across tiles. His breath on my face was warm, like blowing into cupped hands on an icy day. We were so close that our eyelashes touched. The weight of him pinned me in place and I wrapped my arms around him, trying to do the same. Looking up into his eyes, I wanted to shrink the world so it was only as large as the two of us, ask him if this could be love, but he was already moving his head, turning his eyes south to calculate the bare minimum of clothes that needed to be shed. We ended up having sex on that roof, minimal moving, fumbling, functional, rubber-infused sex. His interest in me quickly shrivelled once he had finished.

I lay there, as cold and hard as the tiles underneath me. Wordlessly, he began pulling up his jeans. A scraping noise came from the roof cavity below. Rogan grabbed the torch and shone the beam around. 'Did you hear that?' he asked.

I shook my head, not trusting myself to speak.

'Come on then. Let's go. I'm freezing.'

We left each other in the stairwell on my floor. He didn't try to kiss me. 'Good night,' he said, before I could mention the rally again.

Saying nothing, I turned down the corridor. I could feel his eyes watching my retreat but refused to turn around. I had that much pride at least. There was no one in the breakout area so I didn't have to smile and pretend everything was OK, which was lucky because nothing was. Any happiness I had felt earlier evaporated. I was broken. Guilt covered me like a thin layer of grit.

That night, I had the dream again. I was standing on the bank looking at the river and someone was floating in the water. Even though I couldn't see a face, I was certain it was Rachel. I called for her to get out, but she ignored me so I got in. The water was much deeper than I expected and I floundered out of my depth and became tangled in the weeds. The girl swam up to me, her face blue in the moonlight, and it wasn't Rachel after all, but Tracey, and she held my hand. I smiled at her and began to say sorry. Raising her arm, she grabbed my hair and pushed my head under. I woke up in the darkness with a half-scream stuck in my throat and the taste of the river in my mouth.

Chapter 17

I could hear raised voices as I came in to dinner the next day.

'I know you did this,' I heard a boy yell. As I walked through the doors, I saw Toby standing there, looking amused, and Kesh next to him, looking anxious, waiting to be served their food. Joad was in the middle of the room, shouting. 'They're fucking everywhere.' He was shoving some paper under Leiza's nose.

'What's going on?' I asked quietly. Toby passed me a folded leaflet. I opened it up to see a headline of STOP THIS SEXISM with a photocopied black and white picture of Joad, a rough speech bubble coming from his mouth. It said,

'That Screwdriver Man has the right idea.' Underneath was information about the rally.

'I picked it up over at the Union,' whispered Kesh. 'There's other quotes from Joad about rape, gays, racist stuff. It is all over campus.'

'What are you saying, Joad?' replied Leiza, in her best ringing tone that carried throughout the unnaturally quiet room. 'Are you claiming you didn't say these things?'

Joad's face contorted. He was so angry that he half spat, half screamed at her. 'How dare you? I'm going to get you for this, you stupid stuck-up bitch.'

'He's going to regret he said that,' said Toby, in an undertone. 'If he's not careful, he'll get booted out of college.' From the contented look on Leiza's face, I guessed she might be thinking the same thing.

Joad looked around at everyone watching him, forks frozen between plate and mouth. Even the cook had come out from behind the counter to stare.

'Fuck you all,' he said, and then he picked up the edge of Leiza's table and tipped it over. Dishes, glasses and cutlery went sliding down lengthways, allowing some people to make a grab at their dinner as it slipped past, so the mess wasn't as bad as it could have been. Still, there was a satisfying smash as a water jug and some unattended plates hit the floor. Then he marched out of the hall, only stopping to rip another of the leaflets out of Annabel's hand.

Leiza stood up on her chair. Looking completely composed, she addressed the room. 'Remember the rally starts in an hour in front of the bar.' She then stepped down and began to organise the cleanup.

'Couldn't Leiza be in big trouble for those leaflets as well?' Kesh asked. 'I mean, aren't they defamatory?' She looked at me.

'Well, not if he said those things, which I bet he did,' I answered.

'And who's to say Leiza made them?' said Toby. 'The official posters, which I plastered up with my own fair hands, were completely different. I bet she didn't physically do any of it. It's just the sympathetic sisterhood getting their pound of flesh. And now, after that spectacle, Joad's goose is gonna be cooked. C'mon, let's grab some dinner before this rally.'

'Do we have to go?' I asked, moving towards the counter. 'It will be all cold and dark.'

'It's Take Back the Night, Pen,' said Toby, reprovingly. 'Not Reclaim Morning Tea time.'

But as I turned, balancing my tray, I stopped listening to him. I had caught sight of the table directly behind where Leiza had been sitting. Rogan was there, and the way that eyes can meet across a crowded room, ours did. A long moment. Then slowly, deliberately, he placed an arm around the shoulders of the girl next to him. It was Emelia.

Rugged up in a coat and scarf, I stood next to a concrete pillar advertising house shares, upcoming bands, second-hand bikes, university elections and one enormous-sized poster of Joad. This one gave his response to the AIDS crisis. Toby and I were standing at the top of the stairs that led down to the Quadrangle. It was a cloudy night but the street lights gave off alien-like tractor beams of harsh fluorescent so we could see people gathering for the start of the rally. From our vantage spot we also overlooked the beer garden attached to the bar. Staff wearing black polo tops came in and out picking up glasses. A few customers drank beer. In the garden, Pete, the vampirish ticket guy, was having a cigarette.

A loud distorted voice cut through the noise. 'Attention, attention. Marshals to the front.' Leiza, talking into a megaphone, was standing on a large temporary wooden platform, which had been placed right across the bar's entrance. Girls shuffled behind her, wearing t-shirts with 'Marshal' scribbled on in marker pen. They began to unfold one long banner: STOP THE VIOLENCE, the words painted in alternating purple and green letters. Kesh was holding one end of the banner and, to my surprise, Michael was also up the front and had grabbed on to the sheet at 'V'. There were

243

suspicious shadows around the 'i' and 'o' in 'violence', suggesting that they had originally been in opposing places. Other girls began to hand out candles stuck through paper plates to those who hadn't brought their own.

The space began to fill. This was more than just a loose confederation of Leiza's cronies. Sandal-wearing Christians jostled for position, hemmed in by Marxists on one side and hippies against nukes on the other. They all glared suspiciously at one another as they fought for prominence. More people came and still more until the place was crowded. I began to pick out faces that I recognised: the girl who got caught stealing a book from the Law Library by the grumpy librarian in my first week; the boy who was always late to every lecture; a couple of Marchmain boys, dressed all in white, standing off to one side; and to my surprise, Joad, at least I thought it looked like Joad, standing in the middle of the crowd with a beanie pulled down to just below his eyebrows.

'Leiza has actually pulled this off,' said Toby. 'Either people care a lot more about these issues than I thought or they all really hate Joad.'

Out of the darkness, tiny flickers of yellow flame multiplied as people lit their candles, quivering like the reflection of stars in the sea. They warmed and softened the square concrete buildings that surrounded the Quad. It was beautiful and the crowd became hushed as if surprised by it.

Leiza stepped forward on the platform. 'Tonight we remember,' her amplified voice began, but she was almost immediately drowned out by a couple of motorbikes roaring up the street. The crowd turned as one to see them park on the footpath on the far side of the rally from where I stood. The two riders got off their bikes and began to push their way through the crowd. In the half-light they were a mixture of leather, flannies, denim and beards. I stood on tippy-toes to see if one of them was Tommy of the metal tooth and wandering hands. Some in the crowd began to boo but Leiza held up her hand to quiet them.

'Just wanted a drink,' yelled out one of them, as they got up to the front. The other jumped up on to the platform next to Leiza and took a bow. His comrade slow-clapped him in a show of bravado. They were equal parts menacing and childish. Leiza stood her ground and waited them out, not resuming until they had sauntered inside. But the spell had been broken and even though her speech was passionate and articulate, something had been lost by the intrusion. When the next speaker was introduced, the crowd was restless, humming with their own conversations. Toby was no better.

'There's Nico,' he said, checking out a boy with a head of carpet-like stubble, standing several people away from us.

Wearing his grubby white suit with a backpack slung over his shoulder, Nico turned at the sound of his name.

There was a nasty rash on his neck and he looked like he had lost weight. He put down his backpack and began to fiddle with the zipper.

Toby moved towards him. 'Nico, mate, I haven't seen you for a while.' A woman next to us with short hair and large sculptural earrings shushed and waved her candle crossly in our direction. It went out and she fussed around for a neighbouring flame to relight it.

'You still dossing at the Gulag?' asked Toby.

The Gulag was a series of corrugated huts up behind the Forestry Building that had been condemned by the university. Rumours were they would be pulled down at the end of the year. Infestations of students squatted in them occasionally.

'Been there ever since they took my Alice away.' His voice was rough and congested like he had been sick with a bad cold. He pointed in the direction of the bar. 'They hurt her and now her parents won't let me see her.'

'Who hurt Alice?' Toby asked.

'He did,' and he pointed to Pete, out in the beer garden. The two bikers had joined him. Pete was one of those people who gestured with his hands when he talked. His hands didn't seem happy.

'Pete,' I said, surprised. 'You're saying the guy in charge of the bar was the one who attacked Alice?' The lady with the earrings had just been about to ask us to be quiet, but even she got distracted at the turn of conversation and stopped listening to the Health Clinic woman, who was clutching the loudhailer in one hand and a bundle of notes in the other.

'He's not in charge, just acts like he is,' said Nico. 'Those Death Riders, they're the real power. Them and some guy they call The Master. They hurt people who get in their way.'

Toby tried to judge if he was serious. 'Who else have they hurt?' he asked.

'That nosy one asking all the questions. Came to see Alice in hospital. Rachel something. They killed her for sure.'

The mention of Rachel was enough for me. Nico was deluded. I turned away, but he kept talking. 'Leiza better watch out. She's nosy too, asking for police investigations. They'll hurt her.' He was getting more agitated and began talking louder. 'I'm going to make them pay for what they did to Alice.' People started to look over as he, shuffling sideways, knocked over his backpack. There was a metal clang and a glug of liquid as something shifted and fell inside it. Hastily, he grabbed it and then left, shoving his way through the crowd, towards the platform. The Health Clinic woman was finishing up.

'Can you smell something?' asked Toby. He knelt down to where Nico's bag had been sitting and the shushing lady crouched as well, illuminating the area with her candle.

'Careful,' said Toby, pushing her back. 'I think it's petrol.'

247

'He has petrol in his backpack?' I asked. Straightening up immediately, my eyes scouted through the crowd. Nico was moving towards the platform but not only that, boys dressed in white were pushing through the crowd from all directions. I could see at least ten. It was a Marchmain reunion.

'This isn't good. People could get hurt,' said Toby. 'Get to Leiza and grab the loudhailer. Tell people to get out of here. I'll try and head him off.' We both started running down the steps.

Leiza was talking again, introducing the next speaker, the Student Union's Women's Officer, but she stopped midway, sensing something was not right.

Nico had fought his way through and leapt up next to Leiza, looking like a cross between an escaped convict and a mad preacher.

'Forget Reclaim the Night,' he shouted at the crowd. 'Let's reclaim the bar!'

There was a ragged cheer of surprise and approval at this but Nico didn't wait to listen. He ran towards the front door, only to find it had been locked. Someone inside must have assessed the situation and acted quickly. Slamming his hands on it in frustration, he then began to open his bag. By this time Toby had reached him and was trying to pull the bag away. I had worked my way to the front, yelling at the non-comprehending people around me to

'Move back, move back.' I was about to reach Leiza and the loudspeaker when a couple of the Marchmain boys, their faces covered with bandanas, began to kick at the glass panels of the door with heavy Doc Marten boots. An odd kind of aggressive excitement rippled through the crowd. While I'm sure that some people sensed danger and started moving away, more began pushing forward. Other fists began to slam on the glass, which shuddered under the weight. The Marchmains were chanting 'let us in, let us in', and 'occupy', and people took up their cries. A brick hurtled over my head and the sound of smashing glass mixed with screaming.

'No!' yelled Leiza, as the glass panel gave way, and a boy clambered through, unlocking the door from the other side and trying to jam it open. She began to wrestle with the boy to stop him and I lost sight of her. I was wedged in on all four sides by people I didn't know. I couldn't see Toby or Nico and I felt panicked about the possibility of a fire starting in front of us. I tried to fight my way back, but instead I was propelled on by the bodies on either side of me. We were moving towards the doorway and here the crowd funnelled. Pushing started to come from the back, surging those at the front forwards. When the next wave came through, I was dragged several metres towards the building, though my feet weren't on the ground.

As the push lulled, I tried to plant my feet down and

moved my arms out in front of me, desperate for some space. The next surge would take us through the door, and I was worried I might be slammed into broken glass. I braced myself and then the wave came through. I had almost made it when I started to fall. I reached out to the nearest person and tried to grab on to something to regain my balance. But they slipped past and I landed hard on the floor. Pushing myself to all fours, I tried to get back up but legs and feet kept knocking me down. I covered my head with my arms as the world turned airless. Then I felt my body being pulled upwards. When I was half-standing, half-crouching, I was grabbed around my middle and dragged towards the opposite wall, next to the bakery roller door.

I sat there, dazed and terrified, trying to get air back into my lungs. It was a few seconds before I could even work out who had saved me. Michael sat next to me on the floor.

'Are you OK?' he asked.

I nodded my head, unable to speak. Resting my arms on my knees, I let my head hang, my mouth still gulping for air. I had been close to blacking out, perhaps even dying. All I could hear was the rasp of my own breath and I wondered if this was what it felt like to drown. Is this what it had been like for Rachel? Had she tried to fight it? She had been all alone, struggling to breathe with no one to help her. The thought almost overwhelmed me.

It was a couple of minutes before my breathing slowed

enough to take air in through my nose and close my mouth. Michael had already disappeared back into the melee and several other people had been pulled out. The girl next to me was excited, as though she had been on a show ride. 'They just picked me up and dragged me along,' she said in a tone of amazement. 'Nothing I could do.'

It was a strange combination of riot and party. Crowds kept pouring through the front door. Another door was opened further down and people came through that as well. Someone got to the stereo system and turned the music up full bore. There were yells and screams and it was hard to distinguish the range of emotions involved, everything from jubilation to fear. I tucked myself into a tight ball, out of the way, and stayed still for a long time.

When I finally decided to move, every part of me feeling battered and bruised, I pulled myself to standing, using the wall behind me for support. I was wobbly but I was OK. I wanted to get outside but there were still too many people between me and the entrance, so I began to follow the herd and made my way down the internal stairs towards the bar, keeping to the edges as far away from the crowd as I could. I never wanted to be stuck like that again. It took a while for me to make my way down and even longer to get around the corner. The music was changed from an aggressive fast metal to something more mellow, and the place began to settle into something of a carnival. Marchie boys were behind the bar, handing out free drinks. People were dancing to the music, starting to migrate towards the pool tables and beginning to look back at the outside world and wonder how on earth they ended up here. There were some injuries. One girl was crying on the floor, cradling her wrist. No one paid her any attention. There were other people with cuts from the broken glass, being mopped up by their friends, but on the whole most people seemed to have got in unscathed. I couldn't see the bikers anywhere.

'Pen,' I heard a voice call from behind me. It was Toby, sitting at a table, drinking a beer, with Nico's backpack at his feet. He was holding another unopened beer to his face.

My adrenalin started to slow. I felt shaky like I couldn't walk any more and collapsed on the seat beside him. 'You got the petrol,' I said.

'And saved Nico from a whole heap of trouble, not that he appreciated it. He punched me right in the head.'

'You OK?' I pulled the beer away to have a look. His eye was already closing and around his cheekbone looked puffy.

'I'm gay and Asian. I've had worse beatings than this, believe me.'

'You going to report him?'

Toby shook his head gingerly. 'Poor bastard, he'll have enough people at him. Anyway, how about you? Feeling peachy?'

I nodded wearily, too tired to explain.

'I'll drink to that,' he said, and handed me the beer that had been chilling his face.

'Really?' I asked.

'No greater sacrifice.'

We clinked bottles.

'Well, Rachel would have loved this,' Toby said, as he chugged down his beer. I nodded my head, not trusting myself to talk. It was impossible not to think of what had happened last time I was at the bar. Looking around, I kept expecting Rachel to be in the thick of it, grabbing the free alcohol, trying to break the storeroom open.

'Where are the bar staff, or for that matter, those bikers?' I asked.

'The staff are over there.' Toby pointed to a group of black polo tops playing pool at a nearby table. Like the experienced bar staff they were, they seemed to be turning a blind eye to the mayhem and going with the flow like this was just a normal shift. Occasionally, one of them looked over towards their white-suited replacements and sort of gave a shrug. 'Pete and the bikers beat a retreat via the fire exit.'

'Those bikers just left?' I asked, surprised. I had visions of pool cues as weapons and people getting chairs smashed over their heads.

'A strategic retreat. They've played it smart and won. No

one can accuse them of this. Tonight, we are seeing the last glorious stand of the Marchmains. Tomorrow they will be no more.'

I looked over to see Nico jubilant, standing on the bar, holding a stolen bottle of champagne in his hand, reminiscent of the first time I had ever seen him. He was joined by a pimple-encrusted boy wearing a faded yellow Che Guevara t-shirt, yelling something about a new world order.

'How much trouble is Nico going to be in?' I asked, trying to catalogue the list of offences that had been committed, outside of assaulting Toby.

'I've seen more damage on an average Friday night here,' said Toby. 'Some broken glass, some broken bones. Mind you, there usually is a full till in compensation. That ain't happening now.' A couple of enterprising Marchies were trying to jimmy a register open.

'Pete will call the police, won't he?'

'Na, they'll just patch everything up and reopen tomorrow like nothing happened. If I was Nico I'd be more worried about Leiza catching up with him.'

'Where is Leiza?' I asked.

'Haven't seen her,' said Toby.

Toby managed to finagle another couple of beers, as we watched what seemed like the whole university parade past. A student band turned up and began to give an impromptu concert, their politics more developed than their musical ability. The crowd began to thin in response. We had probably been sitting there at least an hour when the sirens started. One siren joined another and then another until there was a perfect circle of noise in the room.

'The police,' I said, to state the obvious. People pushed towards the large glass floor-to-ceiling windows that overlooked the Quadrangle to see what was going on.

'They're coming for us,' squeaked a nervous girl sitting at the table nearby. A boy with long black hair tied in a lank ponytail started shouting that we should all be prepared to go to jail for the cause, but wasn't specific as to what cause he thought this was.

'I can't believe they called the police,' said Toby.

Around us, Marchie boys had already begun to mobilise by building barricades. I could see Nico was leading the charge.

'Let's get out of here,' I said to Toby.

'Right behind you,' he said. 'I'm much too pretty for a police cell.'

The boy with the Che t-shirt was yelling out instructions to link arms on his command, and even the bar staff seemed to be involved in a discussion about whether you could drag the pool tables over to wedge in front of the broken windows. A stream of people had already started towards the fire exit.

'I have an alternative,' said Toby. He led me over to the window that I had seen him use the night Rachel had died. Fiddling with the lock, he pushed it open and scrambled through. My body had seized up from sitting for so long and I was still a bit woozy, so I nearly fell through it, but Toby was waiting for me and half caught me, half guided me to the ground. We were in the beer garden.

'What about the petrol?' I asked.

'Forget it,' said Toby. 'We don't want to be caught with that. Anyway, let's go down the back where the fence is lower, jump it and head home.'

It sounded like the best plan I had heard. We were climbing over when we heard: 'Police. Don't move.'

We froze, me straddling the fence, Toby already over the far side.

'Put your arms above your heads.'

We did and I wobbled. From up on top of the fence I had a clear view of the road. There was a red glare from a jumble of cars blocking it, blue lights on roofs lazily ticking over. Figures in uniform gathered around them. Behind us, I could hear a different voice on a loudspeaker, a man's voice, telling people to evacuate the building. 'Immediately through the front doors. I repeat, through the FRONT doors.'

A policewoman came towards us, blocking our way. She was in the process of cordoning off the area.

'You can't get through here,' she said. 'Turn around and go back the way you came.'

I recognised her and at the same time she recognised me. 'Wait a second, I know you. You found the girl who drowned.'

It was Constable Morriset.

'What are you doing here?' she asked me. But it was Toby who answered, spinning her a line about having a quiet drink at the bar when all of a sudden there was an invasion and we had no idea what was going on but decided to sit tight and drink more beer.

'We're just going back to Scullin now,' I said as meekly as possible, and then because I couldn't resist, 'What's going on?'

The action seemed to be concentrated in front of us, in the direction of the river, rather than behind us at the bar. The constable followed my gaze. 'This is a crime scene. You are going to have to go back the way you came.'

Just then, another car came up the road, but not a police car this time. It parked on the grass, not far from us. We watched as a pudgy man in crumpled clothes got out. Constable Morriset swore. 'Right, you two, you can go through but follow the path straight back to your college.' She motioned us past her and moved towards the man.

'You can't enter here,' she said to him. 'I'll ask you to return to your car ...'

But the man kept walking. 'What have you found, Constable?'

'There will be a statement in due course.' Constable Morriset blocked his way, pulling out her torch and shining it directly in his eyes. 'Sir, I must ask you to—'

'Four cars, must be serious,' said the man, taking out a notebook. 'Not just some student protest getting out of hand now, is it? Another attack, I'm guessing.'

Other police were closer now. 'Here already, Joe?' called out one. 'Another lonely night with only a scanner for company.'

'Doing my job, Sergeant, just like you. What have you got this time?'

Constable Morriset took a step away from him, and noticing us still standing there, frowned. 'I told you to get going. Move it.'

All the lights were on at college by the time we got back. A knot of people was standing in reception. We tried to slip past but heard someone yelling my name. Kesh came running over.

'Thank God,' said Kesh, hugging both of us and crying. 'You're safe. You're safe.'

'What are you talking about?' said Toby.

Kesh's pale face became even paler.

'There's been another attack. A girl's dead. People are saying it's Leiza.'

Toby asked more questions and Kesh began to cry but all of it was slowly drowned out by the pounding of my heart. I felt a chill on my arm, as if someone was taking hold of my hand and dragging me down into deep water.

*

'A lot to talk about today,' says Frank, and there is a faint sense of accusation that I've lumped all of this in together. 'Let's start with the crush. Were you scared?'

I think about it. 'There wasn't enough time to be scared. It happened so quickly. I felt angry afterwards, sitting there looking at the people still coming through, thinking you nearly trampled me for this.'

Frank nods. 'So you felt angry.' He ponders this as if it is something significant. 'Do you often get angry?'

I wonder if he's deliberately trying to make me angry now, because that seems the only rational response to such a dumb question.

'You're not allowed to feel angry when you almost get crushed?'

'That's not what I said.' Frank gives me one of his long-suffering looks. 'A threat can generate a fear response or an anger response. Some people might panic being in large crowds after that, other people might shut down and avoid shopping centres or sporting events. Some people's first response will be to react angrily, to lash out. Does that sound familiar?'

'No,' I lie. 'I'm the more panicky-in-crowds type.'

Frank clicks his pen, which means he disagrees. 'Who was it who pulled you out of the crowd? Who rescued you?'

But I don't want to cooperate any more. 'Don't know.'

'You don't know who saved your life?' he asks. 'Don't tell me it's another stranger.'

I frown because I am not sure what he means.

'You know, like the person who kissed you that night at the bar crawl.'

And for a moment everything is still. No man from the gift shop to distract us. I can't hear Ivy's heels click-clacking down the hall. There are just the two of us in here, playing games with my life.

'That's right,' I say. 'He was a perfect stranger.'

'University must have been a big place with all these perfect strangers,' Frank says.

There is something funny about the way he says this. He means it as an accusation, but at the same time it is also the truth. Being amongst strangers was exactly what I had wanted and it's definitely what I got.

It is a long wait before Frank speaks again. I look down at my diary. I had worked so hard on it this week, underlining the sections I was going to read to him and practising it at home so that the jumps seem natural, so it sounds like I am telling him the whole story.

'Did you go to Leiza's funeral?' he asks, eventually.

'Only the memorial.'

It had been held in the Examination Hall, a barn-sized room that smelt of paper and disappointment. Despite it being the largest space on campus, so many people turned up that we were packed in together and latecomers had to stand outside.

For some reason, Frank doesn't seem to think the memorial was sufficient because he reminds me that I didn't attend Rachel's funeral either. He doesn't ask for an explanation or a response, but instead leaves the comment to hang in the air for me to contemplate.

Sometimes I wonder if Frank is very good at his job or whether he is just a doctor who didn't like the sight of blood. Once I asked him what his actual job description was and he told me it was to ask intelligent questions, which sounded like a complete cop-out. Surely, intelligent answers would be much more useful.

I shuffle in my seat and glance out the window. The shopkeeper is still not outside. He must be tucked away under the beady eye of his mother.

'Did you cry?' asks Frank.

'What?'

'Did you cry at the memorial?'

'No.'

'There must have been people around you crying,' he comments, another implied criticism couched in deliberately non-judgmental language.

I think back to Emelia and her cronies who had sat in front of me, crying just enough to hold tissues under their eyelashes so their mascara wouldn't run. Rogan sat next to Emelia, looking worried. I heard she went straight to her Accounting tutor afterwards to try and get special consideration on her assignment because of it.

'Leiza's parents didn't cry,' I say.

They had sat in the front row dry-eyed, staring at Marcus while he made his speech. Within two weeks, their lawyer would serve papers on the University.

'Did you think they should have cried?'

'Not if they didn't feel like it. People should act how they feel.'

'How do you think they felt?'

Her father was angry. It sparked off him as he stalked down the aisle when the ceremony was over. He had left his wife stranded, having to deal with the long line of well-wishers mouthing platitudes before they returned to their safe lives. I remembered her face clearly. She was beyond crying. She was listening to each person tell her how sorry they were, and many of them were in tears, as though she was comforting them. But I understood that she had been hollowed out from grief, and that her egg-shell veneer was all that was left.

I try to explain this to Frank.

'How did you feel?'

And I know I am expected to have some insight into my own lack of crying, that somehow I am hollow or angry, but I am sick of all this. So I don't tell him I felt a mixture of fear and guilt, or that very deep down I was almost relieved because I thought no one would even think about Rachel's death now.

'Sad,' I say. 'Just sad.'

Frank frowns but he doesn't push it. Instead he asks, 'When was the last time you cried?'

I shrug my shoulders and think about making one up, but I can't find the words, so I sit there. I know exactly when it was. The day the policeman told me that the trial wasn't to go ahead. That they wouldn't need me as a witness. The day I decided I wouldn't do any more counselling.

Frank senses I am not going to talk about it, because he changes topics.

'Have you written down anything about the events of three years ago in your diary, Pen, like we discussed?'

I don't answer him. Instead I stare at the fleck of white paint. I am sure it is getting bigger.

I can feel his eyes on me.

'We don't need to talk about that. That isn't why I'm here.'

'I disagree. I don't believe that what occurred this year is some kind of coincidence, that "bad things" just happen to you. I believe we need to explore what really happened before with that policeman. To talk openly about what your role was, not just put all the blame on Tracey. You need to face what you did or this pattern of behaviour may keep on repeating.' The words tumble out of him as if there is a lot more he wants to say.

I move my gaze from the wall to his face.

'What pattern?' I ask.

There is a moment of silent confrontation, a battle of wills, before he looks away and starts scribbling something on my file. He doesn't answer me but instead talks about revisiting places from that night with Tracey. 'It could assist you. Perhaps walk up The Hill,' he says.

When I leave, I tell Ivy that I can't make the next appointment and that I will call to reschedule.

I'll keep writing in the diary but I don't want to do this any more.

Chapter 18

'How did she die?' I asked Dale.

He sat there, a slight frown on his face, but not surprised. When you're a policeman, you probably have peopie asking that sort of question all the time.

Leiza's death was the only thing being talked about at college. Officially, all anybody knew was that it was suspicious and the police were investigating. Not even the residential assistants had been told more, Toby said to me over breakfast. We sat across from each other, food untouched. That morning alone, the day after her body had been found, I had heard three different stories about what had happened, each one worse than the last.

To get away I decided to do some study before my Torts

lecture. I was getting behind in all my subjects, and at least in the silent area of the library, I could escape the conversations. So, when the first person I saw was someone who would actually know what really happened, I was in two minds if I should say hello. A bear of a man hunched over a small wooden table, tapping a pen on its surface, while pressing rewind and fast forward on a cassette deck in front of him. Dale. He had been missing lectures so I hadn't seen him since that night at the bar.

He took off his headphones in disgust and popped the deck. As he pulled it out, a long ribbon of tape dribbled from the cassette. He gave a grunt and looked up.

'That's had it,' I said.

'Got six more hours to listen after this one,' he said. 'I need some coffee.'

While Dale chatted to the guy behind the counter, I sat on the decking outside. The sky was an almost-white blue. You could taste winter coming. The coffee shop, a demountable building next to the car park, was quiet. Before 10 a.m. was the student equivalent of dawn and most of the tables were empty. A stripy-shirted stockbroker of the future was demonstrating to his fellow striped-shirts how he managed to get airborne in Daddy's Porsche. Two lecturers were having breakfast while slagging off an article they hadn't written and a table of girls were discussing the front page of the newspaper. I could read the headline: CAMPUS MURDER.

'I heard parts of her body were sliced off,' a dark-haired girl said.

'It doesn't say that in the article.'

'No, it's true. And there was a mark on her forehead, a cross or something.'

'A ritual kind of thing?'

'The Death Rider's cross,' said the first girl, and there were nods of agreement from the others.

'Or it could be that psycho Screwdriver Man who ripped off that girl's ear,' said another girl. 'Why isn't anyone talking about him?'

Their conversation was a mixture of horror and voyeurism. I wondered what would happen if I leant over and told them I knew that dead girl. Would they feel embarrassed? Probably ask me if I knew more about what had happened.

'I don't care who it was,' said one with her back to me. 'I'm never walking around campus by myself again.'

'Me neither.'

'I mean, it could have been any of us.'

I didn't know if that was right. None of it felt random to me. It felt very personal. Terrible things happening, getting closer. I slumped in my chair.

'Forgot to ask how you wanted it, so got them strong and black,' said Dale, walking up to me, balancing two mugs. 'In my job you learn not to risk milk.'

'Let's move,' I said.

The girls fell silent and stared at us as we walked by, and once we passed there was furious whispering again. 'He's a policeman,' I heard one say. 'Wonder if he was there. If he saw her body?'

We sat out on a bench between the tennis courts and the soccer oval, tall gum trees surrounding us. Sipping the coffee, I almost choked.

'Copper's special,' said Dale.

'How much sugar?'

'Enough to get you through a night shift or, alternatively, six hours of law tapes. You look like you needed it.'

He smacked his lips together as a joke. And that's when I asked him how Leiza had died. I hadn't meant to but I couldn't go on listening to the possible, the probable and the absolutely wrong. Better to know the truth.

'You knew her well.' It wasn't a question, more of a statement.

'Well enough,' I said.

'Could tell by your face. These types of deaths leave their own kind of mark.'

I took a cautious sip, grateful we were sitting side by side. If he could really read faces, he might work out that a lot of the damage had actually been done by Rachel's death.

Dale blew on his coffee. 'Too hot,' he said. 'Usually put a bit of cold water in so you can drink it straight away.'

He scratched his nose and then rubbed his eyes with the palm of his hand.

'Night shift,' he said. 'Should be asleep but I've missed too many lectures.'

I wondered if he was ignoring my question, and if I should pretend that I never asked it and we could talk about essays being due or how exams were only around the corner. But after a pause he said, 'She was knocked unconscious by a blow to her head. Then she was cut with a sharp implement, probably a . . .'

'Screwdriver,' I finished. The one detail all the different versions had in common.

He nodded.

'But it was the bikers, wasn't it? The Death Riders must be the ones who killed her.'

Dale grimaced. 'Where's the evidence? And why would they? Something like this is bad for business. They've been pretty smart, flying under the radar mostly, until now.'

'But who then? Screwdriver Man?'

A slight shake of his head. 'Up to now, I had my doubts that this Screwdriver Man even existed. I thought it was kind of like the university equivalent of the Boogie Man, a convenient scapegoat.'

'What about all those attacks? What about Alice?'

'I'm not saying they didn't happen. I just don't think one person did all of them. Outside of the balaclava and the screwdriver, nothing else was the same. He was big. He was small. Spoke with an accent. Had no accent. And the attacks themselves, they weren't that serious. I had them chalked up to the Death Riders' turf war, to be honest.'

I started to speak but he interrupted. 'I know, I know, Alice was badly injured. But I've read the report. There was only one cut and she remembers him watching her and then letting her run off. Now, that's completely different to what happened last night.' Dale gave a sigh and stopped talking.

'How did Leiza die?' I asked.

'It would have been quick. She was unconscious.'

I knew by the way his voice changed that he was lying. I was getting the bereaved parents' version of events, breaking the ugly truth into smaller, more palatable parts to be digested over time. He was being the policeman who rings your doorbell and gives you the bad news, censored. In that moment, I realised I didn't want to know the answer to my question. Some things were too awful to imagine.

'How do you cope with your job?' I asked.

'It has its moments,' he said. 'Murders like this take a layer of skin off. You don't forget them, that's for sure.'

'But you sleep OK?' I had been thinking of my own lack of sleep, but looking at him I realised there were smudges of grey underneath Dale's eyes and even his moustache seemed to droop with fatigue. As he drank his coffee I noticed he was no longer wearing his wedding ring. I wondered what that meant, but now didn't seem the time to ask.

He gave a grim laugh. 'Should be asleep now. Look, most deaths are car accidents, drunks fighting, sometimes a domestic. Not nice, but you can understand them. They don't make you question human nature. This one does.' He took another long drink from his coffee. 'But don't worry. They'll get whoever did this.'

'How can you be sure?'

'Her family for starters. They will make sure the investigation gets all the resources it needs.'

Though none of us had known while she was alive, it had turned out that Leiza's grandfather, dead for some years, had been a prominent politician. Duncan Parnell was a name on plaques everywhere. My own town had the D. J. Parnell Oval where the local footy team played. It was hard to see how that was relevant but the news reports seemed to think it was.

'They'll be turning over every stone and seeing what crawls out. You'll be interviewed.'

A stomach-clenching moment, but not one of real surprise. I had guessed that everyone who had been at the bar would be interviewed.

'I won't be that helpful,' I said. 'I mean, I was at the rally, but so were about half the university. It's not like I saw anything.'

'No, not Leiza Parnell, I mean the first girl. They are opening an investigation into her death as well.'

In the clear sky above us a dart of black plummeted to the ground, only to swoop up at the last minute, and a magpie landed safely on a branch above our heads. It looked around, beady-eyed and judgmental. Saw us. There was a moment of stillness as it tried to work out if we were friend or foe.

'Rachel?' My voice sounded so faint that I had to reassure myself I was actually talking aloud. 'But that was an accident.'

'Possibly.' Dale shrugged as though he wasn't making any judgment. 'A bit late getting started, obviously. Now they've got two girls who knew each other and who are dead within a couple of weeks of each other. There was a Rohypnol tablet found on the second girl's body. The first girl had it in her system. Maybe that's a coincidence, or maybe we are dealing with two murders and maybe they're connected.'

It wasn't just sleeping tablets any more. Now they had a name, a step closer already.

'Rohypnol?' I said.

'Prescription sleeping tablet,' Dale said. 'Strong, addictive. Not widely used. Some suggestion that in the U.S. it's used as a date-rape drug. Pressure is on for the manufacturer to add a dye to it so it can't be used like that. Still, haven't seen much evidence of it being used here.'

'Couldn't it just have belonged to Leiza?'

'She wasn't prescribed it. Haven't found any in her room. It's possible the first girl could have taken it herself. Mixed with cocaine, that's a lethal combination, but still she might have done it for the buzz.' He sighed as he put the empty cup down on the bench beside him. 'But there was no Rohypnol in her bag. Practically everything else you could think of, but not that. Ever heard any talk of girls getting their drinks spiked here?'

It was the way he said this so casually – a little too casually – that made me wonder why Dale was telling me this. Maybe he wasn't my friend. He was a cop after all, not to be trusted. He must be part of the investigation, maybe he was wearing a wire, waiting for me to say something incriminating. I was a suspect, of course I was. I found Rachel and I was at the bar at the time Leiza was killed. I didn't have an alibi for the whole time. Did the police think it was me? I stared at his clothing: a tracksuit and a t-shirt, like he had been working out in the gym first. Could you hide recording equipment under that?

But Dale wasn't looking at me. He was watching a couple of boys who had started kicking a soccer ball on the oval. One began to bounce the ball against his knee and then his head before gently tapping it over to his friend.

'Before now I wouldn't say that we've seen any evidence of it being widely used. Campus doctors don't prescribe it. Women's Health Centre hasn't dealt with anything out of the norm. Nor the drug clinic. Doesn't make sense.'

He stood up, interlaced his fingers and stretched his arms behind his head. I heard muscles and joints pop and creak beneath his t-shirt stretched tight across his frame. There were no square-shaped bulges, no unexplained lumps, just the start of a tyre of flesh around his middle. 'Anyway, that's all for the A-Team who are getting imported in. Them and the Drug Squad.'

'So, you're not investigating?'

'No, a murder investigation's much too important for us local yokels.'

'How do you know all that stuff then?' I asked.

'Everyone knows it. Already on the radio. Be in tomorrow's paper. That Joe McCardle is a bloody leech, but he's a good journalist and he's got his teeth into this one. No better gossips than cops.' His arms dropped to his sides. 'Still, one crisis at a time. Better go try and fix the bloody tape.'

And then I remembered that I had run into him. He didn't know I was going to come along. He was catching up on lectures, as I should be. I had asked him questions about Leiza's death. He was telling me what I had asked for, even giving me a heads-up about being interviewed. He was looking out for me. Protecting me.

'I can't face the library. I'll see you at Torts,' I said, almost wanting to apologise. I felt a surge of relief but my legs still felt weak.

'Yep. Take care of yourself, Pen.' The half-salute goodbye and Dale was gone. The magpie was spooked by his leaving and took off from the branch. It jumped into the air, an act of faith, and then, wings beating fast, the displaced air audible, it began to move higher, heading to the trees on the far side of the oval.

I sat there for a long time, thinking about my Rohypnol. I had been prescribed them a couple of weeks before Tracey's committal and a month before my hearing. I had to stand up in court and blame everything on her. Then I would get a slap on the wrist as an accessory. That was the deal. It was Bob who had organised for me to see Frank, partly because it would look good for my case, but mostly because I was falling apart.

'For Christ's sake, you're a bloody doctor. Do something,' Mum had said. 'She's a basket case.' And he had prescribed these little tablets with his serious face on as he gave me warnings about the potential for an overdose.

The moment I held them in my hand I felt better. I kept them with me always, in my bag at school, on my bedside table at night. If it all got too much, I would just swallow the lot of them and go to sleep forever. I didn't need to give evidence if I didn't want to and knowing that actually gave me the courage to do it. I stood up in the court room and told them Tracey shot the gun, that I had told her not to, begged with her, pleaded, but she wouldn't listen.

'Why didn't you tell someone straight away? If not the police or your mother, what about a favourite teacher?' asked Tracey's expensive city barrister, going through the motions in a case he obviously thought was hopeless.

Tracey and I had been kept apart since we were arrested. She hadn't been at school. I heard rumours she'd been kept in detention. Other people claimed she was staying with relatives. I hadn't been game to ask anyone directly.

I shot a quick glance at Tracey. She had a half-smile on her face at the ridiculous idea of having a favourite teacher. Teachers were the ones who got you into trouble, not out of it. No one went to teachers for help. There were girls who were throwing up their lunch every day in the toilets, getting beaten at home, cheating in tests, and the teachers never heard any of it.

'I was too scared,' I answered, and the prosecutor gave me an encouraging nod. I expected her barrister to ask, 'What of?' but instead he said, 'Did she explain why she shot him? What did she tell you?'

Tracey's face was all I could see as I struggled with what to say. I wanted to yell at her that this was all her fault but at the same time say I was sorry. She didn't look at me, just stared at her own barrister, folding her arms as she leant forward. I didn't have the words to describe that night, so I did what I had been told. Tracey *said not to tell anyone. Bob said the same thing as well. It was too late to start now.*

'Nothing,' I began.

'Speak up,' said the magistrate, his eyes almost non-existent in his red fat face.

'She didn't say anything,' I said.

Tracey turned away, her face blank. She was switching off, as if this was a school lesson that wasn't worth bothering about.

Giving up.

But I wasn't going to give up. No one could prove that it was my Rohypnol that had ended up on Leiza's body but I still needed to find out what had happened to my tablets. I knew where to start asking. I needed to talk to the only person who had been in my room the night Rachel had died, the person who I had invited in.

Chapter 19

It wasn't until Sunday that I worked up the courage to go to the second floor of Page Tower and knock on Rogan's door. Listening, I heard voices, a girl's soft laugh and Rogan murmuring something in answer to her, and I almost walked away. But then he called out, 'It's open,' so I went in.

It was Emelia. She had slipped off her shoes and was posing on his bed, skirt artfully rumpled to display her long legs, hair distressed in a come-hither kind of fashion, like she was expecting someone to pop out and photograph her.

With her usual lack of imagination, she pouted when she saw me.

Rogan's face went from smiling to serious. A touch of guilt was there as well or maybe I just wanted to see that.

'Oh ... hi,' he said.

'Can I talk to you for a moment?' The 'alone' was not said. I hoped it was obvious.

'I'm kind of busy right now.' He gestured towards Emelia. 'Can't it wait?'

Before I could say no, Emelia got up. She made a production of it, stretching and arching her back. Looking at her watch, she picked up the remote and switched off the television that had been on mute.

'Don't let me intrude.' She gave an arch smile.

'No, you don't have to ...' Rogan began, which was the reaction Emelia wanted. She looked pleased with herself.

'Promised the girls I'd take them for a spin.' Her wrecked Honda had been replaced by a gleaming silver BMW. 'I'll see you at dinner, Joshua,' Emelia practically purred. I could hear the rustle of money in every word. The use of Rogan's real name was for my benefit, I guessed, that ring of ownership to point out that he had been acquired and was now her property. Nothing more to do with me.

She stepped past, and for a moment I thought she'd kiss him. He even moved forwards and gave her an awkward peck, looking sheepish. I wondered if they were sleeping with each other. Rachel had told me that Emelia only slept with her last boyfriend twice, on Christmas and his birthday, claiming that sex was for 'plebs'. I almost had to stifle a smile at the thought. Emelia gave me an appraising look. 'Bye, Penny,' she drawled. I moved into the room to let her past.

Rogan's room was the same shape as mine but furnished differently, a room full of gadgets and clothes. This was a student with money. An impressive-looking camera was placed next to a couple of Walkmans on the bookshelf, a VCR next to the television. I wondered whether I should sit down, as I hesitated beginning the conversation that I had been practising in my head for a couple of days, but Rogan started talking instead, trying to pre-empt what he thought I might say.

'So, I'm seeing Emelia now, so what.' He refused to look at me and began moving books around his desk, perhaps hopeful that I would just disappear.

It should have been easy to start hating Rogan at that moment, dismissing me as if I was nothing, but there wasn't time for that now. I had something much more important to find out. The truth is, beautiful people get to act like that all the time and the world lets them. I had been stupid to think that it would be different.

'Maybe it was bad timing with Rachel's death. And now Leiza. Christ, that's just awful.' There was a catch in his throat and he coughed. 'This whole year's been awful. I might transfer back home at the end of it, rather than stay.

Get away from this fucking mess. My parents want me to.'

He walked over to his stereo. A CD was out of its case, resting face down on the top of the player. He cradled it with his fingertips while he flipped open the cover and put it in.

'I mean, I didn't even know Rachel that well. Barely spoke to her, really. And then there were all the lies, making up stuff about people. She said terrible things about Emelia and her parents.'

It was almost laughable that he thought I should feel sorry for poor little rich girl Emelia with her brand-new car. I remembered Rachel sitting on the bank of the river, telling me about Emelia's father and his cook. I had thought she was making it up at the time, but actually I was more inclined to believe it now. As far as I could work out, the only lies Rachel had told were about herself.

As I stood there, watching Rogan work himself up to a display of righteous indignation about me even standing in his room, I tried to remember what Rachel had said about Rogan. She had been vague in her reasons why I shouldn't date him, but she had said he was weak.

Slotting the CD case back into the rack, he looked at me for the first time.

'She killed herself, and that's all very sad.' I could almost see the 'but' forming in the air in front of me. 'But life moves on and I have as well.'

It surprised me that he could believe it was going to be that simple. This was a person with little experience of bad things.

'Well, aren't you going to say something? Why are you here?' He was getting angry and something flared in me in return.

'Actually, what I came to tell you,' I said, not troubling to keep the sarcasm out of my voice, 'is that the police are investigating Rachel's death and they will want to interview you.'

Rogan recoiled and I could see him grappling with the words like he wanted to argue with me.

'But Rachel was an accident.' The same words I had said to Dale, as though by repeating it, we could change what had happened, and make it true.

He leant back, his head resting on the wall, limp. I could still see how beautiful he was, but there was something pathetic as well. He was soft.

'She died from a combination of Rohypnol and cocaine,' I said. This was the important part. I watched for a reaction.

His head jerked back up, alert now. 'Roofies? Are you sure? How the fuck did that happen? Where did she get those from?'

As far as I could tell he seemed genuinely surprised. Or he was a much better liar than he had been in the police interview. Either way, there didn't seem any point telling him about Leiza as well, so I turned around, walked through the door and very carefully closed it behind me.

The television was on when I walked into the Rec Room. I had come to watch the early news about Leiza and the crowd suggested that other students had the same idea. Toby was on duty. 'Turn it up, turn it up,' he said to Joyce, who was sitting next to Michael, and nearest to the set.

Mourning today for the death of Leiza Parnell. The popular student was found murdered on her university campus.

I experienced a strange feeling of dislocation, because the footage on the screen was of our college. A couple of girls were standing near the front wall of Scullin. I didn't recognise them, their faces hidden as they put flowers on the ground, arms around each other for comfort.

The eighteen-year-old granddaughter of political elder statesman Duncan Parnell had participated in a demonstration protesting a series of recent violent attacks against women.

The camera panned to take in a couple of police walking out of our main door. Dressed in blue coveralls, one holding a large paper bag, they moved towards a police van.

'Forensics,' someone said at the nearest table. 'They were back in her room today.'

Police say investigations are ongoing and today her parents made an emotional appeal for any witnesses to come forward.

The image cut to two people sitting flanked by police-men. The camera was on a woman with perfect hair and expensive clothes leaning forward towards the micro-phone. 'If you know anything about that night, if you saw anything at all ...' then her crystal-clear voice wobbled, her head dipped, and the man next to her put his arm around her shoulders. She looked up again and the camera zoomed in. Underneath the make-up, her face was haggard. 'Please, we just want to understand why ...'

I turned my eyes down at the floor, unable to watch any more. By the time I started listening again the next item had already begun.

... could have thought we were in for a thunderstorm, but the rumbles were only that of Death Riders Motorcycle Club in town for a charity event. A new initiative for the club, the event is designed not just to raise noise but much needed money for the children's wing at our local hospital ...

An enormous guy with a red cross tattoo on his t-shirt grimaced at the camera holding a pink teddy bear in his hand. Stoner, who had been sitting by himself, got up quickly and turned the TV off, a scared look on his face. No one challenged him.

'That told us nothing,' complained Toby. 'I could do with a drink.' He grabbed a beer from the fridge. 'Leiza's father was here again today, shouting at Marcus.'

'Shouting?'

'Carol told me all about it. All this stuff about how he should have been sacked from his last university.'

'What for?'

'She didn't hear that bit but Mr Parnell was threatening to sue him.'

'What for?' I repeated.

Toby opened the beer, which fizzed over. Swearing, he picked up a cloth and wiped down the counter. 'Search me, you're the law student. Ask him this afternoon.'

'What are you talking about?'

'Note in your pigeonhole. Didn't you get it?'

I had got out of the habit of checking my mail as no one ever wrote to me. 'Do you often read other people's messages?' I asked.

'Rach and I used to do it all the time. Notes, postcards, anything not in an envelope, really. How do you think I keep myself so well informed? Go now and then come back and tell me what you find out.'

'Finishing off my speech for the memorial,' Marcus explained, as I sat down on the chair opposite his desk.

Though the paint smell had long disappeared, there was still a sharpness to the room, a newness that hadn't yet been absorbed.

'Such a dreadful business,' he continued. He concentrated on the paper in front of him, made a dramatic cross with his fountain pen, and wrote a few more words.

'There, that's it done,' and he put down the pen. 'Must be time for another drink. Care for a whisky?'

I shook my head. I could tell this wasn't going to be some cosy fireside chat. He picked up the empty glass on his desk and went to the half-full crystal decanter on the side table. As I always did when I was in this room, I found my eyes being drawn to the picture of the broken boy, but when I looked it wasn't there. A blank wall.

Marcus noticed where I was looking as he walked towards me with his drink. 'Gone. Sub-Dean took it upon himself to take it down for the Parnells' visit. Thought it might be upsetting.' Then, as an afterthought, 'Have you met the Parnells?'

I shook my head.

'Duncan Parnell was one of the biggest crooks around in his day. Went into Parliament with barely a cent to his name, retired a multimillionaire and a national treasure. Interesting how life turns out.'

Standing there, he swirled the whisky in his glass.

'One must be sympathetic towards the family at such a dreadful time, but every word I say to them seems to be reported on the front of the paper, and then there is this . . .' He threw over a magazine with a double spread inside of the family. 'Came out this morning, so Carol tells me. The family must have hired some PR hack to get this in so quickly.'

'They seem very upset,' I said, looking at a picture of Mrs Parnell crying.

'Of course, of course, we are all upset. Poor Bryan hasn't been the same since he had to identify the girl's body. Mind you, that might be for other reasons. He had taken a keen interest in Ms Parnell's activities and she complained to her parents about his over-zealousness. I am told there were several heated conversations over her role as organiser of the rally. The police wish to interview him as well.'

The chair sighed as he sat down. 'Apparently, he doesn't have an alibi for the time.' Marcus paused for a beat too long before continuing. 'Of course, not for one moment do I think he had anything to do with this tragedy.'

A clock chimed bell-like from the mantelpiece.

'Aah, dinner time. I wonder what culinary delights are in store for you tonight?'

'Mince, I expect.' Grey mince with watery tomato sauce had become a common feature of Scullin dining, with the result that more and more students were becoming vegetarian. Toby thought it was the actual strategy of the cook in order to save on the budget.

'Well, to the matter at hand. You are going to be interviewed by the police Wednesday afternoon at four p.m.

287

They have taken over an administration area on campus for the time being. The details are here.'

He pushed a piece of paper over to me. I folded it and without looking put it into my pocket.

'Now, Ms Sheppard, I know from your student file that you've had ...' he searched for the right word, 'experience with the police before. Therefore you understand that they don't deal in nuances and subtleties. More of a tick-a-box mentality. A contradiction here and change of emphasis there and they may think you have something to hide. Consistency is important. It is important that we corroborate one another. I'm sure you understand.'

It was said so reasonably, so smoothly, that I found myself nodding.

'Good,' he said, and there was a snap to his tone as if I had been caught. 'So you will tell them that Rachel was dealing drugs in college, that she had been warned about this by me personally and that her death must be a tragic accidental overdose. You will be consistent. Joshua will be consistent and I will be consistent.'

He sat back and took another drink from his whisky and I knew if I nodded again, then there would be a couple more pleasantries and I would be dismissed, a little plaything being put back in its box. That wasn't nearly good enough.

'You want me to lie?' I asked.

There was a moment of incredulity as Marcus stared at me. The skin around his jaw hardened and the facade of jovial benefactor slipped.

'You disappoint me. I thought you understood how the world works. There is no such thing as a free lunch. There are always strings attached.'

Marcus rapped a finger on the desk, like a talon sharpening on a rock.

'This college's reputation must be protected. To have one student murdered may be regarded as a misfortune, to have two is carelessness. I am not a careless person. Already, we have parents worried for their children, threatening to find accommodation elsewhere. If they hear another death is being investigated, some will leave. If students leave, our budget will be put under pressure. I would be forced to make some unfortunate decisions such as cutting some of our extra programmes.'

He was too subtle an operator to specify my bursary, without which I couldn't stay at college and possibly not even at university, but we both knew that's what he meant.

Slowly, I nodded my head.

'We understand each other,' and with a smile he drained his drink. 'I knew we would.' With that, the mask was replaced, the atmosphere warmed and the faint air of menace that had been hovering disappeared.

He tapped the side of the glass as if everything had been

decided, and then said as an aside, 'Your mother hasn't phoned me.'

Puzzled, I looked at him.

'She hasn't rung up, demanding to know if her child is safe, telling me that you may leave.'

'My mother doesn't watch the news,' I said. 'And I wouldn't go anyway. I'm never going to live with her again.' The idea that I could really be forced to leave suddenly hit me, and I was surprised by how upset I felt about it.

He nodded at me, all genial now. 'I understand. I was packed off to Australia from England by my mother when I was ten. Escaped the war for oranges and sunshine as they say. The truth being somewhat different.'

'I thought that you had to be an orphan.' I had heard of kids from England being used as cheap labour on farms or sent to children's homes. Tracey's father had emigrated that way.

'Most were.'

'Did you ever see your mum again?'

'Never,' he said. 'For those of us for whom a home has proven elusive, we make do. Having been lost, you find shelter where you can. Another reason why we must both safeguard Scullin's reputation.'

A complicated moment of recognition passed between us, a shared vulnerability.

Marcus stood up. 'Your mince will be getting cold, I expect.'

As he opened the office door, he put out his hand for me to shake. He had set out a bargain for me, from one survivor to another. I hesitated as I looked at him, searching for the scared ten-year-old boy he must have once been, but there in his tailored suit and expensive sky-blue tie, it was hard to believe such a boy had ever existed. Reluctantly I held out my hand and he took it, almost lingering over it. The feel of his skin was papery but there was power in his grip.

Chapter 20

Ros is fussing around me, pulling out various dresses. There is an entire bouquet of floral to choose from.

'This one would be good.' She holds up a frilly pink one. 'Bob said he wanted something youthful.' Underneath the manicured exterior, Ros is as tough as nails. Her hair is a shiny grey helmet. You don't mess with Ros.

'How about the navy?' I ask, grabbing one that Ros has already discarded. It is plain and something a nun would wear, but that's preferable to looking as if I'm off to a five-year-old's birthday party.

'This one's perfect,' Ros insists, steel in her voice, handing over the pink one. 'I've got to run to the bank but Donna can keep an eye on you until I get back.'

The shop smells of steam and synthetics. Donna's perfect apricot talons click as she moves the iron back and forth over a perfectly pleated dress. She has frosted blonde hair, a neatly pressed apricot dress and, no doubt, apricot bra and knickers on underneath.

I sometimes think people in this town age in dog years. Go to sleep late teens, wake up middle-aged in pastels. As Ros walks past, she whispers something to Donna and nods her head in my direction. Bob proclaims his clients' innocence, Ros still locks up the silver.

I sneak a look at the price tag on the pink dress. No wonder they don't have any customers other than me. I drop it on top of the pile lying at the counter.

'What's the occasion?' asks Donna, once Ros is safely trotting up the street. 'Are you going to court?'

I shake my head. I never want to go to court again, not unless I'm the lawyer.

'No offence. Just we get all sorts in here from Bob.' She leans towards me across the ironing board and lowers her voice to a pantomime-type whisper. 'Ros says once she had to dress a murderer. Can you believe it?'

I almost ask for more details because she is bursting to tell, and then I realise she is probably talking about Tracey. Unless she means me. Three years ago, Ros wouldn't have either of us in the shop during daylight hours. Instead, she opened up late on different nights. Didn't want the town to think she was taking sides, even though I was her husband's client. Might be bad for business.

'Haven't seen you before,' Donna says. 'You local?'

'I've been away. Grew up here.' Nearly suffocated here would be more accurate.

'Only moved into town three months ago. Finished school and thought it was time to see the world. Here's all right.' She wrinkles her nose like it's touch and go but she's trying to be polite. Doesn't want to upset a customer, even one from Bob.

'Wanna hand choosing?' she asks, as she shifts the dress to its front, sprays a mist of water on it, and presses down on the pleats.

'All right,' I say, because she can't be any worse than Ros.

'Great. I hate bloody ironing. This lot is for the Festival's fashion parade next week. We're having a try-on tonight. You keep looking. I'll be done in a sec.'

There is a jungle of dresses to choose from. I start shuffling half-heartedly through the rack nearest me.

'Don't bother with those ones,' she calls out. 'That's mostly mother-of-the-bride stuff. Look from the red onwards.' She points towards the back corner. I begin to flick through.

The shop is decorated with scrunched-up bits of pink and white tissue paper to celebrate the Blossom Festival. Ros was once Blossom Princess. There is a black and white photograph of her on the counter next to the till, a sash cut-ting her in two as if she's a prize heifer at the show.

'The last mother of the bride we had in here chose a dress that made her look like a jellyfish, but you can't help some people. God knows what Julie will think of her mum.'

'Julie Cuttmore?'

Donna looks up and bites her bottom lip. 'How'd you guess? Shit, you're not going to it, are you? Sorry, no offence.'

I shrugged to show I wasn't bothered.

'But then you'd know all about it. I only said weddings are nice to have the family all together and she began to cry and told me all about her other daughter. Terrible. A police-man and everything. She says she visits every Sunday but her husband doesn't. Can't even bring himself to say her name.'

I had heard that as well. On the night Tracey got charged he had disowned her. According to Mum, he told everyone he no longer had a second daughter, as though his family was so large he could afford to throw one away.

'But why would you do that? I mean jail's not that bad. Not even jail, more one of those juvenile correction thingies. I had a cousin in one. They're not as terrible as you think.'

She pulls the dress off the ironing board and gives it the critical eye. It passes the test, is put on a hanger and then back onto the rack next to her.

I take out a yellow patterned dress. Someone could have thrown up on it.

'Try it on,' Donna says. 'Nice detailing around the collar.'

She comes round and takes it from me. 'I'll hang it in the cubicle. You keep on looking.' She walks across the room and goes behind a curtain, talking the whole time.

I pretend to be enthralled in the next row, green dresses hanging like limp seaweed. I find one that is the least objectionable.

'How about this one?' I ask, heading towards the change room. I should have acted like I didn't know Julie.

The first cubicle has the dress Donna chose, so I go into the second one and pull the curtain shut.

'I'll just get the curtain right for you,' Donna says. 'Got to be careful, or you can be standing there in the altogether and half the shop can see you.' She twitches the material, first one way and then the other. 'Do you know why she shot him?'

I wonder how Tracey's mother would describe what happened. Would she say that her daughter killed someone in cold blood as the prosecution said? An 'unprovoked attack' was the phrase used over and over again.

I know that's not right.

'You're not to tell anyone,' she said. 'Promise. Not a word. I don't want anyone knowing what he did to me.'

She turned and faced me, the gun pointing in my direction and for a moment I was worried she might shoot it again. I could barely see her face in the dark but felt her eyes watching.

'Promise?'

'OK,' I said. My voice was shaky and weak. I thought I might throw up. 'I promise.'

Tracey stood over the body. I could hear the radio crackling from inside the car, static voices talking half sentences. I focused on that, which was why I didn't hear Tracey kicking him at first. She was kicking and swearing, crying too. I ran around the car and pulled her off but it didn't really matter. He was already dead.

We walked home on dirt tracks, avoiding the roads, two ghosts in the moonlight, falling into bushes if we saw any headlights coming near. Down the back of The Hill with the smell of gum leaves and the howling of a dog in the distance, Tracey clutching the now unloaded gun in her hand, we made our way back to my house. My bedroom window was still open, the television still on. Mum had fallen asleep in front of it again. Later, she'd tell the police that we'd never left that night, that she was home the whole time with us, but no one believed her. If she'd been a different sort of mum they might have.

Balancing on top of the outside tap, which squeaked in protest, Tracey leant her arm through the window and flung the gun onto my bed. Then she heaved herself up to the sill. As I stepped on the tap, she turned and grabbed my hand tight in hers, digging her nails between my bones.

'It was my fault what happened. I won't forget what you did tonight. I'm going to take care of everything.'

I nodded my head and then she helped me to scramble inside.

'How ya going for sizes?' Donna sticks her head in, saying the words in a way that makes me think she is repeating herself and I haven't been listening. Up close I can see hard speckles of hairspray and the freckles under her make-up.

'Doesn't suit me.'

'Try this one then.' Donna has the pink dress. I bow to the inevitable. At least I can tell Bob that I put on everything Ros suggested. I get out of the dress and leave it on the floor.

'Must be nice catching up with old friends since you've been back.' She passes the pink one to me.

'Been pretty busy,' I say, trying to be vague about how many old friends I have. I feel exposed standing here in my non-matching bra and knickers. 'I ran into Kim Stephens.'

'I know Kim. Always down the pub. Did you hear she's pregnant?' asks Donna. 'Only found out last week. Was seeing the guy casual. She says it was an accident, but I reckon she might have done it on purpose. He'd spun her a line about building this massive house on a property out of town and she's desperate to get out of her mum's. Turns out it wasn't even his property, just his mate's.'

'What about Lee?'

'He knows nothing about it. Kim's decided better the devil you know and wants to work things out with him cause he's moving back here in the summer. Got a job at the butcher's. She'll get rid of it.'

I nod and she gets out of my cubicle after grabbing the green dress. I take the pink one off the hanger. It looks worse close up. Stepping one leg into it and then the other, I pull. It's tight on the hips and I have to wiggle it higher. As I struggle to get my arms in, I look at myself in the mirror and shake my head. Not even Ros would make me buy this dress.

'Show us when you've got it on,' Donna calls out.

'Doesn't fit,' I yell back.

'Bugger, only one left.'

I thank my lucky stars as I peel it off, careful not to rip it and have Ros try and charge me. Then I remember what Jan said about seeing Kim at the pub with Terry.

I peek out of the curtain. Donna is at the counter untangling the bead necklaces.

'Who was the guy with Kim?'

'Dunno his name. Tall, tanned. Kim says he's skinny cause he doesn't eat meat. Bit of a joke really, seeing Lee works in an abattoir.' She starts walking back over to me, holding a dress and a pair of shoes. 'Course this new bloke doesn't want anything to do with her now. She's told him that he needs to pay for the abortion and he said he'd only pay half, the cheapskate.' She shakes her head. 'Now, what about this one? Still a dress but it comes with a jacket. A suit really. Need to try it with heels. Not too business?' She is holding up a slate-grey outfit that will make me look like a professional ball breaker.

'No,' I say, smiling, 'that's just perfect.'

At the cash register, grey suit neatly wrapped in tissue paper in a bright pink bag, I sign the receipt for Ros's records, having managed to avoid Donna's attempts at accessorising with cheap gold necklaces and big colourful scarves.

'Thanks for all your help,' I say to her, grateful to have finished this before Ros got back.

'You won't tell anyone what I said about Kim? Probably shouldn't have said anything. Supposed to be secret and that.'

'Don't worry,' I say. 'No one will hear it first from me.'

Terry is sitting on the couch alone in my living room when I walk in. His head jerks up when the door opens, a six-pack of beer at his feet, an empty rolling on the floor.

'Thought it was your mother,' he said. 'Getting takeaway for dinner.' He grunts and turns back to the idiot box which he has stopped pretending he never watches. A game show host, slicked hair and a plastered-on smile, is telling an anecdote about greyhound racing to his bored blonde sidekick.

Normally, I would head straight to my room and lock the door. I haven't been alone with Terry since the day he was laying traps. It's my turn today.

There's a coffee table between me and him. I should have just enough time to get to my room if this turns ugly. Under my mattress is a kitchen knife. There is another in my backpack. It's attached to its own sharpener, so that it wouldn't make a hole in the side. Only for emergencies.

I put the bags carefully down on the floor at my feet, another obstacle he'd have to get over. My backpack's zip is not fully closed.

His eyes flick towards me when the show breaks for a commercial. He scratches his balls and smiles. 'You playing nice today. I can be friendly too.' He grabs his crotch with his hand, waiting for my reaction. I look at him and he shrugs, picks up another beer and frowns at the bag with the suit in it.

'You been shopping? Thought you were broke.'

'About as broke as you are,' I say.

He shifts in his seat as if he gets the scent of a fight.

'Your lawyer money turn up then? You can stop freeloading now.'

'So there's more for you?'

He grunts in denial. 'I'm going to be doing some building here. Soon as Shirl gets some cash together.'

'What do you need to buy?'

'This and that.'

'Like Kim Stephens's abortion.'

Immediately, he's on the alert. 'What did you say?'

'You heard me.'

If he makes the slightest twitch in my direction, I'm grabbing my bag and running down the hall. I'll finish this when Mum gets home.

Instead, he puts his beer down, his eyes expressionless. 'That Kim's a stupid slut. Could be anyone's.'

'Not what she's saying. People have seen you at the pub with her. Leaving together.'

He rubs a finger along the side of his nose as he thinks through his response.

'So?'

'Mum's not going to like that. Getting someone her daughter's age pregnant. Then I'll tell her about finding you in my bedroom, going through my undies, pushing me onto the bed. How I didn't want to tell her but then I heard about Kim. Might even cry about it.'

A muscle pulses in his jaw. His fist clenches around his beer. He's weighing up his options. Hurting me is definitely one of them. I lay out my terms.

'I'll give you twenty-four hours to tell Mum you're leaving. Give her some excuse. Fruit picking up north, your grandma died, whatever, I don't care. But before you leave town, if I was you, I'd pay Kim the money. The full amount.'

'You're gonna make me?' He laughs like I have made a tactical mistake, overreached myself.

'That's up to you. I just thought what with Lee coming back ...'

'Lee?'

'Kim's boyfriend. Father of her two kids. Works up at the abattoir. Don't want him filleting you once he hears what you've been up to with his childhood sweetheart.'

'She said they'd broken up.' A plaintive note creeps into his voice. Not as confident now.

'You can be the one to tell Lee then, because I'm not sure Kim's bothered.'

He stares at me and licks his lower lip, but not in a sexual way this time. He's nervous, trying to assess the damage. 'That's her problem.'

Music bursts from the television and the game show is back on. Terry leans back in the chair, puts his feet up on the coffee table, and pretends he isn't worried. I pick up my bags and leave the room, but I keep watching him from the corner of my eye as though I'm walking past a savage dog.

Chapter 21

The Admissions Building was a single-storey brick, the colour of cardboard. I had lined up there in my first week to get the photo taken for my student card. As I stood in front of a white screen, my rigor mortis smile drooped just as the light bulb flashed. The girl smirked as she handed me the card, still warm from the laminator. It looked like a miniature wanted poster. Perhaps appropriate, seeing the police had now taken over the place.

I tried to convince myself that the detectives would know nothing about my past. I was a juvenile at the time, the court records were sealed and it was a different jurisdiction. All valid and all unconvincing. It only took a chance encounter from someone in my town, a transferred police officer or one phone call to my local station, and everything would be known.

As I opened the fly-screen door, my sweaty hand slipped on the handle. Walking inside, I was surprised to see Nico. He wasn't wearing his full suit, only his white jacket, over a t-shirt and jeans. Leaning across the counter, his hands were grasping on to Constable Morriset.

'I need to talk to Durham now . . .' He was so strung out I thought he might hit her. Constable Morriset's face looked worried about that as well. 'Now, now, NOW.'

She took hold of his wrists, trying to pull them off. 'Let go and take a seat. Then I'll see if he is available . . .'

'Fucking can't wait. I said NOW.' His voice was rising as was hers.

'Sir, you must take a seat.' She wrenched herself away from him, her blue shirt crumpled and untucked. I took her advice and sat down on the seat furthest away from Nico.

Nico started scrabbling through his trouser pockets. He pulled out several pieces of paper with blue scrawls over all of them. 'Here . . . see . . . here . . . I've written everything down.' He flapped the pieces in her face. Constable Morriset took a step back. Nico stank.

'Please take a . . .' but before she could finish, he had lunged forward and started smacking his head against the counter.

'Listen to me,' he began screaming.

Sergeant Durham rushed out of an office door and grabbed him, tackling him to the floor. 'Calm down, Nico, calm down. You don't need any more trouble.' Nico tried kicking out with his legs, but Sergeant Durham had him pinned.

'OK, mate. Nice and easy, I'm going to let you up.'

Nico turned his head to one side and I could see the deterioration in his face. His eyes were a crusty red, eczema stretched down from his neck to the collar of his grubby t-shirt and probably beyond. His ribs stuck out under the material. Eventually, Durham got off him and Nico pulled himself to all fours and then slowly stood up. His hands shook as he took out a cigarette.

'No smoking in here,' said Durham.

Nico acted as if he hadn't heard. He put the cigarette in his mouth but made no attempt to light it. There was dried blood on his knuckles and his head was cut from where he hit the counter.

'Think we need to clean you up, mate,' said Durham.

'I'm OK,' mumbled Nico. 'Just need a smoke.'

'Let's take you outside.' Durham opened the screen door.

'But then you'll listen, right?' Nico started to get a wild look again. 'I'll do a deal. Give you information about the bar ... how they're killing people ... and you'll drop my charges. I've got it all written down.'

'Sure, sure,' said Durham, and Nico walked out the door. A smell of sweat and urine lingered.

Durham looked over to Constable Morriset. 'You OK, Sam?'

Her face was strained but she nodded. Durham gave her a wink and picked the pieces of paper up off the floor. 'Christ, the smell.' He flapped his hands in front of his nose. 'Make a cup of tea for yourself,' he said. 'I'll deal with him.' As Constable Morriset moved up the corridor, Durham hopped behind the counter and I heard the sound of a drawer opening and shutting. Then he came back, kicked open the door and walked outside.

I waited until Constable Morriset returned before I went up to the counter. Her shirt was now tucked in but a lock of hair had escaped from her slicked-back bun.

'Can I help you?' she said in a clipped tone that made me think she was embarrassed by what had happened.

'I've got an appointment,' I said. 'Pen Sheppard.'

'I know who you are,' she said, sharply. 'Take a seat.'

'Do you know how long . . .?' I began to ask.

'No.' She turned away and walked to the back of the counter and out of sight.

I was going to have to wait, something I had hoped to avoid. Waiting is when the lies start to sound weak and the truth sits in your throat waiting to tumble out. You sit there telling yourself not to look guilty, which only makes you seem more so. Cops always make you wait.

There was a window next to where I sat down, a grimy

grey that almost matched the wall colour. The glass rippled so you had to put your face right up to it to see through. It overlooked a small concrete alcove outside that was sheltered from the elements, a smokers' corner currently occupied by Nico and Sergeant Durham.

His cigarette now lit, Nico looked almost sane and Sergeant Durham had his back to me. Twisting, I angled my head to the window. Sergeant Durham was listening, occasionally nodding as Nico talked and talked. Durham had rolled the pieces of paper he had picked up from the floor and held them loosely in his hand.

As Nico threw his cigarette butt down, Sergeant Durham quickly moved forward, blocking my view. It wasn't until Nico stumbled backwards that I could see him again. He was holding something in his hand. I couldn't see what it was but Nico clutched it tightly. The surprise on his face turned into another emotion I couldn't read. Anger. Fear. Greed. He moved too quickly to tell. And then, without warning, Nico ran away.

Durham stood still, watching him go. Then he turned and I could see him in profile, smiling to himself. The glass distorted it into something cruel. I had seen looks like that before, from the police in my town, and suddenly, I felt as if I had been spying through a keyhole. I shrank back from the window and quickly changed seats. Mouth dry, I picked up a university pamphlet lying in a pile next to me and started reading, waiting for Durham to walk through the door, but he didn't.

As I pretended to read the list of the university's achievements I watched the clock turn slowly. A quarter of an hour passed and then half an hour, before Sergeant Durham came back in. At the sound of the door, Constable Morriset popped up as well. She must have been sitting close by but out of my sight. I wondered if she had noticed me at the window.

'How did you go, Sarge?'

'Another day, another junkie scared about their day in court,' he said. 'Told him to head off home and come back when he's making sense.'

'Took a while.'

'All part of the service, Sam. Important to go that extra mile.'

As he turned to walk past, he stopped and looked at me. 'You're that girl from Scullin, aren't you?' He was back to being amiable.

I nodded.

'You still waiting for your interview? Sam,' he called over his shoulder, 'they finished up the last one yet?'

'No, Sarge. Haven't come out.'

'Taking their time.' Durham smiled over at me. 'Must have a lot to chat about. Wait a sec, this could be them now.'

A door scraped open and I could hear voices coming towards me.

'Listen, my client wishes to be as cooperative as possible, but I think we need to take a break.'

'Tell him to start cooperating or he'll be arrested.'

Two tall men appeared. The only difference between them was the price of the suits.

The one in the expensive suit pursed his lips and looked at his watch. 'Let me take him outside for a smoke.'

The other, a tired man with almost no hair, frowned, and then said, 'All right. I'll give you ten minutes. If you want a coffee, tell the constable here and she'll get it for you.'

Morriset's mouth twisted at this. Expensive suit went back up the corridor.

'Finally getting somewhere,' Baldy said to Durham. Durham nodded in my direction, and Baldy quickly shut up. He then turned his attention to Constable Morriset.

'Hear you had an admirer, Sam. Couldn't keep his hands off you.'

Constable Morriset shot a dirty look at Durham and muttered something under her breath that I didn't hear but he did.

'Now, Constable, is that any way to talk to a senior officer?'

She opened her mouth but the lawyer in the expensive suit was back and this time his client was with him. It was Joad. He flicked his eyes in my direction, and immediately looked away, two triangles of red burning on his cheeks.

His lawyer directed him through the door, calling out, 'Two white coffees. No sugar.'

Baldy snorted at this. 'While you're up, Sam, I'll have one, perhaps with a doughnut on the side as well. Chocolate icing and those nice sprinkles.' Constable Morriset stuck up her middle finger as she walked away.

I should have guessed Joad would be suspect number one. I tried to think what they would be questioning him about. The detective had spoken about threats being made and that he might be arrested. The confrontation before the march, I guessed. Joad's words were coming back to haunt him. Even the comment made at breakfast so long ago about the Murder Game, when Joad had joked about being the Screwdriver Man, was now plastered around university.

I watched him slouch past, his face pinched and scared. Joad hated Leiza and I wondered if his comments about slicing off body parts could be more than just talk. But it was Rachel he had talked about killing and I knew her death had nothing to do with him. Had someone else heard it and murdered Leiza that way to put the blame on him? The same person who knew about my Rohypnol? I tried picturing who had been sitting round that table the morning he said it. But all their faces blended into one. Rogan. Had I badly underestimated him? The thought made me dizzy and I closed my eyes. When I opened them again, Sergeant Durham was standing over me.

'Penny,' he said, and I almost jumped. 'We'll have to postpone your interview for today.'

A moment of non-comprehension and then, 'Do I have to come back tomorrow?'

'We'll let you know.'

I got up, trying to look the right level of grateful. 'Thanks, Sergeant Durham.'

'You head off now,' he said. 'Want to get home before dark.'

On the far corner of campus, hemmed in by trees on one side and the highway on the other, was the Gulag. Its real name, borrowed from another dead prime minister, was never used. Burning in summer, freezing in winter, full of asbestos, it was the cheapest accommodation at university. Sergeant Durham said that Nico was heading home, so that was where I was going to look for the only person who seemed to know what was happening at the bar and who had realised Leiza was in danger. I just hoped that he was sane enough to tell me what was going on.

Shadows were beginning to lengthen into night as I walked up to the three long corrugated-iron huts making up the Gulag. A couple of t-shirts were blowing in the breeze on a temporary washing line, hooked up between the last hut and the only nearby street light. I had never been inside and the buildings looked even more derelict than I had remembered, with broken windows and splattered paint. I headed to the only part that had a light on.

It must have once been the kitchen. A single bare light bulb illuminated the shell of cupboards and benches. A boy had his back to me and was chopping onions on a cracked and peeling counter. Dirty dishes piled up in the sink next to him, a camping stove on the other side. A small padlocked bar fridge hummed.

My feet squeaked on the lino and he turned towards me, a large knife in his hand. I put my hands up in the universal I-come-in-peace gesture, keeping eye contact with his face instead of what he was holding. It was Nico's mate from the rally, the owner of the Che Guevara t-shirt. Today he was wearing a t-shirt with a large pot leaf on it.

'Oh, hi . . .' I began.

'I know you,' he said. 'I saw you at the bar the other night, sitting with Toby.' His acne made a beard-shaped rash across the bottom half of his face. He didn't lower his hand.

I tried to smile, the skin around my mouth feeling brittle. 'That's right.'

'You left as the police raided,' he said. His voice wasn't accusing but the knife gave the comment some edge. 'That wasn't very helpful.' He dropped the knife into the grey scummy water with a clatter.

'How long did you stay?'

''Til they dragged us out and charged us.'

'And how did that help anyone?'

He gave a grin. 'The Marchmains went down fighting. That night could have become university legend but it's hard to compete with a homicidal murderer.' He turned away from me and bent down next to a low cupboard. It was missing a door. He grabbed a saucepan and straightened up.

'Actually, I'm looking for Nico.'

'Nico?' He gave me a cool look. 'He doesn't get so many visitors these days. Used to get lots, rich college kids especially. What do you want? Something to get through your exams?'

'I'm not looking to score,' I said.

'Lucky. He's been a bit temperamental since Alice left. Did that this morning.' He pointed to a large dent in a wall behind him.

I studied it carefully, wondering if he was making it up to frighten me and then remembered the marks on Nico's knuckles.

'Saw him round not so long ago. Try the next building.' He pointed to his right. 'There's a sign on his door but he's pretty much got it to himself anyway.'

'Thanks.'

'Got a torch?'

I shook my head.

'Better borrow mine then. Some idiot fucked the fuse up again this afternoon. I'll try and fix it after I've had my dinner.'

He passed over one of those heavy black security ones that double as a truncheon. My hand dropped with the weight of it.

'Thanks,' I said. 'I'll bring it straight back.'

Outside was dusk and beginning to get cold. When I opened the door to the next hut, I automatically scrabbled for the light switch. My hand found three and I clicked them down. Nothing happened. The boy hadn't been joking. I stood there at the door, listening. All the sounds seemed to come from outside, the hum of traffic, the occasional voice in the distance, some bird calls. I tried to adjust my eyes, as waving a torch around where people lived felt a bit rude, something a rich college kid would do. My courage disappeared as I stared hard into the dark, black turning grey, shapes slowly coming into focus, a cavern becoming a room. I moved forward, hesitating.

'Hello,' I said to a couple of empty chairs, who ignored me.

A few more steps.

There was something mournful about being in a place that would have been busy and noisy all its life. Before it was a home for students it had been workers' quarters, on site at some big infrastructure project, a dam or a mine or something. But now that was all finished. It would be flattened and some new architectural monstrosity for educational purposes would turn up and people would forget it had ever been there at all.

'Nico,' I said. I thought I heard something and took another step. A sudden bang above my head, a scream from me, and then an old-man cough and the sound of something scuttling away.

A possum on the roof.

I almost laughed with relief as memories of summer nights with Tracey, lying in our beds listening to possums tap-dance across the tin flashed through my head. I felt braver.

I walked along the corridor, the space only wide enough for one. The floor sagged underneath my weight. Bedrooms ran along the right-hand side. All empty now, I was sure of it. Halfway down the corridor, there was the outline of a piece of paper stuck to a door. I could see it had been ripped out of a notebook, one edge ragged with perforation. The words 'Nico – Keep Out' were just legible in the gloom. It reminded me of the notes he had been carrying, two or three sheets with lots of words scrawled on them. Sergeant Durham didn't have them when he came back inside. Maybe Nico had taken them back? Maybe Nico had left them in his room? Maybe I could read them and see if Nico really knew anything about what was going on.

I tapped lightly on the door. It swung open. The room was twilight in comparison to the darkness of the corridor. Light and an icy breeze came from outside through a cracked window.

'Hello,' I said again.

Still no reply.

Perhaps Nico had never come back this afternoon and his Marchmain friend had lied to a girl he thought was a rich college kid. He was probably laughing into his dinner right now, or perhaps, he was going to creep up in the darkness and jump out at me. The thought of that made my skin prickle and I switched on the torch as I peered behind me. But he was back in the kitchen, burning his onions. I was alone.

I turned back to the room. Something white was crumpled on the floor. It was Nico's jacket. He must have come home after talking to the police. I couldn't see any pieces of paper lying around but I wanted to be sure. Swallowing, I stepped into the room.

My torch caught a photograph stuck to the opposite wall. I stumbled forward to get closer. It was of Nico with his arms around Alice, how they were before the attack. Alice was looking directly towards me, laughing, beautiful, her eyes narrowed in good humour. Nico was looking at her. Wearing his stupid white suit, his blonde hair curled around his head. He was almost unrecognisable.

317

I was too focused on the picture to realise he was there behind me. It was the smell I noticed. Behind the door, caught in the shadows, he was lying on a filthy blanket. A small plastic bag and needle were beside him, a spoon and lighter discarded next to the mattress.

I knelt down next to him. A trickle of brown trailed from his mouth. I didn't want to touch him so I put my hand just under his nose, hoping for the slightest movement of warm air on my fingers as I watched his chest. Nothing. My hand began to shake and I accidentally touched his lips. A kiss from a corpse. It felt like a stain on my skin.

Chapter 22

It's been raining for three days, ever since Terry left. Gentle drops from grey skies giving way to biblical amounts of water gushing down. It is still falling this morning.

Mum is in her dressing gown, listening to the radio in the kitchen. She's on day shift this week so she should have already left for work, but she's banking on the road to the Cannery getting washed out.

'Last time the road was cut off for two days,' she tells me. 'Imagine getting stuck out there.'

'Pack an emergency can opener and you wouldn't starve,' I say.

'I'd get pretty sick of tinned asparagus,' she snorts.

She has taken the Terry break-up better than I expected.

Michelle from work is already trying to set her up with someone.

The radio announcer comes on with the list of today's cancellations and closures. He can't decide if this should be in his usual cheesy manner or something more serious. In the end he goes for the latter and reads it out as if he is compering a funeral. The road to the Cannery has been shut since daybreak. Mum looks relieved.

'Lucky, they don't run a nightshift until corn starts,' she says. Then on reflection, 'But think of the overtime,' and, 'I should see if they'll let you work during the corn season. Casual on nightshift, that's good money. Could save up and the two of us go away on a cruise or something. Wouldn't that be nice, a mother-daughter holiday?'

I ignore her because that would be my worst nightmare and I won't be here anyway.

All roads out of here have been cut off.

We are an island.

Mum keeps smiling until she remembers that the nursing home is across from the school and nearer the river.

'They won't evacuate it, will they?' she asks me. 'Make us take Dad back for a bit?' She is debating whether to phone them or not but just decides that no news is good news when the phone rings.

'You answer it,' she says. 'If it's the home, tell them I'm stuck at the factory. They'd never make you come and pick

320

up your grandfather even if the water was up to their necks.'

Tracey's cousin runs the nursing home. I am banned from entering.

Walking to the phone, I pull a face, which Mum misses because she is heaping sugar into her cup of tea.

She yells from the kitchen, 'If it's someone called Kevin, you're my younger sister.'

But it's not Michelle's cousin's best friend who's getting divorced but has a great sense of humour. It's Ivy. Frank wants to see me.

'Frank has availability tomorrow,' she says.

I wonder why. Ivy always claims that Frank is booked out months in advance.

'If it's so urgent I can do today,' I say, curiously.

'He's assisting with the relief effort today,' says Ivy, in a voice that implies I should know that already.

I wonder what assistance Frank is giving. Perhaps counselling all the idiots who forgot they bought a house on a plain that floods every couple of years, but will remember the story of two girls killing a policeman and how one of them got away with it, for the rest of their lives.

'Tomorrow, eleven a.m.'

'All right.'

I'm curious, but I would sooner rip out my tongue than ask her why. Anyway, that works for me. I've decided I should at least say goodbye to Frank, I owe him that much.

As soon as the highway reopens, I'm leaving. The university made an offer the day after I bought my suit.

I walk back into the kitchen and tell Mum it was only Ivy, but she shushes me so she can keep listening to the radio. Sipping her tea, she is packing bits and pieces into a cardboard box. The remnants of Terry.

'Another festival ruined. Won't be a single blossom left in the district after this rain,' she says, when the next song is played. 'Races cancelled and the peak hasn't come yet. Those poor buggers on Pye Street already have it lapping over their doormats.'

She tries to look sympathetic but we both know she is enjoying it. Usually disasters involve us. This time we are high and dry.

'Already gone over the last one. If the rain stays this heavy overnight, might get as high as 1923 and then the levees will be breached and all bets will be off. Your grandfather knew what he was doing when he bought on a hill. Crafty old bugger.'

She walks out of the kitchen, my slippers on her shuffling feet. I peek inside the box to see if there is anything worth pinching: a Grateful Dead cassette, a pair of grubby thongs and a well-thumbed paperback of *The Kama Sutra*, which makes me feel ill. Mum is back before I can go through it all properly. She's holding some LPs, a couple of t-shirts and a toothbrush.

'Might want to make yourself scarce this morning,' she says.

I look out the window at the pelting rain and ask why. I had planned to spend the day in bed.

'Terry is coming over to pick up the last of his stuff.'

'Is he still here?'

'Staying out at Mick's,' she says with a shrug, like what does she care, but she immediately goes to her handbag, searching for her nicotine gum. 'He'll head off when the road reopens, I guess, to whatever is so important up north.' Bitterness flavours her voice.

'How's he getting in to town?'

'Lyall Bridge hasn't closed yet. I told him that if he doesn't pick up his crap this morning, it will be on the front lawn by midday, rain or no rain.'

Terry's going has been easier than I thought but still I don't want to push my luck. I leave Mum flinging a bunch of his clothes out of her wardrobe onto an untidy heap on the floor.

Outside, the world is blurred and softened except for the rain, which is needle-sharp. At the end of our street you can follow the road all the way down to the river. There is a thin glaze of water over the black tar. But I want to go higher, to take one last look at the town. It's been on my mind since Frank mentioned it, so I decide to go up The Hill.

I haven't been to the top of The Hill since that night.

There's a road that leads straight up to it, but I don't want to go that way. Too close to the cemetery. Instead, I go around the golf course, past the last lot of houses on the edge of town and then up the dirt track that cuts The Hill straight up the middle, like a centre part. The cutting is supposed to be used only during bush-fire season, but I jump the locked gate.

Climbing is hard work. I'm wearing Mum's gumboots which barely have any tread. The track is slick with mud, and I have to stop several times, just to breathe and question my sanity.

On a clear day, you can see the entire town sprawling through the valley, from the saleyards in the south to the fibro government housing in the north, and then the open plains stretching up to the mountains on the horizon.

When I get to the top, half-drowned, legs heavy, I sit down on a bench and see the damage. No mountains today, the clouds hang too low, but the rain is easing and I can still see the town. The river surges so fast that there are patches of white foam on top of it like the sea. The brown water has burst its banks in places and leaked across the fields below me. Trees have fallen and the town is cut in two. I wonder if Terry has made it across.

I can just make out the activity around the edge of town. The school hall has been opened as a relief centre. It was supposed to be the Welcome Parade today with bunches of kids dressed in crepe paper over their t-shirts and shorts to represent blossom season, the high school brass band playing out of tune and the local dance academy putting on the entertainment. Instead, everyone is wet and making sandbags or cups of tea.

Rain begins to pelt down again as I cross the road to the car park and the reserve up the top. The ground is swollen with water. It seeps out with every step. I want to find the place where Tracey lit the fire that night. She made me pick up twigs in the dark while she got it started with a pile of dried grass and paper. The fire was how he found us. There was always a police car at the bottom of The Hill to catch the joy-riders and drunks, to issue speeding tickets or to offer rides to underage girls.

'We've got to head back,' I said. 'Mum's expecting us.' A lie because Mum was watching TV, thinking we were tucked up in our beds.

'C'mon, I won't be long. You keep the fire going.' She got into his car, the red and blue twinkling above the dash like lights on a Christmas tree, the only unmarked police car in town. Tracey's face was visible through the window. A wave goodbye. The wheels spun on dirt which flew up and stung my face. At the crest of The Hill, I watched the backlights drop down through the sharp turns and then disappear behind the trees. I heard the sound of braking and I waited, looking for where the road turned again to see the car tracing the curve, taking her for a ride around The Hill's circuit just for

fun, but the car never reappeared. Accidents were notorious on that stretch. Usually tourists who didn't pay attention to the tight corners, but anyone can hit a tree, especially at night. I stood there, waiting. Silence. Maybe I had missed them. But still no lights.

I waited for what seemed ages but I kept telling myself that time plays tricks in the dark. Coming up here had been Tracey's idea and now she'd got a better offer and probably wasn't coming back. I had to get home by myself. I put out the fire that Tracey had made. That would show her. Puffs of ash rose as the embers gave a dying gasp. I stamped down hard, suffocating it of air. The cutting was too dark to walk alone, so I decided to follow the road.

The car had pulled into an old track, still high up on The Hill, before houses got too close. An isolated spot. You couldn't see it from the road because he had turned off all his lights. It was the crackle of the police radio I heard. He was supposed to be on duty.

I didn't understand why it was there. They were only supposed to have gone for a quick spin. He was going to let Tracey drive for a bit. I thought I should check to make sure they were all right and then yell at Tracey for leaving me. The car had both right doors open, and I could see some movement. He was speaking as well, but I couldn't make out the words over the radio.

I walked towards the car, uncertain.

Tracey's arms were caught above her head and handcuffed to the door handle. He was lying on top of her, squashing her. She lay there naked, a broken doll, with his large hairy hand pressing her neck, a blank look on her face.

As I stood there, she looked at me. I found a rock at my feet and held it up in my hand. She shook her head with the barest movement and then moved it to the right, turned back, looked at me and repeated the motion. On the front seat of the car was his gun and holster. As I crept towards it, he was already turning, sensing my presence. In his haste he smacked his head into the roof and stumbled forward, falling out of the car. Standing there, pulling his trousers back on, he looked at the gun in my hand.

'Now, give that to me. You don't want anyone to get hurt.' He was back to being the nice policeman who did the stranger danger talk for primary schools. But I looked at Tracey naked in the car, red blotches across her body where he had been hitting her, and I took a step away from him and held the gun tighter.

He followed my gaze.

'OK, OK, I've got the keys. Only a bit of fun. Tell her, Tracey.'

My mind was speeding up like it was on fast forward. Mum's boyfriend Shane with his guns, Tracey taking me rabbiting. I'd used a shotgun before but this was different. I held the revolver in front of me with one hand and braced my wrist with the other, just like television. A flash of red rage overwhelmed me as I thought of all the dickheads my mother had brought home. Dickheads like him.

He reached into his trouser pocket, held the keys in his hand, dangling them so I could see. With a sudden movement, he threw them past me and moved forward. Panicked, I squeezed the trigger hard. A crack, and he was on the ground, clutching his chest.

He looked up at me. 'Stupid bitch,' he murmured. I could see his shirt beginning to darken.

Scrabbling in the dirt for the keys, I ran around to the other side of the car and unlocked Tracey. She wobbled as she stood. Her voice was hoarse but calm. 'Give me the gun.' I handed it to her without question. I didn't want to touch it any more.

Tracey walked around the car to face him. He was making these soft keening noises of pain. I knew what she meant to do. Put him out of his misery. She raised the gun, holding it steady with two hands. He realised as well and began pleading, his voice wet with blood. I shut my eyes and put my hands over my ears.

I sit there until I cramp, my body heavy with the memories. It takes a long time to trudge back.

At home, I pull off the gumboots and leave them outside on the verandah that will never be a sunroom. The rain can wash the mud off them. I hang up my coat in the bathroom but I am wet through so I walk down the hall into my room to get changed. The house is quiet and I wonder if Mum has gone back to bed.

I open the door to my room and see clothes all over the floor. Every drawer has been emptied. My university books have been pulled out of the bookcase. Some of their covers have been ripped off. Scraps of grey are everywhere. I pick one up. My new suit shredded. So is the pink bag it came in and the receipt for good measure. Immediately, I run to the cupboard, empty of clothes and shoes. Boxes have been shifted but my hiding place has not been noticed. The plank is undisturbed and my book is safe.

Sitting on my bed, I clutch a piece of the suit in my hands. Running a finger along its edge, I pull at it and see how it frays. Nothing is ever a clean break. Everything has threads, even if you cannot see them.

I take a long time getting dressed before I go find Mum. She is sitting on the couch in the living room, waiting for me. On the coffee table in front of her, next to the ashtray half full with fresh cigarette butts, is a piece of paper, the letter that I had placed in the bottom drawer on top of my suit.

'Smoking again?' I say.

'Can you blame me?' She picks up the letter and waves it like a starter's flag.

'Had to hear it from Terry,' she says. 'My own daughter wins a settlement and I'm the last one to know.'

I should have known she would find out somehow. This is a town that spends its life peering out from behind the curtains at other people's business.

There is a silence that threatens to grow and fill the room. I am waiting to see what she will say but she just keeps staring at me.

'What was he doing in my room?'

A flicker of uncertainty from her.

'Ran up to the shops to buy some cigarettes. Thought I'd give him time to grab his stuff. When I got back he showed me this.'

I stop myself from screaming at her. Terry must have been in there for ages. I try to work out what he was doing in my bedroom again. If trashing my stuff and destroying my suit is his version of a goodbye kiss then I'll live with that. With the amount Bob got, I could buy countless suits. I'm glad Terry knows how much money I'm getting and how he'll never see a cent of it.

'Well,' she says, waiting for an answer from me. 'More than I've ever had in my life and all of it yours.'

'I only found out a couple of days ago.' This sounds weak, even to me.

She flaps the letter again. There are two separate pages. One is the settlement offer on Bob's letterhead. The other has the Southern Cross around an open book at the top of it. The emblem from Marcus's office. I have been accepted into the fancy sandstone university he had worked at before coming to Scullin. Bob sent them letters threatening to publicise the fact that they hadn't investigated Marcus's drug activities but instead let him resign and then arrive at Scullin with an unblemished record. Still, their offer didn't go so far as to include free accommodation or a scholarship. All my settlement money will have to pay for it.

Seeing it in her hand makes me wonder about Marcus.

His court case isn't going to be heard for another year. I have made it through unscathed, and he is the only one being held to account and will probably end up in jail. Despite everything, I almost feel sorry for him.

'Were you going to tell me before or after you left town?' Mum asks. 'I expect you'll be running away the moment you can.'

She flings down the pages on to the table in a dramatic gesture, but paper like that only flutters. They separate and zigzag gently through the air, miss the table and end up on the floor.

'You can't expect me to stay here,' I say, reaching down to pick them up, tucking them safely into my back pocket. 'A place where half the people hate me.'

'They hate me too. Had plenty to say to me over the years. That you were raised all wrong by a stupid slut. Think I don't hear that?'

'You could leave,' I say.

'With what? All my savings went on paying Bob Cochrane to keep you out of jail.'

I have no answer to that, because it's true. I can't even bring up the suit now, because she's got me. Checkmate.

'You know, the day I found out I was pregnant with you, I was actually excited. I mean, I knew that there would be a fuss, but I didn't care. Thought we could be our own little family. And then your dad's parents arrived in their shiny car, taking charge. Money to shut me up and your dad transferred to another boarding school in a different town and none of this ever to be mentioned again. That's when I thought about running away. I was dumb enough to think he'd want to go too. But he was on their side. Said he'd pay to get rid of you. I told him I was having the baby and didn't need his money.'

My father was more generous than Terry, I think. Not the highest standard.

Mum isn't going in for the kill. In fact, she's looking pretty defeated. The fight has gone out of her and she sits back on the couch, grey-skinned without her war paint. I've seen her act this way about a boyfriend, but never over me. Normally, it's all slamming doors and shouted exchanges. I stare at the mantelpiece because I don't want to see her like this. I concentrate on the tarnished silver photographs: my grandparents' wedding photo, the picture of Mum as a debutante. She looks peaky, morning sickness, and then next to it is a photo of a pigtailed preschooler hugging her and she is laughing at the camera.

Once we were happy, just the two of us.

'But I decided the only place to bring you up was here, a proper home to live in, with your grandparents. Had to grow up and make the best of it. That's why I stayed. Everything has consequences. If you don't deal with them, others will have to.'

Her words sting.

'I've dealt with what's happened,' I say.

'Really?' she says. 'I've always told them you didn't do it, Pen. That Tracey Cuttmore was the troublemaker. But I don't know. Tracey's not here any more and you still get into trouble.'

'I'm the victim,' I say. 'That's what this settlement means. That I'm the one who got hurt. That it wasn't my fault.'

'Really?' she says. 'Look me straight in my face and tell me you didn't do anything wrong.'

I don't do that because I can't. Instead, I pick up the china shepherd I gave to her that year for Mother's Day.

'You know, I heard you that night, sneaking out. Tap squeaks when you step on it, climbing out the window.' Rubbing the side of her face with her hand, she looks old. The smoker's pucker has reappeared around her mouth. 'I did it heaps when I was at school to see your father. Didn't go to sleep until I knew you were back home. Two of you next morning, all pale and quiet. Telling me Tracey had to go back to the farm early to do homework. Should have known something was wrong but I thought you were hung over. And instead ...' She shrugs her shoulders. 'Maybe they're right. I am a bad mother.'

I didn't know the answer to that. I'd never thought of her as bad or good, more as an obstacle in my way. Something to get around. Perhaps I should say I'm grateful that she didn't disown me like Tracey's father did, that she paid for Bob, but the words disappear before they can reach my mouth. That just isn't who we are.

'Oh well, off you go then. Better start packing. Terry says the north road may be reopened in the morning. The two of you are so alike. Rats deserting a sinking ship.'

Her voice cracks and I wonder if she is going to start crying, but her eyes are dry and somehow that feels worse.

'I've got my appointment with Frank in the morning,' I mumble.

'Does he know you're leaving?'

I shake my head.

'You tell him the truth. Should tell someone.'

She closes her eyes like she is sick of the sight of me. The room is even quieter than before and I realise that the rain has stopped.

Chapter 23

My hand shook so much that the torch's light danced around Nico's room. When I could get my legs to move, I stumbled back along the corridor, ricocheting off walls. Moving through the front room, something snagged my foot and I kicked out in terror at the hand I thought that held it. But it was only one of the chairs, which tipped over and fell as I stumbled towards the door. I stood there bent over, waiting to be sick.

Nico died the day he went to the police. He had talked about people being killed. There had been no sign of a struggle but the room was so bare it was hard to tell. The marks on his arms suggested that shooting up was a common occurrence. But it would be so easy to get rid of an inconvenient junkie. Give them something too pure or something not pure enough and they'll do the job for you. I tried to picture the look on his face the last time I saw him alive, clutching something in his hands, a perfect mixture of greed and fear.

There was no point getting an ambulance and I didn't want to bring myself to the police's attention over another body. Whatever else I did, I had to make sure that when he was found, I would be far away. But first I had to give back the torch.

I had no idea how much time had passed but the boy was still cooking when I entered the room.

'Find him?' he asked, barely glancing in my direction.

'I knocked on his door but no answer.' I sounded choked, but he didn't seem to notice. 'Thanks for the torch.' I laid it down on the bench near him.

'What college are you at?' he said.

A pause. 'Maggies,' I lied. 'Why?'

'You're a law student, aren't you? Might be needing a lawyer pretty soon to help me with these criminal damage charges.'

'OK,' I said. Relief made me sound over-bright, the way Leiza used to talk when she was trying to get you to do something for her. 'I'm only a first-year, though. You might be better off finding someone who has passed Criminal Law. The student law clinic at the Union might be able to help.'

He didn't seem to think that sounded useful.

As I began to walk away, he started humming to himself and then began to sing out loud. He had a good voice and it echoed through the room. The sound was unexpectedly comforting and I stood there in the shadows listening to him, wanting him to keep on singing. It wasn't until well after he stopped that I stepped alone into the dark.

A thick ribbon of bushland ran along the entire back of campus. Parts of it were expected to disappear by the end of the year with rumours of new buildings, but it was still dense enough to walk through unseen at night. I had to put as much distance between myself and Nico's body as possible without being noticed. I could follow it from where I was until I reached Scullin, about a twenty-minute walk. I just needed to get to the trees.

The moon had already been out for most of the day, overshadowed by the sun. Now it lit the sky to a rich dark blue. The trees were a stark black up ahead. I chose the tallest one I could see and started walking. Running might attract a roaming eye. My legs wanted to do neither. I stumbled as the ground became rougher, feeling every stone under my shoes. When I reached my tree, all I wanted to do was sit down and never move again, but I had to keep going.

Heading east, I stayed within the tangled line of trees. I could smell the tang of eucalyptus and the dried leaves under my feet cracked like delicate bones. I concentrated on

337

a tree ahead and then another, but I was starting to shake.

'*You're too soft,*' came Tracey's voice in my ear.

'*Don't spoil the fun,*' she said, as she pulled a silver hipflask out of her pocket.

'*Where'd you get that?*'

'*Was on special. Five-fingered discount.*'

'*You shouldn't have done that. Not after last time.*'

Tracey had been caught the week before with the china shepherdess in her school bag. The owner had called the police but in the end hadn't pressed charges.

'*I've told you already the copper didn't take it seriously. When we got outside he asked me why I had stolen something so ugly and then said I owed him one. He was all right.*'

I said nothing.

Tracey looked stubborn. 'Stop being so paranoid. Didn't say anything about you. We're fine.'

'*Yeah, I guess.*'

I thought about the stories Mum had brought back from work about that policeman. His wife worked with her at the Cannery. 'She wouldn't say boo to a goose,' Mum told me. 'Never comes out to the pub so we gave up asking. And the bruises on her. I saw them all around her neck when she was getting changed. Asked her about it, but she clammed right up.'

I tried telling Tracey but she didn't want to hear. 'He was a good guy.' She went back to making the fire. 'Should have brought marshmallows,' she said, looking at the twigs beginning to catch with flames and the bigger sticks starting to smoulder. 'Could have made a party of it. Proper fire mountain now. This was a great idea.'

Walking deep in the trees, I heard a rustle of leaves. A twig snapped. I listened but could only hear the blood pounding in my ears like the sound of the sea. I walked on three steps but then stopped, and this time I heard a definite patter continue on, an echo of my feet.

'Who's there?' I called.

Everything was still.

The hairs on the back of my neck told me I was being watched. I turned. Took a step forward. Peered. A black shape between the trees.

Two eyes in the darkness.

And I ran, blindly forward, cutting through the trees, getting back to college by the most direct route, forgetting about not needing to be seen. I wanted people around. Someone to stop and say I shouldn't be by myself at night, to insist on walking me home.

The feet were gaining on me, the tread heavier, not bothering to be quiet now. The noise seemed to change direction, not behind me any more but running alongside, between me and the campus. I was being herded deeper into the bush.

339

Twisting around, I could see a figure moving past a tree but the face was covered. I tripped on a tree root and nearly fell. A branch scratched my cheek in an instant splinter of pain that I pushed aside, focusing everything on the way ahead. Lungs bursting, legs screaming, I still kept running. Almost there, I pushed past the last tree out into the open, Scullin directly in front, hundreds of haphazard rectangular room lights like an elaborate dot-to-dot.

Except that it wasn't.

Disoriented, I turned around. Back behind me, over to the left, I could see it. I had been driven away from safety. No more than a five-minute run but too far. Panic flooded through me as I pitched forward onto the ground, spent.

Dragging myself up, I turned around to face him. I didn't know what was going to happen next but I was prepared to kick, claw and scream. My breath laboured in my chest. Adrenalin raced. Swinging my head wildly from side to side, I waited for a figure to burst out of the bush.

No one.

My breath began to slow. It was impossible that I'd lost my tracker. Perhaps the person had run ahead of me, guessing where I was going, unwilling to attack out in the open.

Numb, exhausted, I stumbled the rest of the way home.

Someone was sitting on the steps outside the main entrance. I was noticed moving under the streetlights and the figure jumped up and came towards me.

'How did the interview go?' asked Rogan. 'What did the police ask?'

He was wearing a dark, long-sleeve t-shirt over black jeans, Doc Martens scuffed with grass.

He frowned when I didn't respond. 'How did it go?'

I wondered how long he had been here. He didn't seem out of breath. Any relief I felt at getting back safely curdled.

'What are you doing out here?' I asked.

'Just been waiting for you.' The aw-shucks kind of smile that he put on was supposed to be cute. 'So, what happened?'

'Want to know if I kept lying for you? Guess you'll have to wait and see.' As I moved away, he put his arm out to stop me, gently held me around my middle and pulled me back to where I had been. A practised move, a sexy one, but the result was still that he prevented me from leaving.

'C'mon, no need to be cross. Let's go for a walk and you can tell me.' The lovely smile again. Beautiful lips. A kissable mouth. 'Somewhere we won't be interrupted.'

I smiled up at him and his face relaxed. He thought he was going to get what he wanted, as usual.

'What are you so worried about, Rogan? You didn't kill her, did you?'

I wanted to puncture his cosy world to match the jagged holes in mine. He grabbed me by the shoulders, a violent, quick move. Shook me roughly so that my head jolted back. His face twisted in shock.

'What do you know?' But he was interrupted by a voice coming out of the darkness.

'Let go of her!' It was Michael, running towards us, hair wild, eyes wide. He got between us, two hands shoving Rogan. Stumbling backwards, Rogan stared at both of us, then abruptly turned away and left. We watched him go.

'I saw him from my room. Are you all right?' asked Michael.

I didn't know the answer to that. I didn't know the answer to anything. I wanted to be alone.

'Rogan doesn't care about you, not like I do.'

I ignored him, turned and began trudging back towards college.

A small bundle lay forgotten on the ground next to the stairs near where Rogan had been sitting. A black woollen shape. Dried leaves and twigs caught in the stitches. It felt damp, a warm sort of damp as if it had just been worn. It unrolled in my hand, two eye holes I could stick my fingers through. A balaclava. Revulsion shook me.

Michael put his arm around me. It was clumsy, with none of Rogan's polish. A teenage boy moving in for the first kiss and ending up with a slap.

I said to him the words that had been rattling in my head for Rogan.

'Leave me alone. I hate you.'

Chapter 24

A siren wail woke me. As more sirens joined it, I imagined Nico's body being found and all the fingerprints I had left. A trail of evidence that would link another dead body back to me. I shut my eyes tight and put a pillow over my head, trying to block out the awful things beyond my room. Hours seemed to pass before the noise stopped and I began drifting into an exhausted numbness that was almost sleep until the fire alarm went off.

I got out of bed and stuck my head into the corridor. Kesh was already up and, wearing a yellow plastic Deputy Fire Warden hat, banging business-like on doors. There was a determined grimness to her as she ordered people out of their rooms. I could barely remember the shy girl

Rachel used to torment, who blushed as often as she spoke.

Catching sight of me, she said, 'Head out to the car park and find Toby to get your name ticked off. False alarm, I expect.'

I quickly ducked back into my room and as I grabbed a cardigan to put over my pyjamas, I saw the balaclava lying on my desk where I had left it. It was evidence of something, what I wasn't sure, but it felt important. It wasn't going to go missing like my Rohypnol. I tucked it into the waistband of my pyjamas.

The stairs were full of people in various stages of dress. No one else seemed particularly worried. There had been a spate of false alarms, though never this late before. I caught parts of the conversations around me.

'It will be someone pulling an all-nighter deciding to make toast in their room at two o'clock in the morning,' Annabel said, walking in front of me.

'Shouldn't take long anyway,' said Tess. 'Not with half the fire brigade on campus already.'

'I went up to the Gulag,' said Annabel. 'Completely destroyed. The smoke was toxic. One of the firemen said if anyone had been in there, they wouldn't have had a chance ...'

I thought of the Marchmain boy and his camp stove. A surge of panic. I had to get outside and see for myself.

'Sorry,' I mumbled, pushing past.

'What's the rush? Where's the fire?' someone called out and I heard people laughing at the joke.

'Are you OK?' asked Annabel, but already she sounded far off as I elbowed my way down.

I got to the bottom of the stairs and along the corridor which was even more crowded as the people from the other tower joined the flow. Pushing my way towards the door, there was a definite haze and the smell became stronger, a mixture of a bonfire and something more acrid. When I got outside the night was tinged red.

A fire engine was parked on the grass out the front of our college, a police car a little further away.

The Sub-Dean, attempting to get people into their floor groupings, directed me to where the car park met the road. Toby was sitting on a bench with a list in his hand.

'There you are,' he said, ticking off my name.

'I'm going up to the Gulag.'

'Why? Not much left to see. Lucky no one was inside.'

'No one?' I asked, my heart racing.

'The firemen had time to go through the buildings and they didn't bring anyone out. They seemed pretty relaxed. Paramedics sitting around doing nothing.'

I sat down next to him. The boy in the kitchen must have got out. But what about Nico? They should have found his body and now his building was destroyed. Maybe it wasn't

345

just me who was worried about evidence.

'This'll be a false alarm,' said Toby, looking up at our building. A fireman came out of it and started to talk to the Sub-Dean. 'Maybe the smoke from the Gulag set it off. It's strong enough.' He held the list up to his face, the words difficult to read in the hazy light. 'Who else? Seen most of the others.' He scanned the document. 'Only Joad.'

I was about to say that Joad was locked up in a police cell somewhere, when Toby said, 'There he is. That's everyone.' He jumped up yelling, 'Bingo!' and wandered over to the Sub-Dean. I turned to see Joad standing there, staring in the direction of the red glow. Not arrested. He must have cooperated with the police, whatever that meant.

A rustle behind me and I felt as if I was being watched. Turning, I saw him.

'I wanted to say sorry ... about before ... the way I acted,' said Rogan.

Instinctively, I jumped up and moved away from him.

'Don't be like that,' he said and instantly the apology changed to impatience.

'What do you want?'

He gave an angry shrug. 'To say sorry, that's all.'

There was no one close enough to hear our conversation but people were close enough to keep me safe. He couldn't do anything to me out here.

'I think you need to say a bit more than that.'

'Like what?'

'Like telling me exactly what has been going on.'

Rogan shook his head. 'You don't want to know.'

'Don't tell me . . .' I began, but the Sub-Dean began clapping his hands and then his voice cut through the crowd.

'I have been informed that we are able to go back inside. Stay in the dining hall until the college has officially been given the all-clear.'

Rogan used this interruption to walk away, not even waiting for the end of my sentence. He moved through the crowd, joining the queue to go inside. All I could feel was anger. It was OK for me to lie to the police for him but it wasn't all right for me to know exactly what I was lying about. He had chased me through the dark for no good reason at all. And now this patronising dismissal. It wasn't until we were walking past the telephone cubicles that I caught up with him. I was going to confront him with the balaclava and see what he said.

'What?' he snapped, as I grabbed his arm.

'I hadn't finished,' I said.

He pulled me into a cubicle as we waited for the people to pass us by. Voices were quieter now. Some were threatening to head straight for bed. But it was only talk. Everyone was heading into the dining hall as they had been told.

'So, what's so important?' But almost immediately the door opened.

'Gotcha. I thought I saw you making a dramatic exit.' It was Toby. 'Now, you two, I'm all for kinky sex but there's a time and a place and I have to be invited. You heard the man, into the dining hall.'

'Go away, Toby,' I said angrily.

'Don't be so touchy,' Toby began, but was distracted by something along the corridor. 'Who's that with Marcus?'

Marcus was talking to men in suits. Suits I recognised. Suits that looked even cheaper after a long day and night.

'Homicide detectives,' I said. 'I saw them this afternoon.'

'What would they want with him in the middle of the night?' asked Toby. 'Is he being arrested?'

I felt Rogan sway beside me. Without thinking, I put a hand out to steady him. He pushed it away.

They began to walk towards us, Marcus behind the two policemen. The detectives moved past, but Marcus stopped when he saw us.

'Tobias, Pen, I was wondering if you would assist me.'

'Of course,' said Toby, his camp cockiness momentarily evaporating.

'Good, good.' Marcus was being his usual smooth self. 'Could you be so kind as to let the Sub-Dean know that I have gone to the city police station for a discussion with these two gentlemen? He should contact my lawyer to meet me there.'

Neither of us moved, shock delaying our response to his request.

'Straight away, if you don't mind.'

'Of course,' Toby said again. He turned the corner quickly, heading towards the dining hall. The noise from there had a fractious quality to it now as if the party had gone on for too long. I started to follow, but then turned back to tell Rogan that we weren't finished yet and that's when I saw it.

It was only a look. Nothing was said. But Marcus had waited for us to leave and the detectives to walk ahead before he turned to Rogan and gave a slow, controlled nod. I knew it was a deliberate signal. A command. The older detective turned back, and Marcus gave another of his charming smiles, and joined them to continue walking up the corridor as if he was escorting them rather than the other way around.

'Are you coming or what?' asked Toby.

'You go, I'll catch you up.'

Toby left, impatient to share the news.

I stayed close to the corner, watching Rogan. He had not moved. In fact, his body was so tense he could have been frozen, until he took a long breath and began to turn. I huddled close to my corner so he couldn't see me. I wanted to know what he was going to do next. He passed by, his face strained.

He moved quickly, almost running, up the corridor towards Marcus's office. I followed at a distance, listening, aware of the gentle slap of my bare feet against the floor. He must have had a key for the office because as I got closer I could hear a door open and then close. But in his hurry, he hadn't snibbed it properly, and the door swung back just a fraction. I peeked in.

Rogan had sat down in Marcus's chair and switched on the lamp. A puddle of muted yellow light spilt over the desk and illuminated a nearby vase of lilies. He dragged down the sleeve of his top over his fingers and began opening drawers. He took out two packets of white powder from the second drawer and laid them on the desk. The next drawer had some pills. He then moved out of sight, and I could hear a rustling sound. Trying to see where he went, I pushed the door open a little further. Suddenly it jerked inwards, and I fell into the room. Rogan slammed me against the wall and pressed a sharp point at my throat.

'Be quiet,' he hissed. He pulled back, his face a mask of shadow and light, and then shut the door, an insect-like click in the darkness.

'You're lucky all I could find was a fucking letter opener. I didn't know who was there.' He showed me an engraved sliver of metal, the size of a nail file, more decorative than functional. 'What are you doing here?'

'Shouldn't I be saying that to you?' I asked.

Rogan moved away, a disgusted look on his face. 'Haven't you guessed yet? I'm cleaning up after our precious *Master*.'

It was the peculiar emphasis that made me pause and then remember the conversation with Nico that I had been so quick to dismiss as delusion.

'You mean Marcus ...'

'Of course Marcus. It's why he nearly got booted from his last university. He's the Death Riders' man on campus. It was supposed to work perfectly. He'd make sure no one in authority asked questions and cover up any accusations. You can see how well that's been going.'

'He's behind the drugs on campus? Taking over from the Marchies?'

'Oh yes. He had dreams of a whole network of dealers, and not just obvious ones like Stoner either.'

'You?'

He seemed to take this as an accusation. 'You as well. What sort of part-time work do you think he wanted me to talk to you about?'

'But you ... never ...?'

'No. By that stage I knew I'd made a mistake and I didn't want to drag you into it. I didn't want that on my conscience as well.'

351

And for a moment, I wondered how easily it could have been me sitting at the Master's desk, getting rid of the evidence.

'Besides, after Rachel died, there was too much police attention on you and so he came up with the idea of Emelia and me. Thought she would give us access to a cashed-up clientele.'

I could only stare at this. 'That was Marcus's decision?'

Rogan shook his head. 'You don't get it, do you? He's all charming at the start, handing out wads of cash, talking about mutual benefit, but once he's got you, he's completely ruthless. I even tried to leave but he said he'd get me kicked out of university and tell my parents I was a dealer.'

I attempted to rewind past events to see how this information changed things but it was too complicated.

'But Rachel?'

'Rachel found out about Marcus. Found coke in his desk when she stole his keys. Found out about Marcus and found out about me.'

His voice was not so confident now, more like a harsh whisper.

'That night at the bar she was showing off. Decided she needed coke right there and then. I tried to make her understand who she was dealing with. These guys control everything. They've got police on their payroll. But she didn't and she ended up dead.' I flinched inside at this, but said nothing.

'Just like those bikers killed Leiza,' he continued. 'At the start, I pretended to myself that this wouldn't hurt anyone, that we were all adults here. Guess I got that completely wrong.' There was contrition in his voice but there was an element of self-pity as well.

The problem was I knew that he hadn't told me everything.

I pulled the balaclava out from under my pyjama top and held it in my hands. It was warm but from my body this time.

Recognition flooded his face. His voice was harsh. 'Where did you get that? Did Rachel give it to you? What did she tell you?'

'Enough,' I lied.

It was as though I'd punched him. He folded up and slumped onto a nearby couch. 'I didn't mean to hurt her. You've got to believe me. We all had to take turns being the Screwdriver Man and it was mine. Marcus said I was in too deep to get out of it now. The Marchies wouldn't accept reality. So Screwdriver Man had to teach Nico a lesson. I wasn't strong enough to attack him so I thought of Alice.'

I looked at the balaclava in my hands. The wool felt greasy, as if his guilt had seeped into it. As I thought of the blood flowing out of Alice, the floor seemed to be moving

353

up towards me, the room tilting. Did Alice even know Nico was dead?

'I thought it would be easy, just scare her. Tell Nico to back off. But she struggled, I panicked, and then the screwdriver ... it was an accident, I swear. I stayed there in the bushes until I was sure she got help. That's when Rachel saw me. Then she snuck into my room on the Academic Night and stole the balaclava and the screwdriver.'

How Rachel must have enjoyed our secrets, pulling our strings to make us jump, never realising how desperate we were.

His face was bitter as he picked up the bin near the desk and swept the packets into it.

'How did the drugs get into Rachel's bag?' I was trying to put together the final pieces of that night.

'Stoner freaked out when he saw that cop at the bar, and insisted I take his supplies back to college. When we found Rachel, I forgot about it until I heard the sirens, so I stuffed it all in her bag. When I told Marcus, he decided that we'd pretend she was the one dealing. Put all the blame on her.'

Marcus. It always came back to him.

I watched Rogan lean down and open the last drawer. He found another bag and dropped it into the bin and I decided this was enough. I needed to get out of here. But then he straightened up, listening hard. I heard it too.

Footsteps outside the door.

He clicked off the desk light. Coming around to where I was sitting, he grabbed my hand and pulled me up. Silently on the thick carpet we crossed the room and stood flat to the wall next to the door.

The handle turned.

A shuffling outside. Someone pushing. The handle moved, harder this time. But the door didn't budge and the person didn't have a key.

Along the corridor came the echo of voices and hundreds of moving feet. The firefighters had given the all-clear.

The footsteps darted away.

Rogan interlaced his fingers in mine, and we just stood there. A soft hand that had never worked hard.

'I'm sorry about this,' he whispered. 'I'm sorry about everything.'

My treacherous heart leapt as if it had been deaf to what I had just heard.

'I try to tell myself I'm not a bad person, but after all that's happened ...'

Rogan might not be bad, but he was weak, and I knew that was just as dangerous. Weak people will always find an excuse.

There was one last thing I needed to know.

'Why did you come to my room that night?'

I could almost hear his reluctance. Eventually, 'Marcus told me to.'

'To have sex with me?'

'He didn't say that . . .' But it was the hesitation that gave me the real answer and I allowed the pressure of silence to build until it forced the truth out of him. 'He said it was important to keep you on side.'

And finally I had heard enough and the spell was broken. I withdrew my hand but Rogan barely noticed. He was busy grabbing the bin liner. He might have been weak but he was a survivor as well. Marcus knew how to pick them.

I moved towards the middle of the room. Looking up, I noticed that the broken boy was back up on the wall. The shadows were even darker than usual. Definitely dead, I thought as I watched him, and for the first time I was almost envious. He was safe now. The worst thing had already happened.

Chapter 25

Carol was sitting hunched at her desk. It was clear she had been crying. When I pointed my finger at the door, she said nothing, merely nodded me through. Marcus's nameplate had already disappeared. The Sub-Dean was inside, talking on the phone. Up until then I had only been focused on what last night's revelations had meant for me. With him sitting at Marcus's desk, I could see that everything was going to change.

The Sub-Dean was saying something about not wanting to be presumptuous and 'innocent until proven guilty' but the look on his face said otherwise. When he saw me at the door he waved me forward. 'A safe pair of hands ... no, thank you, Chancellor,' he concluded the phone call.

'Ms Sheppard,' he said. 'Sit down.'

'You said you wanted to see me.'

I sat down on the other side of the desk, in the same chair as last night. Lying between us was today's newspaper, folded over to page six. 'ACADEMIC ARRESTED' was written in small type across the top of the right-hand column with a small picture of Marcus underneath.

'I have had discussions with the police this morning. They no longer wish to interview you.' My heart skipped a beat. The relief I felt was mirrored in his face. He didn't need to be interviewed either. Both of us were in the clear.

The telephone next to him buzzed, and he pressed the speaker.

'Carol, I said hold all calls this morning.'

'But it's Joe McCardle for you.'

The Sub-Dean leant back in his seat, getting a feel for it. 'You can tell him that the college will be issuing a public statement to the media this afternoon.'

A tinny version of Carol's puzzled voice came through. 'He said he was returning your call.'

With a quick dart forward, he snapped up the phone and turned away from me. 'I'll ring him back shortly.'

Putting down the phone a little harder than was required, he glanced at me. No smile now. 'Was there something else, Ms Sheppard?'

I wanted to know if Rogan was going to be interviewed,

but instead I asked, 'What has Marcus been charged with?'

'I'm not at liberty to say any more than what is already in the public sphere.' Frowning, he pushed the paper over to me. It was short on specifics other than saying it was related to the murder investigation that was underway. A police spokesperson talked about enquiries being ongoing, but hopefully this arrest would lead to others.

'Extremely damaging for the college,' he said, taking off his glasses and polishing them with his tie. He was addressing the room at large, rather than me specifically, something Marcus was fond of.

'Unfortunately, no matter what the outcome, there will have to be changes at Scullin. Marcus Legard will never be able to return to his position at this college. The Chancellor has appointed me to take over his duties immediately.'

Without his glasses, his face was mole-like, but the naked triumph was obvious. Perhaps sensing he was giving too much away, he put his glasses back on, a stubby white finger pushing them up onto the bridge of his nose.

'I feel I should warn you in particular, Ms Sheppard, there will of necessity be changes to some of the unorthodox financial decisions that he set up during his short time with us. But that is a discussion for another day.' And I knew that the next time I saw this room, the pine-framed fruit bowls and flocks of sheep would have returned, the walls would be back to a nice safe cream and I would no longer have a bursary.

'Now, if you will excuse me, I have a very busy morning.'

Carol looked up as I shut the door behind me.

'He talks to that journalist all the time and he's already ordered new business cards,' she whispered. 'Hateful man.'

College was a half-asleep world, unaware of the Sub-Dean's coup. Most students, tired from last night, were ignoring the fact that it was a weekday and sleeping in. When I walked past the dining hall few people were in there. Only one person was walking down the stairs as I climbed up them. Returning to my room, I decided to keep my decisions simple, to take one step at a time. I didn't have the energy to worry about the Sub-Dean's threat to my finances. Not today. I didn't have all the answers to what had been going on, but I thought I had enough to navigate my way through safely. The police weren't interested in me now. For the first time since Rachel's death, I wasn't living with the fear of imminent exposure. I had my own quiet moment of relief as I walked down the corridor. Until I saw my door was open, a door I knew for certain I had locked.

The article was on the floor, neatly folded, a copy of the one I had found the night Rachel had died. Next to it was a set of bangles. Rachel's bangles. I picked them up and put them on my wrist. They tinkled as I looked around my room. The balaclava had been taken.

Last time I had assumed Rachel had left the newspaper article in my room. Whether it was to show she could harm me or was protecting me, I could never tell. I picked up the paper. Words had been scrawled above the headline, above where Rachel had written my name. 'Meet me on the roof.'

Maybe the first article had not been left by Rachel at all. Maybe I had been wrong about that. I had been wrong about so many things, especially that there would be an end to this. There are always threads.

For a moment, I wondered if I could ignore it, go have a shower, eat my breakfast, pretend I had never got it. But that wasn't possible. I had to do what the note said, but first I ripped it into little pieces and flushed it down the toilet so no one else could find it. I pushed the bangles halfway up my arm, tucked in place by the cuff of my jumper. I would get rid of them later.

My floor was still empty. I could hear quiet music behind some doors and the occasional muffled voice. But the kind of cozy sleepiness of the place had changed to something harder. Isolation. I could have passed a hundred people and it wouldn't have made any difference. I had to face this alone.

I climbed the stairs and walked along the corridor until I came to the room with the only bath in the tower. Unlocked.

The chair was waiting for me on the top of the counter. No face looking down at me or putting out a hand to help. I wondered what would happen if I couldn't pull myself up. A tiny giggle flickered inside me for one moment but I snuffed it out immediately. There was a hysterical edge to it.

I stared into the black square above my head, the manhole cover already removed, and then down at my slip-on shoes. I took them off, thinking that at least bare feet would have a better grip out on the roof. I clambered on to the chair. It felt flimsy this time and I held on to the square's edges to stop my legs from shaking. My head was already through the hole. I stood there for a while, half in, half out, letting my eyes adjust properly to the dark before I moved.

Taking hold of the sides of the manhole, I jumped. My legs only half pushed, my feet slipping on the chair. Arms gripping, legs kicking furiously, I was swimming in the air, trying to propel myself upward. I kicked hard again, lurched forward and my hands thrust into the space, reached a beam and I scrambled up. I was through.

The air was hot and so thick with dust that I gasped and coughed as if I had taken in water. The only light came up through the hole. Cautiously, I moved an arm around, feeling for the torch that had been there last time.

But there was no torch.

The air swirled in clouds, disturbed by my movement.

As I sat there with my legs dangling through the square trying to remember the way, I noticed a pair of footprints on a beam near me, as crisp in the dusk as on wet sand at a beach, a trail to follow into the dark.

The square of light lit up a few of the vertical beams around me. They stood there as dark as the trees from last night. Then, I had run away from danger, but now I was walking towards it, and it was probably the same person in both instances. Logic and time were disappearing and something more primitive had taken their place inside me: the honing of senses, the pulse of adrenalin.

I could have jumped back down into the world below and taken the consequences but instead I began walking along the horizontal beam, carefully putting my foot into each footprint as if pretending I wasn't there, as if none of this was really happening.

As I reached the first vertical beam, I hugged it tightly, swaying slightly. I held my breath and listened. I could hear the scurry of tiny feet. Rats perhaps, trying to work out what the disturbance was. I could almost feel their teeth on my skin, and my heart began to thump.

The roof got lower and I ducked my head further and further. Finally, almost bent double, I could see the chinks of light, the lighter grey in the black of the wall. Something scuttled down my arm and I jerked forward, almost falling off the beam but catching a rafter at the last moment. In straightening up, I smacked into the side frame. Pain flashed red across my eyes. Steadying myself, whimpering, I put my hand to the top of my head. My hair was sticky. Blood smeared my fingers.

I needed to get out. In desperation I banged my hands against the side of the roof and caught my palm against a metal fastening. Pushing the hatch open, I heard the dull clang on the tiles outside. The sky appeared and I half fell, half stumbled onto the roof.

Chapter 26

The world was the colour of milk.

I shut my eyes and slowly opened them again, squinting in the light. The white discoloured and shapes began to form. A fog wrapped the building like gauze. The air smelt of leftover smoke and wet pine.

I blinked again.

Tiles the colour of weathered wood. Moss and dew making them slick.

Michael sitting on the roof, watching me.

I scrabbled across the tiles and perched myself at the other side of the hatch. A careful distance. I felt my head. Blood spotted on my hand. Scrapes on my arm, a couple of nails torn ... not so serious.

I waited for what was going to happen next.

'Have you ever been up here during the day?' he asked.

I shuddered. Cold was seeping into my bones. 'Only once. At night. Weeks ago.'

'Oh, I know about that.' His voice was bitter. 'I followed you up here. I've followed you everywhere.'

And I knew that was true. The ever-present flicker at the corner of my eye. The dark shadow in the bush. The face across a room. But I was not ready to bring him into sharp focus yet so I looked at a small black bundle lying nearby. The balaclava, I guessed.

'Did you take that from my room?' I asked.

A nod.

There was something thin and sharp next to it. A screwdriver.

'Do they really belong to Rogan?'

'I think so. I mean, I took them from Rachel's room, but I am assuming she took them from his when she worked out that he attacked that girl, Alice. They've been useful, but don't worry, I'll return them to their rightful owner in time for the police to discover them.'

Carefully, he picked up the screwdriver in gloved hands, angled so that a sudden spike of sunshine pierced through and illuminated the stained black edge.

'Hard to believe that it could do so much damage. That you could literally chisel the life out of someone.'

My chest felt tight. 'You left the balaclava there last night for me to find. You weren't in your room at all. It was you who chased me.'

A nod.

'And you're going to frame Rogan for Leiza's murder?'

'That depends on you. If you keep fucking him, like you did here that night, as you probably did last night in Marcus's office, then yes, I will. But to be honest, even if I don't, he's in enough trouble already. Isn't he?'

The sun disappeared again, as if it had seen enough.

'The problem is, Pen, I don't think you understand all that I've done for you.'

I took a deep breath as though drinking in the sky.

'Why don't you tell me, then?'

So Michael told me his version of the last few months. Events I knew but now saw again distorted through his dead-eye gaze. The story of a boy who stole into someone's room to set an alarm clock for the early hours and found a rolled-up balaclava, a screwdriver and a newspaper article about a murdered policeman with the name of the only girl who had ever kissed him scrawled on top. What I worried would repel people only attracted Michael more. He watched me even more closely. So closely, that he noticed me storm out of the girls' toilets one night at the bar and crush something over Rachel's beer.

'It was how you smiled when you handed it to her. A beautiful, genuine smile. Nothing fake about it. No pretence. I wanted you to smile at me the same way.'

He followed Rachel outside and watched her stumble to the river. She fell down and sprawled on the bank, possibly overdosing already, possibly not. It was hard to tell, he said. It was taking so long. He wanted to watch her die, this girl who tormented him. Partly, because he hated her, but also because he was curious. What did death look like? How did it feel?

In the end, he became impatient. He dragged her into the shadows where the river was deep and held her face under and in that grey water, synapses sparked and a neural pathway was completed and Michael's world was changed forever. It was like hearing music or seeing colour for the first time. A revelation, he said.

He ran to college, got changed, climbed into my room to leave the article so I would know I was safe. He saw the Rohypnol sitting out and took that with him. All my secrets protected. Heading back to the bar to find me, he saw Rogan and me kissing, holding hands and walking out the door. Following us, he watched as we discovered Rachel's body, saw Rogan stuff Rachel's bag full of drugs and realised that with Rachel gone, he was the new finder of secrets. Rachel's mistake had been that she couldn't keep them. Michael was sure he would.

'I decided not to tell you. Punishment for Rogan. But then that day in the laundry when I was washing the clothes I had killed Rachel in, I overheard Leiza threatening you.'

'Not threatening,' I whispered. 'Talking to me.'

He looked at me dismissively, a snarl in his voice. 'Leiza was a threat. Her whole campaign was a threat. Any police investigation was. They nearly caught you last time. I couldn't risk losing you.'

'You killed her.'

Michael nodded. 'I didn't just want to kill her. I wanted to send a message. Everyone else would think it was part of the attacks. Blame the Screwdriver Man or the bikers at the bar. But really it was for you. That's why I left the Rohypnol. I was the only person who knew what you had done to Rachel. I wanted you to realise all that I had done for you. That we killed Leiza together just like we had killed Rachel.'

He sat there and smiled at me, the savage smile of someone who truly believed that. What he had done was more than a gesture. My tablets tied me to both deaths.

He kept talking about his plans but I couldn't listen. I didn't want to hear any more. I thought about the people who had been caught in Michael's web. Rachel. Leiza. Even Nico. He had thought, like everyone else, that the bikers killed Leiza. He went to the police and ended up dead. Even Rogan and Marcus, guilty of their own crimes, were now wrapped up in something far more sinister.

I thought about them and I thought about me. How responsible was I for all of this? How guilty should I feel? I had spent all semester studying subjects that professed to have discovered the formula to allocate blame, to apportion guilt. But courts never find people innocent. They find them not guilty. There is a difference. Here, I was not innocent. I was not blameless. Most of what Michael thought had been distorted through the fairground mirror of his mind, but he had seen me clearly, perhaps more accurately than I was willing to admit. For a fleeting moment I had wanted to kill Rachel, and I, out of everyone, should have understood the repercussions of acting on a murderous impulse, on decisions made in the blink of an eye.

A breeze picked up, moving through the trees, poking holes in the mist. It tasted cold on my tongue.

The day Tracey and I had stolen from the gift shop had been cold.

'Let's get something to eat.' Tracey pulled my arm as she walked into Cook-a-Chook. The thick-necked owner looked up in anticipation when the bell rang. His sweaty face soured when he saw it was us.

'Let me guess, one chips with gravy to share.'

The cheapest thing on the menu.

'Two Cokes as well,' added Tracey.

'Youse are big spenders.' He grunted, reaching into the fridge behind him.

'Pay the man, Pen,' said Tracey. She was broke as usual.

Annoyed, I handed over the money. 'I'm supposed to be saving for Mother's Day. If I don't get something, she's going to nag me for the rest of the year.'

Tracey laughed. 'She's going to nag you anyway.'

She picked up the aluminium foil container, careful not to squeeze it so the gravy wouldn't spill. The door dinged on our way out.

'Maybe we should try the gift shop?' I asked.

'Dunno,' said Tracey. 'You'll look guilty and give the game away.' She fished out a chip, swore when a blob of hot gravy landed on her wrist and thrust the container at me.

'I won't.' I balanced it in both hands, feeling the heat radiating outwards. 'Besides, you said it was easy. That the guy's too busy reading his newspaper to notice.'

Tracey sucked the gravy off her skin and said nothing.

'You're chicken,' I said. 'Dare you.'

There was a red welt where the gravy had been.

'All right,' she said. 'But only because I haven't got anything for Mother's Day either.'

I began all this.

Michael stood up on the roof.

'Now you know my secrets and I know yours. We'll keep each other safe,' he said.

'No.' My voice was as thin as vapour. I wasn't sure he heard what I had said, but he turned and looked at me.

I spoke louder this time, the wind catching my words, hurling them at him.

'We're never going to be together.'

He began to slowly crawl towards me across the tiles like a spider. The door to the roof lay between us but all my courage had been used up. I couldn't force myself to get any nearer to him.

Suddenly, he began to move unbearably fast.

Too late for the door now. My only thought was to put space between him and me.

I began clambering up to the top of the roof, my numb feet sliding on the wet tiles. But momentum was on his side and as I reached the top, his arm stretched out and grabbed my foot, a gloved hand against my icy skin. Clinging to the roofline, I kicked back viciously and felt something give way. He let go and I threw my body over the far side. My clothes and feet snagged on loose tiles as I slid down away from him, grabbing at an old roof turbine to help stop my fall. I only just managed to slow down before the edge. Tiles cascaded over the side and I could hear them smashing down the four storeys.

I thought I could hear movement below us. A sluggish world was beginning to wake up.

I stayed as close to the edge as I could, trying to brace

myself on the uneven wet surface. Michael came over the ridge. As I watched him move down the roof, part of me couldn't believe that Michael would actually hurt me. But the screwdriver in his hand told me otherwise.

Indistinct voices began floating up towards us, curious and puzzled. I tried to scream but the sound caught in my mouth. No one could help. I watched him come nearer. His nose was broken. I had done that much. I felt a surge of hopeful anger, a moment of exhilaration. This wasn't some monster and I wasn't a scared fifteen-year-old. I hunted around for something to use as a weapon. A cracked piece of tile broken by my fall was lying near my feet. It fitted in my hand perfectly. There was a weight to it, a sharp edge.

'You're smarter than this,' Michael said. 'You don't need to be scared of me.'

In a single movement, he knocked the tile out of my hand and pushed me backwards onto the roof. My head slammed against the surface and, pinned together, we juddered towards the edge, my feet scrabbling to push back on the gutter and not slide off the roof.

He lay on top of me now. I could feel his heartbeat in my chest. In the struggle, the screwdriver had sliced a large cut near my eyebrow. A flap of skin. Warm blood trickled out of me.

I looked straight into the light-blue eyes that I had tried to avoid. Blood began to cloud my vision but I saw the truth at last. There were similarities between Michael and me that couldn't be denied, but fundamentally we were different.

I was a survivor and he was not.

Michael shifted slightly and his weight lessened. Distracted, he reached out to touch my face. 'I didn't mean to hurt you,' he said. 'I love you.' He dropped the screwdriver. It rolled down and fell into the gutter, out of his reach.

'I've got something that belongs to you,' I said. I lifted up my arm with the bangles. He sat up and pulled back my sleeve and I slipped them off into his hand. Then with my heels braced against the gutter, I pushed him as hard as I could. Two great shoves to his chest. The first pushed him off me, arms flailing. The second pushed him right over the edge.

Lying on my stomach, I peered over. There were holes in the mist and the ground was visible in large patches. Michael lay there.

He could have been asleep.

Chapter 27

I am sitting in the waiting room looking at Ivy's red circles on the wall. Today, for the first time, they really are balloons, floating away, free. Escaping like me. The train ticket is in my blue diary which sits on my lap. Most roads are open. My bags are packed. I am leaving again, as I did before, except I am heading to a different university in a different city. I've got time to settle in and find a place to stay. After Christmas, I'll catch up what I missed at summer school and by the time first semester begins, everything will be back to how it should be.

The town is cleaning up now that the flood has started to recede. We didn't beat the 1923 record and Mum was disappointed. The whole place stinks of dirt and the river, as though we were buried alive and have just been dug up.

Frank had to be a 'real' doctor during the flood. He delivered a baby and treated a couple of broken legs, one concussion and Bob, who had a suspected heart attack trying to help move racehorses to higher ground. It turned out to be angina. There is a picture of Frank on the front page of the newspaper, standing next to Bob's hospital bed. Bob is looking paler than usual, but maybe that's just the printing because Frank is looking a little green. I'll send Bob a card when I get settled.

Frank the Hero. Our local paper deals in absolutes. Ivy bought multiple copies and has put them around the waiting room. But I'm the only person here to enjoy them, which I find a bit odd. I would have thought everyone would be wanting an appointment but they must still be sweeping mud out of their houses.

Ivy is distracted by her new computer today. It's a light-grey beehive of a box that hums all the time. I can tell she's a bit on edge by the way she presses a key and then pulls her hand back as if it's got teeth.

In my mind I am saying goodbye to all of this. To Ivy. To the balloons. To the newspaper. To the waiting room. I didn't get a chance to do that at Scullin.

By the time they got me off the roof I had lost a lot of blood and was fading in and out of consciousness. As I was bundled into the ambulance, I could see Scullin disappearing forever.

Kesh and Toby visited me at the hospital. Kesh cried a lot and Toby chatted up the cute male nurse. Rogan stayed away. The police were a constant presence but having a head injury helped me avoid difficult questions until I'd come up with the right answers. In the end, I told them what they wanted to hear: Michael had killed himself after admitting he had murdered Rachel and Leiza. I tried to stop him and that's how I got injured. I even made him responsible for the attack on Alice. That was easy with the balaclava and screwdriver on the roof. I figured Rogan had tried to protect me from Marcus, so I owed him that much. It was also neater that way. Real life is never simple, but I've found people like to pretend that it is.

The only person I didn't mention was Nico. But then I thought I didn't have to, because I expected the nice, fatherly sergeant, who I suspected was on the bikers' payroll, and who spoke to me in a gentle voice and occasionally held my hand when my head hurt too much, knew exactly what had happened to him.

When they discharged me from hospital, I was put into my mother's car, and found all my belongings packed next to me. The Sub-Dean had convinced Mum that it was 'for the best', if not for me then definitely for his budget. He tried to get her to sign a waiver against suing the college but she didn't fall for that one.

The telephone rings and Ivy pounces on it. She transfers the caller through to Frank but only after she whispers who it is. It is the whispering I notice. It cuts through the room the way a soft murmur never does. Something about 'insurance' and the 'medico-legal department'. Her head bobs up and down as she puts through the call.

I wonder what trouble Frank is in. Maybe a patient has made a complaint. Must go with the territory when they're mad in the first place.

Ivy sees me looking and she smiles nervously. Something is definitely wrong. But before I can ask any questions, Frank is standing there and he's not smiling at all.

'Thanks for coming in today,' he says, after I follow him to his office. 'I wasn't sure if you would after you cancelled your last appointment.'

'I tried to get one yesterday,' I say. 'But Ivy said you were busy.'

Frank's lower lip juts out and he nods his head slowly, as if he's not sure he believes me.

A little stung by this, I take the initiative. 'I wanted to see you because I'm leaving town on the train tonight.'

If he is surprised, sitting there in his chair, he hides it well.

'My settlement came through. There's enough money for me to start studying again. Bob's organised my new university.'

He asks me which one and I tell him. It's actually his old university, which I had forgotten. He doesn't seem very happy for me.

'Pen, I am obliged to tell you that the police have been in contact with me.'

'What did they want?'

'They wanted to know if you are my patient.'

This is a ridiculous question because everyone in town knows who Frank's patients are.

Unless these police aren't from our town.

'Did you tell them?'

'Do you remember what I explained to you about confidentiality at our very first appointment?'

I do. What Frank doesn't know is that I looked it up again this year. It was mentioned in a lecture and I did some extra reading in the library. I could cite the cases for him. Explain how strict his obligations are in favour of the patient. In favour of me. I have been so very careful not to give him any reason to go to the police.

'I neither confirmed nor denied that you were my patient. I asked them to put their request in writing and explained to them that I would have to discuss the matter with you, if you were actually my patient. They faxed it through yesterday.'

He shows me a piece of paper. A smudged official-looking crest is at the top.

'Their request concerns a murder investigation and they are considering whether to apply to the courts for all my notes concerning you.'

'But . . .'

He holds up a hand to quieten me. 'There's more. It asks whether a certain diary makes up part of my patient notes. They provide a description. A4 size, dark blue, hard-cover, gold embossed writing on the front.' He glances at what I am holding in my hands. 'They describe that book exactly.'

Sun is pouring into the room. There is a spider's web under the eaves.

Who would have told the police about my diary?

I wonder if that was what Terry was looking for in my room. I can't believe he would get the police involved. Others would though. Julie Cuttmore for a start. She'd do it in a heartbeat if she thought it would get me into trouble. She'd ask Terry to steal it and when he couldn't find it, go to the police and tell them I was keeping one. It seems far-fetched but still the police know about my diary. Someone told them.

'I've just spoken to my insurer's lawyer. Your diary isn't part of my notes. It belongs to you, as we agreed at the beginning, so it isn't protected.'

I put the diary down on the table in front of us, carefully, as if with one false move it might explode.

'But what if I give it to you?' I say. 'I could give it to you now and then it's part of your notes.'

Frank puts his hands in his lap, as though he doesn't want to accidentally touch it.

'You would only be giving it to me to attract the privilege, not as part of a genuine treatment. I cannot lie to the police. I will have to tell them that there is no diary in my file.'

There is a flatness to the way he says this, rehearsed almost. He is not outraged or flustered. He's not even surprised. And I wonder how long he has known about this. Did it begin with the phone call from the police or was this something he knew from our first session?

I turn my head away from him and look at the spider's web again as I work through the implications of what's happening. Raindrops still cling to the web like crystal beads, a beautiful deadly trap.

'You said if I wanted to continue with you, I had to put everything down in writing. Did you tell the police?'

He looks straight at me and says, 'Why would you think that?' and I almost laugh that I expected an answer from the man who only ever asks questions. It doesn't matter though. I may not have been as successful a liar as I thought, but I'm better than he is. I stare at him and for a moment I think he is going to say sorry, but instead, he says, 'Pen, what have you done?' Something he has probably been wanting to ask me every session.

I don't answer him. He doesn't deserve it. But that isn't important now. I need to get rid of the diary. I pull it back towards me.

'You can call me anytime. You know that.'

I shake my head. I don't need him. I don't need anybody. I'm starting again.

As I tuck the diary into my bag I'm already thinking of ways to get rid of it. Burning it would be the best. I imagine ripping out the pages and watching them, one by one, fuel a fire. Ashes to Ashes. Rachel, Leiza, Michael, Tracey, disappearing forever. But the cover probably wouldn't burn. Too waxy.

No, that idea isn't practical. The ground is too damp to light a fire outside. But also, part of me knows even if there was a fire right in front of me, I wouldn't put the diary in. I'm not ready to get rid of it, to say goodbye to the people inside it. I can't let them go. If I go straight home perhaps I can hide it under the floorboard. It worked before.

I walk out of the door. Frank is behind me. There are tall people in blue uniforms standing in reception. Frank says, 'What on earth is going on?' but we all ignore him. They surround me. A shorter one steps forward. I recognise Constable Morriset. I scan the rest of the faces. Another man looks familiar, but then all policemen look the same.

'Penelope Sheppard, you are not obliged to say ...' she begins. I don't even bother listening to the rest of it and say 'Yes' before I am supposed to. Ivy stays well back from it all, behind the reception desk.

Constable Morriset puts on gloves and pulls the blue book out of my bag. She slips it into a clear plastic bag and seals it. They put me in the police car, next to her. She is trying not to look too pleased with herself. A good day's work. They never wanted Frank's notes, just the diary. They must have kept a watch on this place, knowing I would bring it in for our session.

People have come out into the street to see what is going on. The man from next door is standing out the front of his shop, gaping like a fish. I wonder if he knows who I am, if he remembers the day that I came in and stole a porcelain ornament. I was sure he saw me. That's why I left so quickly and ran back to the park, clutching it under my jacket. Tracey was more confident and decided to browse for longer.

'It's been a while, Pen,' says Constable Morriset.

'Why isn't Sergeant Durham here?' I ask.

She tries to appear unruffled but her edges get sharper. 'He's not part of this investigation any more.'

'Is that right?' I say. I want to show her that I'm not intimidated.

'Don't worry. Sergeant Woodley knows the way to the police station.'

I look at the rear-vision mirror. The policeman who seems familiar.

'I know Pen as well,' he says.

'Is that right?' says Constable Morriset, tartly echoing my words.

'You forgotten me?' he says. His eyes catch mine in the mirror. 'Pen was the star witness in a big case we had a while back. Didn't get to trial though. Accused killed herself the day before it started. Shot herself with the murder weapon. Remember, Pen? I had to come and tell you.'

The trees are bare in front of the court house. The rain has torn off all the blossoms. Winter is here again.

They put me in the same interview room I was in that night. I tell myself that it is not deliberate, that there aren't that many interview rooms in a country station.

I pretend this is just a waiting room. But it isn't the same as the others. There are no pictures on the walls.

I sit for a long time alone, trying to work out why I am

here. What am I really guilty of? Michael killed Rachel, not me. Just like Tracey killed the policeman. The diary doesn't help, but I think of how to explain it away. It was a hypothetical exercise as instructed by my psychiatrist to help me deal with my emotional loss. My survivor's guilt was such that I blamed myself for others' actions.

Sounds like lies.

The interview starts and it is the uniforms again. Not detectives. They'll be here soon, Constable Morriset tells me. The flood's delayed them.

She says that I am being questioned in relation to the death of Michael Doherty.

'Michael killed himself,' I say. 'He jumped from the top of the building.'

'Did he?' Constable Morriset asks. 'Because the angle of his fall looks like he was pushed.'

I keep my face blank. Expert evidence, that's all they've got. We just need to find another expert to say he wasn't.

She brings out a plastic bag and for a second I think it is my diary, and I begin to ready my excuses. But instead it's a bottle of tablets. The label has been ripped off. I still recognise it.

'Have you seen these tablets before?' she asks.

I retain a veneer of control. I need time to think about what to do next. I tell her I want legal representation. I give her Bob's name and number.

'Of course,' Morriset says.

'Might take a while,' Sergeant Woodley tells me. 'Hear he's back in hospital. Another angina attack.'

Bob not being there doesn't stop them from talking. Morriset holds up the bag with the tablets.

'We found them in Michael Doherty's belongings. These are the same tablets that drugged Rachel Brough and that were found near Leiza Parnell.'

'How can you possibly know that?' I ask. I didn't mean to but it just popped out.

'Because you're not the only one who wrote things down.'

It takes a moment to register what she is talking about. It seems not even Michael could keep a secret. Perhaps no one can.

'This isn't the first murder you've been questioned for, is it?' asks Sergeant Woodley. 'Must be hard having friends die again. Seems to happen to you a lot. Tracey was a friend of yours, wasn't she?'

I look at him and say, 'Tracey's my best friend.'

'Was your best friend.' He sits there as if he has all the time in the world. 'Here's what I think, you want us to know what happened. Why else write it all down? I mean, you hardly kept this diary a secret. We had anonymous calls to the station about it.'

I don't look at him.

I try to think practically about murder and manslaughter,

mens rea, guilt and innocence, but it is like time is winding backwards and everything I have learnt about criminal law has vanished. That I never won a bursary, went to university or escaped this town.

I am a scared fifteen-year-old staring at the blank wall.

But if that's the case then Tracey is on the other side of it. If I get up from my chair and beat on the wall with my hands she will hear me in the other room. We haven't been separated yet. I haven't had to betray or protect her or whatever it is I did.

She isn't really dead.

Sergeant Woodley puts my diary on the table.

'If I tell you, will I be able to have it back?' I ask, gesturing at my book.

Morriset shakes her head. 'I don't think so.'

It isn't my diary any more. It is their exhibit.

I look at it sitting there next to my tablets.

My talismans. Their evidence.

Both were supposed to ward off the darkness, but darkness is here anyway and I am falling into it again, weighed down by all the secrets I carry inside me. Putting my hand up to push back my hair, I feel tears on my cheeks.

'Do you want a coffee?' Morriset asks, not unkindly.

I shake my head.

'I'll make that phone call,' says Sergeant Woodley. He

picks up the plastic bags and they both walk out, leaving me alone to cry.

I thought I would be able to control this more, that writing it down would help me decide who was the hero, the victim, the murderer, the liar, but maybe I have been all of them. It just depends on where you are in the story.

I don't know where this will end or what I will do when they come back in with more questions. All I know is that everything is unravelling and I want to keep pulling it all out until I am right back at the beginning.

So I start with this morning. Frank's betrayal and Ivy's nervous smile fade quickly and are gone. The last few months move past me in reverse, slowly but getting quicker. Blossoms on trees. Mum without a perm. Terry hasn't moved in. My life on rewind. Michael standing on the roof. Leiza and her petition. Toby smiling. Kesh blushing. Rogan, a stranger across the table and Rachel knocking on my door scrounging for a cigarette. A knot and I pause, standing in front of the picture of the boy on the wall for the first time, but a quick tug and that disappears as well. Fast now, I am almost free. A court room, shots in the night, the china shepherdess. The images blur until a flash of the purest blue.

A summer morning on The Hill.

This is where I cut the thread.

It's the dog that I hear first, scrabbling in the undergrowth before bursting out. A furry bullet, he darts away immediately. Nearby, a girl's voice calls out to him. Tracey Cuttmore appears, walking along the dirt track.

The sun has already burnt away the cool of the night. As soon as it opens, I'm heading to the pool where the chlorine is so strong it turns yellow hair green. Tracey is in my class at school. I haven't seen her since we broke up for the year. Farm kids go wild over summer, jumping into dams, riding their horses, hunting for yabbies, not bored like us townies.

'What are you doing here?' she asks, when she sees me.

Shrugging my uncertainty, I continue to pick at a mozzie bite on my leg until a pomegranate seed of blood bubbles up.

'Dad's seeing Mr Phillamey,' she says. 'Thought I'd hitch a ride in. You hiding out?'

'Nothing better to do.'

She flops down onto the dirt next to me. 'Your mum's got a new boyfriend.'

I make a face. He's the reason I stay away from home.

'Gary's my second cousin,' says Tracey. This doesn't surprise me. Half the district is related to Tracey. 'He's a dickhead.'

The dog comes bursting out of the dry grass. A long-eared bundle, more than half his size, struggles in his mouth. He drops it and scoops it up again. A savage shake of his head. The rabbit bleats high-pitched squeaks.

'Let go,' I yell. Whether I startle the dog, I'm not sure, but the

rabbit kicks free and rolls over and over, finding its feet to streak away. The dog bounds after it.

Tracey jumps up, shading her eyes with her hands, trying to follow the movement below us. 'You're too soft,' she says, dismissively. 'Besides, the rabbit's probably injured. Best thing is for Nipper to finish it off quickly.'

Neither of us speak as Nipper disappears back into the bush. I stare at Tracey, sullen from the rebuke. Patches of sunburnt skin, translucent like an onion, are peeling off her arms and legs.

'You got a lock on your bedroom door?' she asks after a while.

'I'll be all right.'

'Take money from your mum's purse and get one. I'll put it on for you.'

A peace offering. I swish a fly off my neck before reciprocating. Pulling out a crinkled packet of cigarettes from the pocket of my shorts, I lay it down on the dust between us.

Tracey gives me a sidelong look, 'Your mum's?'

'Gary's. He thinks he lost them down at the pub.'

She pulls a cigarette from the packet and cups her hand around the lighter I pass to her.

'Careful, don't want to start a bushfire,' I say. 'A spark's all it takes.'

She laughs, 'Let it burn. No great loss.' But she's careful all the same.

I lie on my side, propped up on one elbow, watching her, the long grass tickling my skin. She smokes properly, inhaling in a way that would make my head spin. I don't take one. Nicking them was enough.

The world stretches out before us. Yellow fields give way to dirt tracts stretching up to the horizon of dark-blue mountains that stand between us and the rest of the world.

'Remember what Smelly Kelly called this?' she asks. I'm surprised Tracey remembers anything that Mrs Kelly taught us. She spent most of last year standing under the clock, in disgrace.

'An extinguished volcano?'

'A fire mountain, she said, a fire mountain that had gone to sleep.'

I press my ear to the ground, trying to listen for the fiery heartbeat down in the earth, a throbbing whooshing sound, but it's only the wind in the trees. All is quiet below. 'Still sleeping,' I say, and I close my eyes to pretend I am as well.

I can feel the sun's heat on me. Rolling onto my back, everything turns red underneath my eyelids and it's easy to imagine a world on fire. I force my eyes open. Heartbeat red dissolves into blue and I am looking up at a limitless sky. I think about the fire worlds above my head, the stars that disappear from view because of the dazzle of another, smaller but closer. I wondered if the world is on fire all the time, and we don't notice.

Tracey gets up and stands over me, the sun behind her, and she is dark and light all at once.

I get to my feet and dust myself down to give my eyes time to adjust.

'You coming?' I ask.

'Where?' But she's already stubbing out her cigarette.

'Haven't decided yet.'

She nods, whistles for Nipper who appears further along the track minus the rabbit, but looks cheerful enough, trotting away and then looking back to check we are following. Slowly, we move towards him, heading down The Hill, leaving behind the fire and the stars, to walk back into town together.

A Guide for Reading Groups

All These Perfect Strangers

Aoife Clifford

Questions for Discussion:

1. Do you agree with Pen's decision to re-write her own history in her meetings with Frank? Do you think we all constantly edit and revise our own histories? If so, why?

2. Though the novel is set in Australia, it has a very universal feel. Do you think this was an intentional decision on the part of the author? What does the relative anonymity of the places and setting add to the novel?

3. Near the beginning of the novel, Rachel declares, 'Everyone's got skeletons. Your secrets are what make you different. What make you interesting.' Do you agree with this statement? How does this belief of Rachel's shape her actions at university? How does it shape others' actions?

4. Pen's life at university is a shock for her after the small-town life she had before. Discuss these two settings. How are they the same? How are they different? Does the university, with its insular feel and class hierarchies, really provide the escape Pen was looking for?

5. Pen is ultimately an unreliable narrator – as the reader, we get multiple versions of her story and have to decide for ourselves what we think really happened and how much Pen is to blame. Do you think we're getting the whole story? How much do you believe Pen's version of events?

6. *All These Perfect Strangers* is set in 1987-1990, in a world before emails, mobile phones and social media. How do you think Pen's story would be different now? How would her ability to keep her past hidden be compromised? Do you think her actions at university and her entire story would be different if people like Rachel could find out everything about her online?

7. Pen is not the only one in the novel who is manipulating the truth to serve her own purposes. Discuss how the other characters are each twisting and editing facts to write their own stories. Who do you think causes the most damage in doing this?

8. The title, *All These Perfect Strangers*, works on a variety of levels. How did your interpretation of it change over the course of the novel?

9. We realise early on that Pen, for obvious reasons, has issues trusting authority figures. But underneath her toughness there is a vulnerability and desire for a mentor of some kind. How do you think the actions of both Marcus and Frank will affect this desire? How did you interpret Frank's actions at the end? Do you agree with Pen and think this was planned all along?

10. The main reason that Pen is so attracted to Rogan is that he seems perfect, the antithesis of everything she's ever known. As she discovers certain things about him, this belief changes. How does Pen's experience at university, and the realisation that no one is who they seem, change her as a person?

11. *'The grief you feel – maybe it's even guilt about what happened – is distorting the way you view the world.'* By the end of the novel, we realise that almost every character is guilty of something, and that their guilt informs their actions. Discuss each character's guilt and how you think it shapes them as a person. How does Pen's guilt about her past influence the deaths at the university? Do you think she will ever be able to acquit herself? Should she?

12. Of all the characters, Michael is perhaps the most successful at hiding who he really is and what his motivations are. Were you surprised by his part in events? Did you feel sorry for him?

13. Though we only ever see Tracey in flashbacks, her presence is felt throughout the novel. How does her friendship with Pen shape Pen's current interactions and reactions to the people in her life? Were you surprised when you discovered what happened to Tracey? How did it change your feelings towards Pen?

14. The novel's ending is haunting and so deliberately open that it lingers in the mind. What do you think happened to Pen? Why do you think the author decided to leave the story this way?

A Conversation with
Aoife Clifford

What was your inspiration for writing **All These Perfect Strangers?**

The university setting was my initial inspiration. First year at university is such a perfect mix of excitement, loneliness and self-discovery. People are on the cusp of adulthood, trying to work out who they are without the anchors of home and school.

It is one of the main arcs of storytelling that the protagonist undertakes a journey to a strange land, overcoming threats and struggles before returning home, understanding more about themselves. It is *The Odyssey*, *The Hobbit*, *Brideshead Revisited* and probably every detective novel. I wondered if I could extend this idea so that every main character was a stranger in a new land. First year at university was perfect for that.

What is your writing process like? Do you do lots of research or work to a strict schedule? Where's your favourite place to write?

I can write anywhere and at any time, but if I could choose it would be somewhere quiet in the morning. I try to write every day, but life often does get in the way of that. I only tend to research when I have a specific question to answer otherwise I suspect I would fall into the same trap as I did at university, where I would treat photocopying/printing articles as actually doing work.

At one point Pen writes, 'This is one of the advantages of telling the story. You get to choose where it starts and finishes.' As an author, why did you choose to finish Pen's story as you did?

At the start, Pen tells the reader that this is a story that could be 'told a hundred different ways', because I wanted to give the reader space to come up with their own interpretation of the events that take place and Pen's culpability in them.

The main story of *All These Perfect Strangers* is Pen's time at university interwoven with Pen back in her hometown. This is interspersed with snapshots of Tracey and Pen's relationship, starting at the last time they saw each other and moving backwards in time. So I wanted an ending that brought all these strands together while also telling the story of the beginning of their friendship, which is at the heart of the story. In short, I wanted an ending that captured the essence of the book.

You explore some dark issues in the novel, yet the narrative always maintains a certain hopefulness due to Pen's resilience. How did you find this balance?

University and early adulthood are times of many emotions, including resilience and humour. I wanted to try and capture that in the book, even though the events I am writing about are bleak. Pen, in particular, is a character determined to succeed at all costs. That leads to some terrible decisions but it is also the reason that allows you to hope that she will prevail.

Which authors do you most admire?

A few years ago, I listened to a Mariella Frostrup interview of Jane Gardam, where Jane said that she started writing on the very first day her youngest child went to school. At the time I was home with my babies (pregnant with my third) and could identify with that feeling of not wanting to lose another minute. Only, I thought that I couldn't wait until they all got to school, so I began writing straightaway. So I owe Jane Gardam a debt of gratitude for giving me a push.

Whenever the character Gabriel Betteredge in Wilkie Collins' *The Moonstone* has a problem, he opens a page of *Robinson Crusoe* and always finds an answer. For me that book is Allan Hollinghurst's *The Line of Beauty*. Every page is a masterclass of character, of structure, and of dealing with the issues of the time while grappling with what it is like to be human. It is perfect.

There are too many other writers that I admire to list, but I included references to a few in my novel as homage. These include Raymond Chandler, Agatha Christie and Evelyn Waugh. I even named some minor (and disreputable) characters as a cheeky nod to some of my favourite Australian crime writers Peter Temple, Shane Maloney and Garry Disher. The most unlikely reference in the book (which probably no one will see, other than me) is that the Academic Night chapter owes a lot to Anthony Trollope's *Barchester Towers* and the Sub-Dean is my modern-day equivalent of Obadiah Slope. I tried desperately to fit in Mrs Proudie but I couldn't make it work.

What are you working on next?

Once, at law school, we were studying a particular case in a lecture. By coincidence, in an Arts tutorial on the same day, I met a member of the family who had been the defendants in the case (he had an unusual surname and I asked him). His story about the case was very different to the 'facts' set out by the court and in our lecture. That tension informed *All These Perfect Strangers* and it is feeding in to my next novel, which focuses on the aftermath of a girl's murder in a small country town. The main character is a friend of the victim, the local policeman's daughter. She becomes convinced that her father, a good man, has deliberately charged the wrong person and is determined to find out why and what really happened.

If you weren't a writer, what would you be?

I would love to be a children's book illustrator but I'm not that good at drawing. In fact, my school art teacher said the most artistic thing about me was my signature. Probably I would be a lawyer of some description as that is what I studied at university, but amongst the billable units and an office covered in manila folders, I would still be dreaming about books and writing.

Acknowledgements

This book began in earnest at my kitchen table with my friend Carolyn Tetaz on the other side of it insisting we try out some writing exercises. The exercises didn't last but the writing did.

It was rewritten when I undertook the Faber Academy writing course and I am grateful to my tutor Tom Bromley and fellow students for their insight and encouragement, in particular Ruth Cooper and Julia Brown.

A mentorship from the Australian Society of Authors allowed me to work with Garry Disher, whose writing I have long admired. His wisdom and experience made this a better book.

Clare Forster has been agent and guide on the road to

publication, and her gentle words of advice have always proved invaluable. To her and the rest of Curtis Brown, especially agent Rebecca Ritchie at Curtis Brown UK, I could not have done this without you.

Simon & Schuster, both in Australia and the United Kingdom, have made the experience of being published a joy, in particular my publisher Larissa Edwards, editors Carla Josephson and Roberta Ivers, Dan Ruffino, Anna O'Grady, Elissa Baillie, Elizabeth Preston, Dawn Burnett and Merle Bennett. I would also like to thank book designers Crista Moffitt and Sian Wilson.

In the United States, working with my editor Julia Maguire, Erika Seyfried, Ashleigh Heaton, Marietta Anastassatos, Jennifer Rodriguez, Gina Wachtel and all the team at Alibi/Ballantine Bantam Dell Penguin Random House has been a delight. Thanks to agent Catherine Drayton and Inkwell Management.

I benefited from the expertise of the following people who put up with my questions and were generous with their suggestions and time, especially Glenys Harris, Melissa Lowe, Colin Mandy, Michelle Gotting, Anna George, Sinead and Ciara Clifford. I would also like to thank two great cheerleaders throughout, Jackie Quang and Kerry Ruiz who always had faith even when I did not.

The pram in the hallway is supposedly the enemy of writing. That is not my experience. I started writing this novel surrounded by babies. By the time I ended it the pram had magically turned into school bags. To my children Aidan, Genevieve and Evangeline, without you there would be no book, and above all to my husband, Richard, to whom this book is dedicated with love.